to be a mother

BOOKS BY EMMA ROBINSON

to be a mother

emma robinson

bookouture

Published by Bookouture in 2022

An imprint of Storyfire Ltd.
Carmelite House
50 Victoria Embankment
London EC4Y 0DZ

www.bookouture.com

ISBN: 978-1-80314-394-1
eBook ISBN: 978-1-80314-393-4

For Julia

My cousin and friend

PROLOGUE

My dream child.

You live in those moments between sleep and waking. With eyes that see the world as possibility, a nose which leads you to adventure and a mouth which speaks your own individual truth.

You are made of laughter and mischief and kisses. Brave beyond measure, you love to see everything, do everything, be everything.

Blonde curls and a quick lopsided smile echo your father so that I catch my breath each time you turn towards me.

But what will there be of me in you? What lasting gift can I bestow?

My love. My pride. My dearest hope that you will be all you wish to be.

My dream child.

ONE

HANNAH

Last night, she'd dreamed of Katherine again.

There was no need to call in Freud to work out why. Tonight's dinner with Katherine's old friends combined with all the hormones Hannah had been taking must be wreaking havoc with her subconscious. Still, it wasn't the most comfortable of experiences to wake up next to her husband when she'd spent the last few minutes of REM being yelled at by his late first wife.

In the car on the way there, she almost told David about the dream. How Katherine, stunningly beautiful in a red silk gown, had been a passenger in Hannah's Ford Fiesta. As Hannah drove faster and faster – something she never did in real life – Katherine had been screaming at her to stop until Hannah woke with a jolt, heart thumping so hard she was surprised it hadn't woken David.

No, she wouldn't tell him; it would just sound creepy. Better to start mentally preparing herself for the evening ahead. 'It feels so weird going for dinner on a Wednesday.'

David stopped his accompaniment of David Bowie and turned the radio down. 'I know. I said that too. Apparently, since Ben went freelance, his work schedule is so erratic that they've started to socialise on odd days whenever they can.'

Ben was a cameraman. He and Lauren both worked in TV. Which was where they'd met Katherine. It was a little difficult not to look impressed when they name-dropped some of the celebrities they'd filmed with, but Hannah tried her best.

David reached out and squeezed her hand. 'Are you sure you're up to this tonight? I know you don't always enjoy seeing them, and with the appointment tomorrow and everything.'

She loved him for being so concerned about her. He'd held her hand through all the fertility tests of the last few weeks, rolling along with her erratic moods without turning a hair on his handsome blonde head. 'It'll be fine. As long as they don't get the photo albums out again, I promise that I'll play nicely.'

Though Lauren and Ben lived only a short distance from the High Street, their road was wide and tree-lined; their house enviably large. According to David, there was money in Ben's family, plus they both had very successful careers. This success extended to their creation of a family: some people were just good at everything.

When Lauren opened the wide front door, she had her five-year-old daughter Maisie on her hip. Hannah hadn't been surprised to learn that Lauren had been a model before moving into TV production, and her daughter had inherited the same long lashes and lithe limbs. 'Hello, hello. Come in. Maisie is just off to bed but she was adamant that she had to say goodnight to Uncle David before she'd go.'

'Hello, Munchkin.' David reached his arms out to take the little girl as he stepped into the hall. Seconds later she was screaming with pleasure as he swung her around the room.

'Because that's really going to help me get her to bed.' Lauren rolled her eyes at Hannah, but her smile showed she didn't mind at all. 'Come through, Hannah. I'm sure you'd rather be with the grown-ups.'

On the surface, this was a pleasantry, but Lauren did this every time. Made a big thing about David being great with the kids and then assuming that Hannah wasn't interested. Hannah had told her several times that she was a hands-on godmother to both her closest friends' children, but somehow it didn't seem to get through.

They'd been delayed by traffic on the A12, so Priya and Luke were already in the sitting room with a drink in hand. Priya also worked in TV – she was a producer like Katherine had been – but Luke was a dentist. He was the one person in the group that Hannah felt relaxed around. When he'd discovered she was a speech therapist, he'd made a joke about them both being orally fixated, which had made Priya frown at him. Later, after a few craft beers, he'd whispered to her how relieved he was that she wasn't another media queen. 'There's only so many acronyms about a camera angle that a man can take.'

Priya stood up from the sofa to kiss Hannah on both cheeks. Though she wasn't quite as scary as Lauren, she was equally beautiful; her fragile features and petite frame making Hannah feel like a giant beside her. 'Hannah! So lovely to see you. Where's your gorgeous husband?'

'Currently throwing my daughter around in the hallway and ensuring that bedtime will now take twice as long,' Lauren answered for Hannah as she pushed two bowls of nuts and crisps onto the coffee table, to Luke's delight.

From the hallway, they could hear Maisie's high-pitched laughter. 'Well, it sounds like she's enjoying it. He's always been so good with kids.'

The shake of Priya's head and the sadness to her tone suggested she was thinking what a shame it was that David didn't have his own children to play with. It surprised Hannah that they'd all assumed that she and David wouldn't have children; she was only forty-one – hardly past it. She suspected the sadness came more from the fact that he and Katherine hadn't had children.

Although Hannah had known these people for almost two years now, she still felt almost naked without David next to her. So she was relieved when he came through to the sitting room, followed by Ben who was holding a wriggling – and crying – Maisie. 'Mean old Daddy is taking this one to bed. Unless you'd like to do the honours, Lauren, and I'll get the drinks?'

Lauren laughed. 'No way. I've been cooking all afternoon. You're in charge of bedtime tonight.' She blew a kiss at her daughter and waved him away with a smile.

As soon as they disappeared, she turned to David and Hannah. 'You guys are so lucky you don't have that every night. What can I get you both to drink?'

David sat on the arm of Hannah's chair and reached for her hand, a private show of sympathy for the way he knew this comment would make her feel. Despite their regularity, he would never believe that they were meant in the way Hannah took them. He smiled at Lauren. 'I'm driving tonight, so I'll save myself for the one glass of wine with dinner. Have you got anything soft?'

Lauren raised an eyebrow. 'You have him so well trained, Hannah. Every time you come out with us, David seems to be the one driving so that you can have a drink.'

Another barb. How could he not hear it? She could hardly tell them that it was because David always felt forced into drinking more than he wanted to when he was with them. That he preferred to have an easy excuse *not* to drink. 'It must just fall like that. He gets his fair share of being chauffeured, believe me. A glass of white for me, please.'

Priya leaned forwards to smack her husband's hand away from his fifth scoop of cashews. 'Didn't you and Katherine used to roll a dice to see who drove, David?'

'Did you?' Lauren laughed. 'That was a bad move on your part. She always had the luck of the devil, that one.'

There was a painful silence as she realised what she'd said. Someone who had died in a car accident aged only thirty-five could hardly have been called lucky.

As always, David was the balm to any awkwardness. 'That she did. Turned me into a borderline teetotaller. Anyway, Luke, tell me about this new electric car you've just bought.'

Luke didn't need asking twice. 'It's a hybrid. Absolutely brilliant. Do you know—'

Priya held up a hand to stop him. 'Hang on. Let us two escape to the kitchen before you start discussing range and battery capacity. Come on, Hannah. Let's go and pretend to help Lauren in the kitchen.'

Hannah's heart sank. Anytime they were alone, the subject of Katherine seemed to come up. It wasn't that she objected to it; Katherine had been their friend, and she and David had been married for over ten years. It was just the way they did it. Katherine was so good at this. Or Katherine would have definitely known the answer to that. She'd been funny and clever and beautiful, and Hannah was always left with the impression that they thought she wasn't in the same league. They were probably right.

She could hardly refuse, though, without seeming rude, so she followed Priya's lead and took a stool at the island in the middle of Lauren's large, modern kitchen, while Lauren ferried a glass of lemonade to David.

'You're looking well.' Priya looked her up and down. 'Is that a new dress?'

It was new. She'd been out and bought it with tonight in mind: a new dress was always effective armour. 'Yes. Thanks. I saw it on my lunch hour last week in a new shop by the station. It called to me because David loves me in blue.' The look in his eyes when she'd descended the stairs earlier had made the expense worthwhile.

'Your dress?' Lauren was back in the room with a glass of wine, which she placed in front of Hannah. 'I noticed that too. It looks great.'

Somehow, their attention was almost as uncomfortable as being ignored. That was her issue though, not theirs. And she had promised to play nicely. 'Thank you. You both look great too.'

Priya snorted. 'This dress is ancient. Not that my husband would notice if I had a new dress on anyway.'

Lauren was wielding a large chopping knife as she made headway through a sizeable bunch of tarragon. 'Mine neither. But Hannah and David are still in the first flush of love. It's different for them.'

First flush of love made it sound like they'd just met rather than being married for over a year. It was irritating being made to feel like a short-term girlfriend.

It had happened quickly between the two of them; she wasn't denying that. David had been widowed for less than a year when they'd first met, and it was only five months later that they'd got married. She could understand his friends' concern – hadn't her own cautioned her that he might be on the mother of all rebounds? But she and David were old enough to both know what they wanted.

Speaking of which. 'Can you excuse me? I just need to use your bathroom.'

'Of course. You know where it is.'

Hannah had read somewhere that Oscar winners often kept their gold statuette in a downstairs toilet as a way of appearing humorously humble while actually displaying it in the room that visitors would be most likely to frequent. Perhaps that's why Ben's cameraman award adorned the shelf in here. She had a vague memory of Lauren telling her about Katherine winning a prestigious award. Of course she had. Sadly, there were no such awards for paediatric speech and language therapists for Hannah to display anywhere.

While she was in there, she took the opportunity to freshen her make-up. David made her feel like the most beautiful woman alive, but five minutes with his friends had the opposite effect.

On the way back from the bathroom, Hannah stopped to look at the mosaic of photographs lining the hallway. Baby photos of Maisie, family holidays and there, right in the middle, the large photo of the six of them: Lauren and Ben, Priya and Luke, David and Katherine. She leaned closer to look at her predecessor. Katherine really had been a very beautiful woman: wide smile, great teeth. Maybe Luke was right – she *was* orally fixated.

In the photograph, five people looked directly at the camera, but David's eyes were on his wife. It was a look of pure adoration. Hannah wasn't a jealous woman, but it was hard not to wonder if he ever looked at her the same way.

They made such a handsome couple; like the beautiful people you saw on billboards or on the cover of a magazine. Her long dark curls, green eyes and flawless skin; his thick blonde hair and the deep blue eyes she almost lost herself in the first time they met. It was easy to see why she'd been so surprised that someone like him would fall for someone like her. Maybe that's what had surprised his friends too?

Lauren emerged from the kitchen and paused behind Hannah, looking at the photograph over her shoulder. Her sigh was dramatically loud. 'She really was lovely, you know. I miss her terribly.'

Hannah knew she was being unfair. She wouldn't know what to do with her grief if she lost one of her friends in such a tragic accident. 'I can imagine. It must have been so hard for you all.'

As always, any mention of Katherine brought on an anecdote of another of her wealth of accomplishments. 'She was one of the funniest people I have ever known. She was a really good mimic. Has David ever told you that? There was this one night she did all these impressions of her teachers and Priya and I couldn't breathe for laughing. And we didn't even know her teachers. That's how funny it was.' She sighed. 'It's just not the same without her.'

As if he'd sensed a silent distress signal, David came through the doorway from the sitting room, waving a beer glass. 'Your husband informs me that there's some non-alcoholic beer somewhere in the depths of your kitchen. He says someone brought it to a party and then drank all of his Belgian imported beer instead.'

Lauren rolled her eyes and took the beer glass. 'I know where it is. I'll bring it through.'

As soon as she disappeared into the kitchen, David wrapped his arms around Hannah and rested his chin on her head so that they were both looking at the photograph. 'Has she been laying it on thick about Katherine? I'm sorry.'

The strength of his arms around her always made her feel better; like she could let herself go and he would catch her. 'It's okay. You look really happy there.'

As always, the invisible shutter came down. 'Do we? Come on, Ben is trying to persuade me to cycle the London to Brighton bike ride and I need you to run interference.'

She let him lead her back to the sitting room. In contrast to his friends, he never wanted to talk about his first wife. When pressed, he'd say it was another life, that it was painful, that he didn't want Hannah to feel uncomfortable.

To be fair, it wasn't him that made her uncomfortable, like she was second best. But once they had a baby, were a family, that was going to change. Tomorrow's appointment was going to be the beginning.

TWO

HANNAH

Hartswood Fertility Clinic was only fifteen miles from where they lived, but it was at the end of a long, twisty country lane, so it took them almost forty minutes to drive there. Then they had to wait another ten minutes in the near silent waiting room before the receptionist called out their names. Once they were through the double door, Dr Ellis's office was at the end of a long corridor. If Hannah could have run the length of it, she would have. Good news or bad, the sooner they knew, the sooner they could do something about it. But she had a positive feeling about this. Even if they needed some help to get pregnant, it would be worth it. David would make a fabulous dad, and she was going to do her best to be a good mum too.

It had been a sure sign that she was starting to fall hard for David when she found herself imagining what their babies would look like. Maybe it was because she was already thirty-eight when they met. Or maybe it was because, for the first time ever, she'd found someone who ticked pretty much every box. He was funny and kind, and the way his eyes crinkled when he smiled gave her a funny feeling in the pit of her stomach. The night they'd met, she'd come to the bar with a few colleagues for a quick drink after work; he'd been forced on a night out with two friends. The barman had mistaken them for a couple and, when she'd realised that David had just inadvertently paid for her drink, she'd blushed to her roots. 'I am so sorry. Please let me buy you one back.'

'It's fine.' He smiled, but it didn't reach his eyes. 'It's been a while since I've bought a drink for a woman I've just met. My mates will be proud of me.'

The flutter in her stomach hoped that he was flirting with her, but he turned immediately to rejoin his friends in the corner of the bar.

It didn't matter that he'd refused her offer of a drink; Hannah's father had brought her up to always pay her way. To that end, she kept an eye on his group so that, the moment he got up to buy another drink, she could swoop in with her credit card.

He jumped as she appeared beside him, then laughed. This time he looked a little more relaxed. 'So now I'm having a drink bought for me by a woman I've just met? You do realise how much you're elevating my status right now?'

This time, he didn't go straight back to his friends. It must have been the three gin and tonics she'd now had, because she never would have had the courage to speak to a man as good-looking as him otherwise. When she'd described him to Tessa and Charlotte the next day, she'd said he was 'a bit Ryan Reynolds' and they'd both sighed and wished they were still single.

At Hartswood, the doctors didn't wear white coats. Dr Ellis was immaculate in a creaseless grey suit and low expensive-looking shoes. She welcomed them into her office with a smile and then sat opposite them, behind a large oak desk, a blue card-board file open in front of her. On the printed papers inside, Hannah and David's future was mapped out in a series of test results. Hannah tried to radiate positivity as she smiled at him;

he gave her a wink of support. After everything he'd been through in losing his first wife, this had to be good news. He deserved it.

'I'm afraid it's not good news.'

Dr Ellis's words slammed into Hannah like a bullet. David reached for her hand, but she couldn't move. 'Just say it quickly.'

'Unfortunately, we've gone through the results and we think that it's highly unlikely that IVF will be successful using your eggs. Therefore, that's not a path that we can recommend.'

With every inch of her, Hannah had been hoping for more positive news. After the shock of being told she would need help to fall pregnant, they'd chosen this very expensive clinic because of their impressive success rates. 'What does that mean for us? What do we need to do to them?'

Dr Ellis was always a model of calm. 'Well, there are various options. You would be able to use donor eggs, for example.'

She clearly hadn't understood what Hannah meant. 'No, I mean, what can you do with my eggs? This is only our first try. Don't people do this several times before they just give up?'

David squeezed her hand again. Though he hadn't gone into detail, she knew that he had wanted children from his first marriage. This must be painful for him too. But she needed to ask these questions. Needed to know.

Dr Ellis was very kind and patient. 'We already knew from the blood test that you had high levels of follicle stimulation hormone and oestrogen. We talked about how that can indicate low egg production and low quality of eggs.'

At every stage, Dr Ellis had answered all Hannah's ques-tions – however detailed – and had been particularly sensitive with both of them. But her reminder that 'we talked about this' made Hannah feel like a child who wasn't behaving herself. 'I know that. But IVF means you can extract multiple eggs at once. Surely that increases our chances?'

Gentle, but firm, Dr Ellis gave them the cold, hard science. 'There is no treatment to improve the oocyte quality. Whilst IVF allows us to extract multiple eggs in the hope that some of them can reach the required quality, in my professional opinion, you would just be putting yourselves through an awful lot medically and mentally with very little chance of any success.'

Very little? That didn't mean no chance at all. 'What percentage of a chance is there?'

Dr Ellis's face was so kind, so sympathetic that it was painful. 'We're talking a miracle, Hannah.'

David sagged beside her, and she looked at him through the blur of tears. He had his eyes closed. What was he thinking?

The journey home from the clinic was quiet. David turned off the radio as soon as they got into the car; the chirpy DJ and pop songs too brash and bright for the way they felt. Without discussing it, they'd made a tacit agreement not to speak about this until they got home. For the forty-minute drive, Hannah kept her hand on David's leg, and he would pat it from time to time. She stared out of the passenger window, not wanting to distract him with the tears that wouldn't stop falling down her face. She didn't have the energy to keep wiping them away.

Every part of her ached with loss. She'd wanted a baby – their baby – so much. Had pictured every moment: coming home from the hospital, early morning feeds, walks with the pram. And it wasn't only for her; they were going to be the family that David had been denied in his first marriage.

He'd told her about Katherine that first night in the bar. No details, just that he was a widower, and that his friends were trying to drag him back into society. Though she barely knew him, the crack in his voice and the broken edge to his smile made this so much more than a pick-up in a bar. Both their groups of friends had left them to it long before, and it was almost a surprise when they realised that the bar was closing. He'd insisted on paying for an Uber to get her home safely. Made her promise to text him when she got home. It was nice that he was so considerate, but she'd also hoped that it was a way of giving her his number and getting hers.

The car bumped up onto their driveway and the jolt brought her back in time to wipe her face. She needn't have bothered. As soon as they got through the front door of the house, David dropped his coat and keys onto the floor and turned to hold her, as fresh sobs ripped through her body. When she could finally speak, she said the only thing that had been on her mind the whole way home. 'I'm sorry. I'm so sorry.'

'Hey.' He pulled her gently from his chest and looked into her eyes. 'Don't apologise. Never apologise. This is not your fault, Hannah.'

They both knew that wasn't true. 'But it's my eggs. It's my eggs that aren't good enough to make a baby.'

Tenderly, he wiped tears from her face with the back of his fingers. 'I know it's hard, but it's just one of those things. We can't do anything about it. No one can. It's just really bad luck, that's all.'

How was she letting him comfort her like this? She'd sworn she wasn't going to make this difficult for him. Right from the word go, he'd been unsure about whether to start down this road. Though he hadn't talked about it in any detail, she knew how badly he would like to be a father, so she could only assume that Katherine hadn't wanted – or been ready – to have children. 'I'm sorry I made you go through this. I should have listened.'

From the moment they'd met that night in the bar, their relationship had been on fast-forward. It wasn't as if Hannah had never been in love before, but this was different. She'd always laughed at people who talked about soulmates, but with David, that was exactly how it had felt. The ease of their relationship made it even more of a shock when she hadn't fallen pregnant within a few months of trying. The quiet, intimate wedding they'd planned came and went and there was still no baby. It had been a disappointment, but, like most things, there was no point getting upset about it and wondering why. Far better to meet it head-on and work out what they needed to do. Hadn't that been what her parents had always taught her? *Just work hard and you'll get what you want, Hannah.*

David pulled her close again, into the warmth of his arms. 'You were right that we should try. We had to know, right?'

To know. To know for sure that her body would never be able to produce a baby on its own. She started to sob again.

That night, David collected takeaway food from the Turkish restaurant on the High Street because neither of them could face cooking. The chicken shish and rice came in individual cardboard boxes so they didn't even need to get plates out. Instead, they sat on the sofa and tried to find something funny to watch on Netflix.

Hannah's mobile beeped. The group chat. Tessa's message: *How's things?* was followed by a second beep from Charlotte: *How did it go? Don't leave us hanging.* She smiled. She could screenshot this as a perfect example of Tessa's tact and Charlotte's cut-to-the-chase clarity.

She tapped out a quick reply: *Not good. Talk to you both tomorrow.* adding a sad face emoji that didn't come within the same postcode as her current mood. She couldn't face even typing the details right now.

David dropped the TV remote on the couch. 'I can't find anything we haven't seen before that doesn't include babies or hospitals.'

Hannah picked at the chicken with her fork. 'Don't worry about it. I don't think I can concentrate anyway. I just can't understand it. There must be something they can do?'

David pushed his box of food onto the table; he'd barely touched it. He twisted in his seat to face her. 'I know it's hard.'

Hard didn't even come close. She'd wanted a baby for so long. With David, she'd finally met someone she wanted to start a family with and now she was being told that it would never happen. It wasn't just sadness she felt, it was anger because it was so bloody unfair. 'I don't want to just give up on a baby of my own, David. There must be other doctors we can talk to? Research we can do? There has to be a way.'

David closed his eyes and, when he opened them, they were so unbearably sad that she could barely look at him. 'I don't think I can go through all of that, Hannah. I'm so sorry, but we said we'd always be honest with each other.'

They had said that, but today she'd had more honesty than she could cope with. 'I know that's what we agreed. But that was before. It's my body that we're talking about, and I'm willing – wanting – to do it.'

David was shaking his head slowly. 'I'm not sure... Fertility treatment... It's a big thing. People refer to fertility treatment as if it's as easy as popping a headache pill, but it's a lot to go through.'

She wasn't an idiot. Hadn't she held Charlotte's hand through three failed cycles of IVF? 'I know that, David. But it's worth it, isn't it?'

He reached out and took her hand. 'But Dr Ellis was pretty clear that it wouldn't work. You'd be putting yourself through all of that treatment and there would still be heartache at the end. We've got to be sensible.'

'I don't want to be sensible!' She hadn't meant to raise her voice. The way he flinched made her lower it immediately. 'I'm sorry.'

'It's okay. I'm upset too. And I love you. And if this doesn't happen for us, I will still love you. We've got each other.'

This was what he did. He held her and he made everything okay. But he couldn't make this okay. When he looked at her in the deep, searching way he had, she felt so loved, so cared for. Why wasn't it enough? 'I just want a baby – our baby – so very much.'

Collapsing back onto him, her head nestled in the dip at the front of his shoulder, Hannah tried to regain control of her breathing. David rested his cheek on the top of her head and rubbed her arm. 'There are other ways we can have a baby, Han. We could adopt. Look how well it's worked out for Charlotte and Jim. Those boys are brilliant.'

Adoption had worked out well for Charlotte, but – even though she hated herself for thinking it – that wasn't what Hannah wanted. How could she make him understand that she wanted to have her own child? That she needed to create her own family? She wanted a baby that was part hers and part David's and who belonged to them and them alone. There had to be a way to get that.

'I don't want to give up on carrying a baby. Can we at least book an appointment to talk about our options? To find out if there's another way?'

There was a long silence before David replied. 'Of course. If that's what you want to do. But let's just take a breath before we rush into anything.'

THREE

HANNAH

The staffroom was empty. Alongside the large jar of non-branded coffee for common use were another three jars bearing people's names written in permanent marker. After lying awake for half the night, Hannah needed a large cup of caffeine to keep her awake.

David had suggested she take the day off. He'd made her a cup of tea as he did every morning and brought it to her in bed. 'You've had such a big shock and you've hardly slept. You never take a day off sick. They'll understand, and I can call in for you if you like?'

Sat on the bed beside her, he looked so concerned that she felt guilty. This was happening to him too; it wasn't just about her. She never took a day off sick, because her dad had drummed it into her from a young age that you didn't do that. Work, punctuality and family: they were the three pillars of Brian Hughes. It was times like this that she missed him even more than usual.

But it wasn't her Protestant work ethic that forced her into the shower, her suit and the car. The fear of staying home with only her spiralling thoughts for company was far worse than

going into work today. The numbness of the shock of yesterday
had worn off and now she just felt really, really sad.

She'd started to screw the lid off the cheap coffee when
Charlotte found her. 'You're in early. Don't drink that muck.
I've brought a jar of the good stuff with me. How did you get on
yesterday?'

Charlotte was a whirling dervish in the mornings. With
four-year-old twins to get ready and drop off to the nursery
before she came into work, her morning was a tightly run schedule. Still, she managed to look effortlessly smart with her
cropped red hair and matching fingernails. Hannah watched
her open the dishwasher and rattle through the cups to find
theirs. Charlotte was one of her best friends, but she couldn't
tell her anything right now. One word of comfort, one hug, one
tear in Charlotte's eye and she would be done for. Putting one
foot in front of the other was all she could do right now. 'It was
complicated. I'll tell you later.'

Pausing with a spoon of coffee in her hand, Charlotte's eyes
narrowed. She was sharp, but she was also sensitive. 'Okay. We
can talk about it tonight when we meet up with Tessa.'

Hannah had completely forgotten about that. They were
supposed to be meeting their third musketeer after work. The
last thing she wanted was a night in a noisy bar. 'Actually, I'm
not sure I'm in the mood for going out on the town tonight.'

Charlotte didn't probe. 'No problem. What about if you
came to mine instead? I'm sure Jim would be more than happy
to have a night out instead.'

Her two best friends in Charlotte's comfortable sitting
room? It was exactly what she needed. 'Yes please. That would
be lovely.'

Charlotte smiled as she filled their cups with scalding
water. 'Great. I'll even crack out the good biscuits.'

. . .

Hannah's room was near the main school reception. About a third of the size of a regular classroom, it had a square of desks set up in the middle for group activities, but she also met a lot of the students on their own. Today, her first student was Ethan: almost five and with the kind of grin that always made her smile in return. He'd been coming to see her for the last six months and was really beginning to make progress.

When she first started working with a child, she asked their parents to fill out a questionnaire about them. What they liked to do, or watch on TV, or what their favourite foods were. It gave her a head start in engaging their attention and interest. She knew that Ethan loved *Paw Patrol*, hot dogs and playing football, so most of their sessions involved one of those things.

When he arrived at her door, he had a picture in his hand and he passed it to her without looking at her directly. 'Is that for me? Thank you.'

She took the damp crumpled paper from his hand: a drawing of a boy and a woman with an *almost* round ball in between them. The woman had long dark brown hair and a huge red smile. Hannah laid the picture on the small table. 'This is fantastic, Ethan. Who is this in the picture?'

Ethan sat down on the small chair beside her and pointed at the boy, 'Me,' and then the woman, 'Lou.'

Ys and Ls were still very tricky for him, so she emphasised the Y in: 'You and me? I love it. And what's this?' She pointed at the football.

He looked at her as if she was stupid. 'A ball.'

Fs had been difficult for him too, so she asked, 'What kind of ball?'

She could see him concentrate hard. 'F... F... Football.'

Holding up her hand for a high five, she was also rewarded with the killer grin. 'Yes, it's a football. Great job, Ethan. I'm going to put this up behind my desk and then we can start work. I'll show your mummy when she comes in later too.'

As she pinned the picture up on the corkboard behind her desk, she had to take a minute to compose herself. There was something about it – this picture of her and Ethan – that made her heart ache. She looked at all the other pictures the children had done for her. Her children. That's what she, and the classroom teachers, called them. 'Hannah, your Joseph stood up and talked about his goldfish today' or 'Your Ellie read a whole sentence aloud to the teaching assistant today.' They did feel like her children, but they weren't. Like her godchildren, she only got to spend a little time with them; they were borrowed. And every hour in this job made her yearn for her own child even more.

She swallowed down the sadness and turned to Ethan with a smile. 'Shall we get the *Paw Patrol* cards out and have a game?'

Later that afternoon, she had a meeting booked with Ethan's mother to talk about his progress and discuss how the strategies were going at home. When Hannah collected her from reception, she was bustled up in a thick coat, but she unbuttoned it as soon as she came into the small classroom. 'It's warm in here after that wind outside.'

'Yes. It gets a bit too warm sometimes. There's a hook on the back of the door for your coat if you want to hang it up.'

Hannah walked to her desk to pick up Ethan's file. She always preferred to take these meetings around the small table she used to work with the children, rather than sit across a desk from the parents. It felt more collegiate; they should be a team.

She turned back to Ethan's mother at the exact same moment as she herself turned back from the coat hook. Hannah almost gasped. *She's pregnant.*

When you're trying to have a baby, it feels as if the rest of the world is just about to or has just given birth. Prams full of newborns, dads with baby pouches, toddlers on the end of safety straps – they assail you from everywhere. Hannah had perfected the art of smiling indulgently while her heart tore a little more. This was the look she pasted on now. 'Oh, congratulations.'

Ethan's mother blushed as she stroked the convex outline of her stomach. By Hannah's reckoning she must have been five or six months pregnant. 'Oh, thanks, yes, it was a bit of a surprise. We weren't planning on having another one yet.'

She pulled a comical 'what are we like?' face. Somehow it made it worse when people said they'd got pregnant by accident. As if they were so fertile, they just couldn't help it.

'I'm sure Ethan will make a lovely big brother.'

His mother's face changed to concern. 'Do you think? Because we are a bit worried about it. I mean, he has had our full attention for the last four years and, obviously, he needs a lot of support. That's why we had planned to wait longer before having another one. We don't want him to feel pushed out or like we're abandoning him.'

Her eyes filled as she spoke. Pregnancy hormones were the most likely culprit, but Hannah's heart softened towards her. 'As long as you prepare him, I'm sure he'll be fine. I can talk to him about it in our sessions too, if you would like?'

Ethan's mother beamed at her as she found a tissue in her pocket and blew her nose. 'Oh, thank you so much. I would really appreciate it. And you think he'll be okay with having a baby brother?' She wrinkled her nose. 'We found out the sex because we thought it might help him to know who was coming. I even thought about letting him name the baby, but my husband thinks we might end up with a boy called Rubble or Rocky.'

Hannah was familiar with all the *Paw Patrol* characters from her conversations with Ethan. 'It could be worse – what about Robo-Dog?' She smiled. 'I think he will be absolutely fine.

And it might even help with his speech. Talking to the baby would be good practice for him.'

She could see the relief in Ethan's mum's dropped shoulders. 'And you don't think he'll feel pushed out?'

Hannah wasn't an expert on family dynamics, but Ethan's mother was only looking for a reassuring word. 'I'm sure he'll be great. I mean, who doesn't want a brother or sister to play with?'

She knew that she had. Much as it had been lovely to have had her parents' undivided attention, the older she'd got, the more she'd wanted a brother or sister. She'd had good friends, but on family holidays, she'd been desperate for a playmate on the beach or in the countryside. Even as an adult, she would have dearly loved a sibling to share the emotional load of losing her dad.

Ethan's mother smiled. 'Thank you. You've made me feel so much better. I really am excited about the new baby. I've always wanted two children. It feels like a complete family to me.'

Hannah kept her well-practised smile on her face. 'Yes. Me too.'

The desire to have a family was eating her away from the inside. Yesterday, they'd said that they would let the dust settle, take a breath before deciding what to do. But she didn't want to wait any longer. Tonight, she would talk to David and they would make a plan. She wanted a baby. The only thing they needed to work out was how.

FOUR

HANNAH

When she got home, David was in the kitchen, layering a lasagne.

She'd always loved watching him cook. A natural chef, he enjoyed being in the kitchen so much more than she did, and most of the evenings they spent at home involved him trying out a new recipe he'd googled and shopped for. Sometimes she helped, other times she filled him in on her day, and asked about his, with a glass of wine in her hand.

They'd redecorated most of the rooms in this house – starting with the bedroom – as soon as she'd moved in. But a new kitchen had felt like an unnecessary expense when the granite worktops and high-gloss white cabinets were pretty much what she'd have chosen herself. Only occasionally, she would wonder if Katherine had sat on the same stool, watching David in the same way.

Tonight, she dropped her keys into the bowl by the letter rack and wrapped her arms around his waist, laying her cheek in the space between his shoulder blades. He was so solid, so warm, so dependable. 'What are you doing home so early?'

'I couldn't focus on the numbers so I asked my boss for the afternoon off.'

'Sharon?'

'Yep. She said I could leave this once, but not to make a habit of it.'

Despite her mood, Hannah smiled into his back. David was a partner in an accountancy firm. Sharon was his personal assistant. A sixty-two-year-old grandmother of five who could probably have run the business on her own.

David leaned across the kitchen counter for a towel, wiped his hands and turned in her arms. He brushed the hair from her shoulders and leaned down to kiss her neck, just below her ear, then leaned his forehead on hers, looking her in the eye. 'I wanted to be here when you got home. How was your day?'

Even after being married for over a year, it still made her stomach flip when she looked in his eyes. 'Okay. I was busy, so that's good.'

'Well, speaking of busy, there's a bag of salad over there that needs washing and chopping.' He kissed her cheek and winked at her before letting her go.

Preparing dinner together was an everyday routine, but nothing in their life seemed usual any longer. Their relationship had moved pretty fast – too fast for some people – and it had always felt as if they were building towards something. A family. And now? What happened now?

Hannah pulled the leaves from a gem lettuce and threw them into a colander. She didn't want to just pretend that everything was normal. 'I can't stop thinking about it, David. And about what we're going to do next. I mean, I know that I still want a baby.'

She watched him to gauge his immediate response. Last night, as she'd lain in bed awake, she'd wished she knew more about his first marriage. She'd accepted that he didn't like to talk about Katherine. But in the early hours of the morning, she'd wondered if his reluctance to pursue further fertility treatment was because he'd been through it before? Although, surely he would have mentioned that?

David passed her two tomatoes that he'd just washed. 'I still want a baby too. I'm not suggesting that we just give up on it. I do want to be a dad. I want to be a parent with you. I suppose we just need to work out what route is best for us. Adoption is an option obviously.'

It was an option of course, and this was the second time he'd suggested it. She knew from Charlotte how successful adoption could be. But she couldn't give up on the dream of carrying a child herself. Not yet. 'Dr Ellis mentioned donor eggs.'

David stared down at his hands as he sliced a red onion for the salad. 'How do you feel about that?'

Though she'd thought about it all the way home from work, she still wasn't sure. 'Well, on the practical side, it makes sense. I don't have the eggs, so we get them from someone else. We can still use your sperm then, because there's nothing wrong with you.'

David frowned and took hold of her hand. 'There's nothing wrong with you either. You're perfect, Han. Like I said to you last night, this is enough for me. Us. This marriage. I didn't even know I would get you.'

She loved him for that, but there was no escaping the physical truth of the matter. 'You know what I mean. It's okay. I am disappointed, but I'm a grown-up. I need to think realistically. We can still have a child that is biologically yours, and I can still carry our baby and give birth. Two out of three isn't bad.'

She tried to make her voice upbeat, but she couldn't keep the wobble from it. It *was* a logical decision, and she just had to get her head around it, make it okay. She needed him to be on board with it too. He would carry her through it.

David pulled her in and held her close. For a few moments they just stood there. With her ear to his warm chest, she heard his voice as an echo. 'There is another option which I need to mention, but I don't know if now is the right time. Or, to be honest, if there would ever be a right time...'

She pulled herself away so that she could look him in the face but close enough that his comforting hands still rested behind her shoulders. 'What do you mean?'

He ran his hands from her shoulders, down the length of her arms, until he was holding both her hands in his. 'Shall we sit down for a minute?'

As soon as they were seated in the sitting room, David began. 'This is probably something I should have told you before now. I almost did a couple of times, but I didn't want to – I don't know – bring things from the past into this, into us.'

He was starting to scare her a little now. This was what he always said when the subject of Katherine came up. *That was then; this is now.* She'd been curious, of course she had. But it wasn't as if she didn't know anything about her. Lauren and Priya had made sure of that in their constant references to how exceptional she was in every conceivable way. 'What is it? You can tell me anything.'

He took a deep breath. 'Okay. Well, Katherine and I, we did this too. We started fertility treatment.'

She tried not to let her face register her shock. Much as she had considered this again in the depths of the darkness last night, she hadn't thought it would actually be true. How had he not told her this before? 'Wow. That's a pretty big revelation.'

'I know. I'm sorry. It wasn't that I was keeping it secret. It's just that... well, the whole thing was such a... mess. We shouldn't have done it and... Oh, Hannah, I didn't want to go through it all with you.'

Did she want to know what he meant by a 'mess'? At least

this explained why he had known that IVF could be difficult. 'I see. I still think you should have told me.'

He grasped her hand. 'I know. I know. I almost did a few times but, when it seemed as if history was repeating itself, it just felt as if telling you would make it worse.'

It was the 'history repeating itself' that hit her the hardest. On one level, she almost understood; it must have been tough for him to relive what had happened before. But she couldn't help feeling that he'd been less than honest with her. Not wanting to talk about Katherine was one thing, but this felt like lying by omission. 'I don't know what to say. That's quite a bombshell.'

All of his friends must be aware of this too. Lauren and Priya had known all this time that David and Katherine had been trying for a baby before she died. Her cheeks burned. Was that where all the 'David is so good with kids' came from? Did they feel sorry for him? Another part of his life she was shut out from.

He looked so contrite though that she knew he hadn't meant it to hurt her. 'I'm so sorry, Hannah. I should have realised that you'd have wanted to know.'

And now she did. But she didn't understand how this gave them another option. 'So what made the difference? Why are you telling me now?'

He paused, looking at her as if gauging whether she was ready for the next hit. His grip on her hands got a little firmer. 'Well, the thing is, when we underwent the IVF, the clinic fertilised five eggs.'

He paused as if to let her take that in. She'd done her own research on IVF in the last few weeks – failing to prepare is preparing to fail – so she knew that this was pretty standard. 'Okay?'

Still he was staring at her; it made her stomach tighten. 'And we only used one of them. We had one cycle of IVF.'

She was beginning to realise what he was getting at. 'Which means...'

'Which means that there are four embryos still in storage.'

It took a few moments for that information to make it to her brain. 'Embryos? So Katherine's eggs and your—'

'Sperm. Yes. Four successfully fertilised eggs ready for implantation.'

The medical terminology wasn't making this any easier to get her head around. 'And the plan was obviously for you and Katherine to use them? They were like your children-in-waiting?'

David frowned. 'I don't think it's wise to think of them like that. I mean, there are never any guarantees. Katherine's... issues... were complicated. The first cycle didn't work out.'

'So you haven't got a couple of kids somewhere that I don't know about too?'

She'd meant that to come out as a joke. To lighten the tension a little. But even she could hear that it didn't land like that.

David grimaced. 'I'm really sorry that I didn't tell you. I know this sounds unbelievable, but I hadn't thought about it. When she... had her accident, it was the last thing I could consider and then, I guess I just pushed it to the back of my mind. I'm sorry, Hannah.'

How could he not have thought about it when they'd been talking about nothing but fertility treatment lately? And, if he'd kept this from her, what else was there that she didn't know? Up until now, she'd accepted that he had another chapter of his life that he didn't want to share with her. That he'd turned the page and started a new story. 'I just... it's a lot to take in.'

'Of course.'

They were quiet for a few moments. She focused on his thumb, stroking the hand he held. As his words settled around her, she realised that he hadn't just told her about the IVF. He'd started this conversation by referring to the embryos as an option. She looked up at him and realised he'd been watching her, his eyes uncertain, concerned. He hadn't seemed that vulnerable in a while. 'So are you suggesting that we could use the embryos – yours and Katherine's – for us?'

He met her eye, in that way he had of seeing right inside her. Even when they were with others, he had a way of looking at her that made her feel like the only person in the room. 'It's probably a ridiculous idea, but I just wanted to tell you. That they are there. That it is, like I say, an option.' He screwed up his face. 'It's ridiculous, right?'

Was it ridiculous? She wanted a baby and there were embryos there waiting for them. Embryos that were already genetically his. But not hers. It wasn't the dream; it wasn't what she'd wanted. But it was something. 'I don't know, David. Is it?'

Leaning back in the chair, he let her hand slip from his. 'We don't have to rush into anything. We can just put it on the table, with the other options. You need to see how it feels. It has to be right for both of us.'

She was glad she hadn't cancelled her night with Tessa and Charlotte. A bit of space would help right now. 'You're right. We don't need to rush a decision. But I'm going to Charlotte's after dinner, so shall we eat?'

He smiled as he got up. 'I'll stick the lasagne in the oven. When you tell them all of this, can you make sure they don't think I'm a villain?'

Of course he knew her well enough to expect that she was going to process all of this with the help of her best friends. She returned his smile. 'I'll try.'

Both Charlotte and Tessa loved David, and the way he was with her, but they'd both been more than curious that he never spoke about Katherine. She could just imagine how they were going to react to this latest revelation.

FIVE

HANNAH

Tessa was already at Charlotte's when Hannah arrived. She was the one who opened the front door, her hands full of envelopes. 'Come in. Although I warn you that she might put you to work on a production line.'

'No, no.' Charlotte came down the stairs into the hallway as Hannah walked in through the front door. 'I'll let you stop now that Hannah is here. The boys have finally gone to sleep so we can relax.'

Hannah followed them out to the kitchen where the counter was strewn with paper. 'What have you been doing?'

'Invites to the party. It's become a beast.'

Hannah glanced down at the guest list, an A4 page crammed with names; she was pleased to see hers and David's close to the top. 'That's a lot of people. More like a wedding than a ten-year anniversary.'

Charlotte groaned. 'I know. It's just that there are still a lot of extended family who haven't met the boys yet. It seemed like an easy way for everyone to meet them at once.' She rolled her eyes. 'Although easy is not what it has become.'

Tessa waved the envelopes. 'I've been on stuffing and addressing duty.'

'I can help. What shall I do?'

'No, it's fine. We want to focus on you. I'll just make a drink and then we'll go through to the lounge. Coffee or tea?'

'Coffee please. But let's sit in here and do this while we talk.'

Charlotte knew her well enough to understand that she'd prefer to be doing something. 'Well, that's fine by me. I'll get the kettle on and then I can give you my full attention.'

Tessa pulled out a chair at the dining table for Hannah. 'Charlotte is writing the names on the invites then I'm writing the envelopes. You can put one inside the other, stick them down and put a stamp on.'

There was already quite a sizeable pile completed and only half the list of names had a tick mark next to it. 'It didn't take quite this long for my wedding, did it?'

Charlotte called over her shoulder from where she was making their drinks. 'That's because you couldn't wait more than five minutes to get married. You barely had time to buy the invitations, let alone send them out.'

She wasn't wrong. From that first drink in the bar, David had been open that he was a widower and that Hannah was the first woman he'd dated since he'd lost his wife nine months before. When she threw herself into the relationship, talked about falling in love, her friends had been worried for her. 'Take care, Hannah. Nine months is really recent. It might be a rebound.' And she knew that his friends had given similar advice.

But they'd just clicked. Like he was the missing piece of her puzzle. And it was more than that. They wanted the same things – marriage, children – and, given their ages, it had seemed pointless to wait. He'd proposed that Christmas, three months after they'd met. They'd stopped using contraception that same night and arranged a wedding two months later because, Hannah had said, 'I don't want to have to keep altering a wedding dress because I'm pregnant.' She could cry now for her naivety.

Charlotte cleared a space on the table for a mug of coffee and a plate of cookies. 'They're lemon. Ignore the shape – the boys were helping me. I can confirm that they washed their hands.'

She slipped into the seat to Hannah's right, and Tessa picked up her own cup and nodded at Hannah. 'Okay. Go.'

Both their faces were an open book of sympathy and love. Whatever she told them would be met with kindness and support. But where to start? 'Well, basically, my eggs are rubbish. The chances of being able to use them are pretty much zero.'

Tessa reached out and squeezed her arm. 'Oh, honey. I'm so sorry.'

Hannah had been determined not to cry, but when she looked up at Charlotte, the deep wells of understanding in her eyes made it difficult. Charlotte had been up, down and around the fertility rollercoaster for several years before they'd decided to adopt. She, more than anyone, would know how Hannah was feeling right now.

She reached across the table and took Hannah's other hand. She didn't need to say anything – what could she say? – for Hannah to feel her support. 'It really, really sucks.'

Despite her best efforts, tears rolled down Hannah's cheeks. 'I know this sounds childish, but I just keep thinking it's so bloody unfair.'

That was the overriding feeling. Her desire to have a baby had been growing for years, but it had taken a long time for her to find David. A man that she wanted to be with forever, who wanted to start a family with her, who would make the most wonderful father. And now that had been snatched away.

'It *is* bloody unfair.' Charlotte tilted her head as if she was about to say something profound. 'Shall I forget the coffee and open the wine?'

Hannah's laugh spluttered through her tears. 'Yes please.'

Over a glass of wine, she gave them more details from the appointment and what the doctor had said.

'Have you thought about your options yet?' Tessa had gone back to addressing envelopes, then passing them to Hannah for her to insert the invitation and stick it down.

Hannah took the next one from her hands and slid a silken invite inside. 'I am thinking about egg donation.'

Charlotte was writing names at the top of invitations before passing them to Tessa and she nodded as she wrote. 'That makes sense.'

It was the next part that was going to be tricky to explain. Best to get it all out at once. 'Also, David told me that he and Katherine also went through IVF and there are embryos still frozen that they didn't use.'

Hannah focused her attention on slipping the next invitation into its envelope, licking the glue and then pressing it closed. The silence emanating from her two friends was almost tangible. When she looked up again, they were both staring at her. 'I know. It's a lot to take in.'

Charlotte was the first to recover. 'I can't believe he hasn't told you this before.'

This was Hannah's thought too. On the way over here, she'd turned it over in her mind. Even though they were her best friends, she didn't want them to think badly of him. 'Me too. But you know he doesn't like to talk about her.'

She saw Charlotte glance at Tessa and she knew what was coming. Tessa was at least the more tactful of the two of them. 'I know we all love David, but doesn't it worry you that he still won't talk about Katherine? I mean, the fertility treatment is a case in point. That's a pretty big thing for him to keep to himself. Especially as you're going through it too.'

Charlotte was more direct. 'It's weird, Han. It's not healthy to keep it all locked up like that. You're his wife. Don't you want to know what she was like?'

Of course she'd been curious, but thinking about Katherine always made her feel... lesser in some way. It was almost a relief to pretend that she hadn't existed. And Tessa and Charlotte didn't know David like she did. Hadn't seen the pain that crossed his eyes every time that Katherine's name was mentioned. 'The thing is, it's not even about that right now. I love him and I trust him. And if we are going to have a baby, we need to get on with it. And the embryos are there, waiting.' Their silence spoke volumes. 'You don't think it's a good idea, do you?'

Tessa shuffled around in her seat and glanced at Charlotte. 'It's not our choice, is it? I mean, it's up to you.'

'I know that. But I want your opinion. I want you to be honest.'

Charlotte could always be relied on to give it to her straight. 'It's not the egg donation, Han. That makes total sense. But using David's late wife's eggs? I have to be honest – I can't believe you're even considering it. Is it even legal?'

With the conflicting thoughts vying for attention in the last couple of hours, that was something Hannah hadn't considered. Would this be yet another closed path? 'Obviously, we'll have to look into legalities. But David seemed to think it was an option for us. And they're not just her eggs. They are embryos. They've got David in them too.'

Charlotte frowned. 'But if you used an anonymous donor egg, you would still be able to have David in it.'

How could she make them understand when she wasn't even sure herself? It just felt different to egg donation from an anonymous donor, and not just because it would move them one step closer – and faster – to a baby. 'These embryos are ready and waiting though.'

Charlotte shifted in her seat, turning the invitation in her hand around and around. 'But still. They were for *them*. As a couple. Before you. It's… Look, I feel like an absolute cow saying this, but you want me to be honest?'

She raised an eyebrow, looking for permission to launch into whatever she was going to say. Hannah gripped the table and squinted, pretending to physically prepare herself for the onslaught. 'I do. Hit me with it.'

Charlotte shook her head at her and picked up her pen to write another invite. 'I'm not saying it.'

'I'm joking.' She sat up straight again. 'I do want you to be honest.'

Taking a deep breath, Charlotte looked Hannah dead in the eye, as if she was trying to gauge whether her words would hit too hard. When she spoke, her voice was gentle and weighed with care. 'I'm just concerned, Han. You've spent the last two years worrying whether you're living up to David's first wife, and now you're considering giving birth to her child?'

Like a guided missile, Charlotte's words found the heart of Hannah's own concern. Both her friends had been a salve for the times she'd suffered from the deification of Katherine by David's friends. It was more than understandable that this might sound like an incredibly ill-judged idea.

And yet, she couldn't help but feel a prickle of excitement that this might be the perfect solution for them. 'It wouldn't be her child though. I mean, it would be biologically, obviously. But the baby would be ours. Mine and David's. Surely you of all people would understand that?'

Charlotte's two lads – noisy, excitable Jamie and quiet, sensitive Ben – were the centre of her world. Along with her kind husband Jim, they were practically a poster family for adoption. 'Of course I understand, but for the exact same reason as I understand, I am also sitting here with my eyes open on this. And it's different for me. My kids' biological mother is a name on paperwork. Aside from the letter I'm obliged to write her every year, we don't have any contact. I don't have to socialise with her awful friends or see photographs of her in my husband's photo albums.'

Sometimes your friends knew too much. Charlotte and Tessa had been there through the whole journey with David. They knew all about the framed photo of Katherine that had looked down from David's mantelpiece when Hannah had first started to spend time at his house. That David's married friends would describe Katherine as a cross between Mother Teresa and Elle Macpherson. Charlotte hadn't thought it was a good idea for Hannah to live in the same house that Katherine and David had shared; it was hardly surprising she didn't relish the idea of her also using their embryo.

The embryo. She reminded herself. Not *theirs*. This baby would be hers and David's.

Tessa was less forthright than Charlotte, but she was no less concerned. 'Do you really think this is a better option than an anonymous donor?'

To be honest, Hannah had had less than three hours to work out what she really did think. 'I haven't completely made up my mind. But, well, I suppose it would be reassuring to know where the egg came from. Who, I mean.'

Charlotte raised an eyebrow. 'And who the baby might look like.'

Tessa shook a disapproving head at her and turned back to Hannah. 'I'll do it if you want.'

At first, Hannah didn't understand what she meant. 'Do what?'

'Donate my eggs to you and David.'

Charlotte sprayed wine across the table. Immediately, she

grabbed the invites in front of her and quickly wiped them clean. 'Sorry. I'm so sorry. But really?'

Tessa held out her hands. 'It makes sense, doesn't it? I've had my children. And they are pretty perfect if I do say so myself, so my eggs must be good ones.' She smiled at Hannah. 'Whatever is left in the tank is all yours if you want it.'

Charlotte looked at Hannah with such amazement that she was tempted to pretend she was going to accept Tessa's offer. She had no idea whether Tessa was serious, but it was best to bat it away with humour. 'Well, we always said you were the kind of woman to give your friends the coat from your back, but the eggs from your ovaries seems like a big leap from that.'

It seemed that she was serious though. 'I mean it, Han. I love you. I would do this for you.'

When her eyes filled, Hannah reached across the table to pull her into a hug. 'Oh, Tessa. I love you too. You are the most generous person I've ever known. But I can't ask you to do that. It would be too complicated. For a start, we'd have to tell our child who their biological mother was and you know for sure they'd end up preferring you and your platinum-level baking skills.'

As the words left her mouth, she realised the truth of them. Part of the attraction of using these embryos would be that she could know for sure that her child wouldn't want to go looking for their biological mother one day. There would be no fear of her losing them or having to share them with someone else. She could hardly say that right now with Charlotte – who was legally obliged to keep her boys' birth mother up to date – in front of her, but it was definitely something to be considered.

Before Tessa could offer her eggs again, Charlotte backed Hannah up. 'She's right, Tessa. The baby would be a biological half-sister to your two. It affects more than just you and Hannah.'

Tessa picked up a lemon biscuit and snapped it in half.

'Well, I just want to help you. I don't want you to have to use your husband's ex-wife's eggs.'

This was possibly one of the strangest conversations that Hannah had ever had. And she didn't want this to sound like David was some kind of bad guy. 'First wife. Not ex-wife. And I don't *have* to use them. It's not like this is being forced on me.'

Charlotte nodded. 'Yes. And you have other options. Like egg donation, or adoption.'

She'd expected Charlotte to suggest this. And, much as they were close, she was going to have to choose her words very carefully. 'Yes. Like adoption. That's definitely something we could consider if—'

'If all else fails?' Charlotte narrowed her eyes at her.

Hannah's stomach clenched. The last thing on earth she wanted to do was upset one of her dearest friends. 'I didn't mean—'

Charlotte nudged her and rolled her eyes. 'I'm messing with you. Adoption isn't for everyone. And nor is IVF. Or donor eggs. It's a personal choice. I get that. Short of actually stealing a baby, however your children come to you is fine.'

Hannah reached across the table for Charlotte's hand. As wise and content as she sounded right now, Hannah had been there – along with Tessa – for the rounds and rounds of failed IVF and then the soul-searching as Charlotte and Jim had decided to adopt. In fact, she'd been one of the references for the adoption agency, who had wanted her opinion of Charlotte and Jim's suitability as parents. Thankfully, that was one of the easiest questions she'd ever been asked. Despite Charlotte's frank and forthright manner, she had one of the biggest hearts in the world.

'Hey, I want in on the hand-holding action.' Tessa reached for each of them, and they sat there in a connected triangle.

Hannah looked from one to the other of her best friends. 'So you'll be there for me? If I go through with this.'

Charlotte nodded. 'Of course. If this is what you want, we'll be there. A hundred per cent.'

Tessa smiled. 'Every step of the way.'

She knew that they meant it. That they loved her as much as she loved them. Now she just needed to decide whether it was what she wanted. And the sooner the better. If they chose to use the embryos, maybe she could be pregnant by the end of the year.

But, whatever route they took, finding out about Katherine and David's IVF had woken a curiosity in her. It was a shock that David hadn't mentioned it, even in passing. What else hadn't he told her about Katherine?

SIX

KATHERINE

The Premier Ballroom at the Regent Hotel glittered in navy and silver. Circular tables covered the floor like islands, sprays of silver stars with table numbers at their centre. The Media Star Awards were a long way from the Oscars, but it was still an achievement to be nominated for Best Producer of a Lifestyle Show. Though Katherine had pretended to be satisfied with her name on the programme – it wouldn't hurt her CV, that's for sure – there was the familiar itch of ambition that knew she deserved more. After all, her show had been far more successful than they'd anticipated. Was it too much to expect that she might actually walk away with the trophy?

'I'm unlikely to win.' She'd already told David this before they'd walked in tonight, partly out of superstition and partly because she didn't want anyone's sympathy if she didn't. Even from behind, he looked striking in black tie; she'd been right to insist he hire a designer dinner suit rather than wear the one he already owned. They both looked good; people were turning to watch them as they found their table on the left-hand side of the stage.

Ever the gentleman, he pulled out a chair for her. 'Why

don't you just enjoy yourself? It doesn't matter who wins. And who's to say you haven't won, anyway?'

Lauren chuckled as she took the seat next to David. '"Just enjoy yourself? It doesn't matter who wins?" Have you actually met your wife before, David?'

Lauren looked fabulous in a dark red full-length gown, as did Priya in a beautiful purple sheath dress. But Katherine knew that she outshone them both in her 'go big or go home' gold sequined dress. 'And what's wrong with wanting to win? There's no point in playing unless you're going to try to come first. But realistically, it's going to go to one of the longer-running shows.'

David filled her glass with the Prosecco on the table. 'Well, it's brilliant that you've been nominated. I'm so proud of you.'

That was annoying. Did he not think she was good enough to win? Across the table, Priya leaned in and lowered her voice. 'Our seats are quite near the front. That has to be a good sign.'

Though she'd thought the exact same thing when they'd checked the table plan, there was no way Katherine was going to say it out loud.

Before the opening speeches, the dinner was served: three mediocre courses and a tray of after-dinner mints. Then the lights were dimmed and a young comedian she recognised from a quiz show took to the stage to introduce the proceedings.

David reached for her hand and whispered from the side of his mouth. 'This is exciting, isn't it?'

She leaned in close to his ear. 'Depends who wins.'

Her award was one of the early ones, so she wouldn't have to wait too long. She politely clapped each nominee, until her own name was read aloud and everyone on her table gave a little cheer. Once the comedian – his name was on the tip of her tongue – had read the names from the front of the envelope, he pulled out a card from inside it.

'And the winner is...'

David squeezed her hand under the table; Lauren crossed the fingers on both hands and looked at her.

'Katherine Maguire for *Home to Home!*'

David was on his feet, pulling her up. Everyone around their table – Lauren and Ben, Priya and Luke, her cameraman, the presenters – was jumping around and squealing, shaking her hand or kissing her on the cheek. Everything was a blur as she stepped up to the podium to take her award and thank everyone involved with the show.

The awards ceremony finished by 9.30 p.m. and they'd decamped to the hotel bar an hour ago. 'I still can't believe you've done it! You're amazing!' After passing the glass shard on a plinth to Priya, Lauren clapped her hands.

Priya read the engraving aloud. '"Best Producer of a Life-style Show."' She nodded at Katherine. 'That's you, that is.'

Katherine would be lying if she didn't admit she was absolutely ecstatic about it. 'It's nuts, isn't it?'

'It's not nuts.' David shook his head. 'You've worked every hour that God sent for the last year. You've earned this.'

Was that a barbed comment? Perhaps she *had* neglected him a little, but surely this made a few cancelled dinner dates worthwhile? 'Well, it helps if you're given a dream of a show to produce. And all the people working on *Home to Home* have been amazing.'

'Yes, yes. We don't need to hear the acceptance speech again.' Priya's husband Luke pretended to stifle a yawn, then smiled at her. 'I'm joking. You did good, kid. Although I still can't believe you forgot to mention poor David in your acceptance speech.'

Thanks, Luke. Why did he have to bring that up? In her defence, Katherine had been so fixated on naming everyone in the production team that she hadn't thought to thank David for his support. Not that he'd said anything, but every other winner after her had thanked their significant other. After the third mention of 'my wonderful wife' or 'long-suffering husband' she'd begun to feel a little guilty. But this was her night and she wasn't going to let that bring her down, so she laughed it off. 'I know. I'm a terrible wife.'

Lauren clapped her hands again. 'Right then. Where are we going on to next? My mum is staying over with Maisie, so we are footloose and fancy-free all night.'

David held up his hands. 'Not us. We've got plans for tomorrow. We're off home.'

There was a chorus of disapproval from the rest of the table. Katherine knew they'd agreed not to make it a late night, but that was before she'd won. 'Don't be so boring, David. Of course we have to go out and celebrate.'

She saw his mouth tighten a little. As the others made a lot of fuss finding bags and coats and draining the last of their table wine, he turned towards her so that his back shielded their conversation from everyone else. 'We have the appointment with the fertility clinic early tomorrow to talk about trying again. You can't rock up there with a hangover. You agreed we'd head home straight after the ceremony.'

Damn. In the excitement of winning, she'd forgotten all about the appointment. Though the first embryo hadn't worked out, they still had four others in storage waiting to go. 'Well, I've changed my mind. I want to go out and celebrate with my friends.'

Priya was in earshot of her reply and she laughed. 'Katherine Maguire in change-of-mind shocker.'

Luke was helping his wife into her coat. 'You're just lucky she doesn't change her mind about you, mate.'

David wouldn't argue the point in front of everyone, but his frown was irritating. Why did he have to be so serious lately? 'If you don't want to come, David, I can see you back at home in a few hours?'

After his recent complaints about her never being home, she knew that would do it. 'No, it's fine. I'll come.'

It wasn't the enthusiasm she was hoping for, and she could do without him looking at his watch and suggesting they make every drink their 'last one'. But she'd just avoid his eye and keep moving all night. That usually worked.

Getting stopped by congratulations every few steps, it took twenty minutes to get out of the bar. Outside, she took a deep breath of the cold night air. She'd been trying to think of an excuse not to go to the clinic tomorrow. With his warning about hangovers, David had inadvertently handed her the perfect excuse for the next morning. After that, she'd have to think of something else.

SEVEN

HANNAH

A neat path, front lawn trimmed within an inch of its life: there was something so reassuring about returning to the house she'd grown up in. It didn't matter that the second bedroom was now decorated in duck egg blue with guest towels in the ottoman at the end of the bed; it would always be Hannah's room, even though there were no longer peeling posters hanging from the wall or clothes draped around the furniture. She could let herself in the back door, help herself from the fridge and rifle through cupboards for wrapping paper or a measuring jug or anything else that she needed to borrow. She may not live there any longer, but it was still home.

When she saw Tony's dark blue Ford Focus parked outside though, she knocked on the front door. Much as she liked her mum's 'friend' – Tony refused the word 'partner' and Gwen said she was far too old for a boyfriend – Hannah was glad that her mum had never asked him to move in. It was one thing accepting that her mother deserved another chance at love after losing Hannah's dad, but she wasn't ready to see him living in their family home. Although as the second wife of a widower, her own hypocrisy in that sentiment wasn't lost on Hannah.

Tony opened the front door before she'd even got her finger on the doorbell. He was wearing his trademark pastel casual shirt and perfectly ironed jeans combo, the shirtsleeves rolled halfway up his forearms. 'Hi, Hannah love. I was watching out the window for you. Your mum is just having a little lie-down.'

Hannah frowned – that was strange. Her mum was much more likely to be up a ladder cleaning the windows or vacuuming the tops of the picture frames. 'Have you both been out for a pub lunch or something? Mum never has a nap during the day.'

It was almost a point of honour with her. 'I'm seventy-one, not ninety-one,' she would say at the very suggestion that she might want to rest. Plus, to take a nap, she'd actually need to sit still for more than five minutes.

Tony wasn't meeting her eye. 'No, no. No pub lunch. Just a bit tired, that's all. Can I get you a cup of tea?'

He was already on his way down the hall towards the kitchen, so Hannah followed him, pulling off her jacket as she went. Although he didn't live here, he'd taken on most of the duties of a husband. Hannah preferred not to think about how far that went. 'Yes please. Wasn't she expecting me? I know I'm earlier than I said, but David had some work to catch up on, and Mum had said she was going to be in all day.'

Tony was over at the sink. He twisted the tap, and the water echoed loudly as it hit the metal bottom of the kettle. He was still not looking at her. 'Yes, yes. It's fine. I'll go and let her know you're here in a minute.'

'No need.' They both turned to see Hannah's mum, Gwen, in the kitchen doorway. 'I wasn't asleep – I was just resting my eyes for a minute.'

She winked at Hannah. That was something Hannah's dad always used to say if she caught him dozing in front of the football on a Sunday afternoon after a big lunch.

Tony looked relieved to see her. 'I was just making Hannah a drink. Would you like one, my love?'

The way Tony looked at her mother made Hannah smile. Unlike Gwen, he'd never been married before and he treated her like she was the prize he'd been awarded for his patience. It was one of the reasons Hannah couldn't help but like him.

Although... was she imagining it, or was there another edge to his attentiveness today? There was something anxious in his movement, his expression. Was he concerned about something?

Her mother looked her usual immaculate self though in dark pink, three-quarter-length trousers and a fitted shirt with a flower print in the same shade, finished off with dark green pumps picking out the leaves in between the blooms. She held out her arms to Hannah, and she stepped inside them for a warm Chanel-scented hug. 'So lovely to see you, darling. Yes please, Tony. I'll have a tea.'

Mugs chinked together as Tony took them from the cupboard above the kettle. 'You two go through to the sitting room and get comfortable. I'll bring the drinks in when they're ready.'

The sitting room was as coordinated as her mother. Cream leather sofas were covered in navy and pale yellow cushions of varying patterns. A papered navy-and-yellow feature wall was offset by the three painted yellow ones. The overall effect was both bright and calm: two adjectives that could also be applied to Hannah's mother.

'What's all this napping in the day then?' Now Hannah looked at her properly, her mother did look tired.

'Oh, give over. Can't your mother have a rest without the Spanish Inquisition? I want to hear about your appointment. How come you only told me about it today?'

She hadn't told her mother that the appointment with Dr Ellis had been on Thursday, because she'd known that Gwen would worry. Once she knew the outcome of the tests, she'd been relieved that she hadn't: some news had to be explained in person. She sighed. 'It wasn't great news, Mum. Apparently, all my eggs have gone off.'

Her attempt at a joke fell flat when it was accompanied by the filling of her eyes.

'Oh, Hannah. I'm so sorry, my darling.' Her mum was on her feet and beside her in moments. 'What does that mean? What did the doctor say exactly?'

Telling her mum was harder than speaking to Tessa and Charlotte. Not only because, sitting here, she felt like a child asking her mum to make it all better. But also because her mum had a vested interest in this: it was her potential grandchild they were talking about. And her mum – with her endless supply of cakes, crafting projects and care – would make the best grandma.

'It means that my eggs aren't healthy enough to make a baby. IVF would be pointless.' An open packet of tissues appeared in front of her. Another reason her mum would make a great grandma: a handbag that was prepared for every eventuality.

Her mum rubbed her back as she blew her nose. 'But there's so much they can do these days. Did the consultant not suggest anything? What's the next step?'

Hannah didn't know where to start. 'She suggested egg donation. Well, she didn't actually suggest it, but she did say that would be an option.'

Her mum nodded slowly. 'And how do you feel about that?'

That was the million-dollar question. It wasn't the dream she'd had for so long. The baby wouldn't look like her. Wouldn't have her mum's eyes or her dad's smile. How important was that? 'I don't know. I'm still trying to get my head around it, to be honest.'

Her mum reached out and took her hand in hers. 'Well, you don't need to know yet, do you? You can have a bit of a think.'

This was another reference to her dad. Whenever they asked him anything – Where shall we go on holiday? What colour shall we paint the sitting room? What shall we have for dinner tonight? – he always said the same thing. 'Let's have a bit of a think.'

Tony rattled in with a tray bearing two mugs and a plate of biscuits. He still seemed to be avoiding looking at Hannah. 'I'll leave you two alone for a natter. I need to pop home anyway and sort out a few things.'

Hannah didn't want him to feel pushed out on her account. Although she could understand that the subject of her fertility would not be something he'd want to weigh in on. 'Don't leave, Tony. Mum and I can talk about all of this later.'

Slowly and carefully, he rested the tray on the coffee table. 'Ah, that's kind of you, Hannah, but I really do have a few jobs at home. I'll see you in a couple of hours, Gwen. We'll go to the quiz at the club tonight?'

He leaned over her mother and kissed her so gently that Hannah had to look away; it was so intimate.

'Definitely, love. I'll call Lyn and Mick and let them know we're coming along.'

Hannah coughed into her hand. 'I'll see you next time then, Tony. Maybe you and Mum could come for dinner? David is on a Mexican food kick at the moment.'

Finally he looked her in the eye, and there was a sorrow there which hit her in the stomach. 'That would be great. Just let your mum know when, and we'll be there.' He leaned over her and gave her a dry kiss at the top of her cheek.

As soon as he'd gone, Hannah turned in her seat to face her mother. 'Mum, what's going on? Tony looked like someone just stole his favourite golf club.'

Her mum sighed. 'It's me, love. I've been feeling a bit under the weather so I went for a check-up and my doctor sent me for some tests.'

It was as if all the air had been sucked out of the room. Hannah had lived with the terror of hearing a statement like this for the last five years. Since she'd had the same conversation with her father. She opened her mouth, but nothing came out.

'It's nothing to worry about. Just some shortness of breath, and my chest has felt a bit tight. They've put me on a load of pills, and I've got to look after myself a bit better.' Her mum's voice trembled, and Hannah could see how hard she was trying to be brave, to make sure that Hannah wasn't too scared.

Somehow, she managed to get the words past the lump in her throat. 'It's more than that, Mum. I'm not silly. What did they say?'

Gwen waved a hand as if what she was about to say meant nothing. 'Well, the doctor was worried about my heart. But I think he was just trying to scare me into drinking less wine and eating more salad.'

Humour had always been their family's defence against bad news, but Hannah didn't have it in her to laugh today. She was like a boxer who was already reeling from one punch only to be clobbered from the other side. All she wanted was to hit the floor and not get up.

But she didn't have that option. She might be her mother's daughter, but it was her turn to be the one who did the looking after. 'I'll be there for all of it. Whatever you need. I can't lose you, Mum. Please, I can't lose you.'

Her mum gave her hands a squeeze. 'Hey, hey. That's enough of that. You're as bad as Tony, the soft sod. I'm not going anywhere. I just need to do what I'm told and get myself healthy so that I can be there for you with whatever you decide.'

Hannah let her mother take her into her arms, not wanting to ever let go. Whatever she did decide needed to be soon. She wanted her mother to meet her grandchild almost as much as she wanted to have a baby herself. Surely the universe wasn't so cruel that it would take her mother in exchange for giving her a child? And did it matter where the embryos came from, if it meant she could have a baby as soon as possible?

Another piece of advice her father had been known for was to find out all your options before you make a decision. Did David even know for sure if they would be allowed to use Katherine's embryos? There must be rules and Hannah had no idea who would be responsible for deciding whether they could. At least they could make an appointment with the consultant to talk about it. And the sooner the better. She wasn't planning on leaving her mother's house until Tony was back here to keep an eye on her. But as soon as she got home, she was going to talk to David about making an appointment with the clinic.

EIGHT

HANNAH

Halfway home from her mum's, Hannah switched off the car radio; every song was making her cry.

After they'd lost her dad, she hadn't been able to listen to any slow songs for over a year, especially anything by his favourites: the Beatles or Neil Diamond or Karen Carpenter. Even modern songs with lyrics about loss would force her to change stations. There was something about a ballad that just reached into the pain inside and squeezed it harder.

David's car was on their drive, so she parked on the street in front of it. Neither of them were going out tonight and she could move hers in the morning. All she wanted to do right now was hide herself in his arms, listen to him tell her that everything was okay. Then, when she'd got her strength back, they could talk about the embryos.

When she let herself into the house, David was there in the hallway, closing the sitting-room door behind him. 'You're back. I wasn't expecting you so soon.'

Was it her imagination or was he not entirely pleased to see her? 'Haven't had time to clear up from the party, eh?' She smiled weakly, but then her lip wobbled and the tears started again.

David was in front of her in a couple of steps. 'Hey, what's the matter? What's happened?'

It was such a relief to let herself relax into his arms. When her dad had been ill, she'd lived alone. No one to offload on when she'd got home from a hospital appointment or – after her dad's surgery – visiting hours. 'It's Mum. She's not well. It's her heart.'

David held her even more tightly. 'Oh, Han. I'm so sorry. Poor Gwen.'

Yes, exactly. Her poor mum. Wasn't it enough that her mother had lost her husband five years ago? Now she had to endure this. 'It's so unfair, David.'

'I know. And I'm so sorry. What can we do? What does she need?'

This was one of the many reasons she loved him so much. When she felt weak, he was strong. Beneath her cheek, his chest felt solid and safe. 'I don't know. She said there are tests she has to have. To be honest, I think she's not telling me the whole truth.' The look on Tony's face when he came back for the evening had told her more than her mum's platitudes and generalisations. He was scared and so, in turn, was Hannah.

'Whatever it is, we'll get her through it.' David pulled her away gently, bending his knees so that his face was on the same level as hers. 'You're not on your own, Han. Either of you. I'm here.'

Those were the words she needed to hear more than anything. She hadn't intended to talk about anything else until later that night, but it all felt connected. Why wait? 'And I think we should make an appointment to speak to that clinic. The one where the embryos are stored. We should at least find out if it's possible.'

David straightened up, so he was six inches taller than her again. 'Fairfield? Really? Are you sure?'

No, she wasn't sure. But maybe she would be after they'd spoken to someone there. 'I want to find out more about it before we make a decision. But I do want to get things moving. I do want us to have a baby as soon as we can.'

David looked as if he was trying to read her face, but then he nodded. 'Well, if that's what you want, I'll call them tomorrow.'

'Thank you.' Hannah was halfway to kissing him when she heard a cough from the other room. She frowned. 'Who's here?'

David took a deep breath and lowered his voice so that it was barely above a whisper. 'Okay, so here's the thing. I didn't tell you about this because I wasn't expecting her to come over straight away. But I called to speak to her and she said she was free to talk now and as you were out it seemed like a good time and—'

'Who is *she*?' So that was why he'd pulled the sitting-room door closed behind him. There was a woman in her sitting room? Who was he talking about?

'Yes. She. Katherine's mother.'

It was so unexpected that all Hannah could do was repeat it back to him. 'Katherine's mother?'

'Yes. Look, I know that I'm probably being completely premature, but after our discussion, I mentioned it to her on the phone because, well, because I wanted to see what she thought. About us using the embryos, I mean.'

Hannah knew that David had kept in touch with Katherine's mother after her death. She'd taken it as another example of what a good man he was. She'd never met her though. It had never felt like the right time.

But now she was here, in their sitting room. After the afternoon at her own mother's, this was the last thing she needed. 'You could have warned me, David.'

'I know, I know. I'm sorry. I hadn't planned to talk to her about it – it just kind of came out. I'm sorry, I really am. But she's sitting in there now. Come and meet her. She's a really nice woman. I know you'll like her.'

Meeting her was way down on the list of things that Hannah wanted to do right now, but she could hardly disappear upstairs like a stroppy teenager. Besides, there was a part of her that was curious. Who better to tell her about Katherine than Katherine's own mother? 'I'll go and wash my face and then I'll be in.'

David breathed out in what sounded like relief. 'Thanks. I'll go back and let her know you'll be in shortly.'

She nodded. Then trooped upstairs to wash away the sticky dried tears and smeared mascara.

Her face was not a pretty sight in the bathroom mirror. Even after splashing it with cold water, it was red and blotchy. She wasn't someone who wore much make-up during the day – a squirt of BB cream and a few flicks of mascara were usually enough – but she didn't want to appear in front of Katherine's mother looking like she'd been dragged through a hedge backwards. Even as she rubbed tinted lip balm onto her mouth with her finger, she realised how ridiculous this was. Was she seriously trying to impress the mother of her husband's first wife?

She had to admit she was a little curious about what she would be like. Katherine always looked so glamorous in the photographs she'd seen of her. She was expecting an older version of her, really.

Which was why she was so surprised when she walked into the lounge to see a small, shrunken woman who plucked at her mauve cardigan as she stood to say hello. 'Nice to meet you, love. I'm Marie.'

'Hannah, obviously.' Hannah laughed, but she could have

kicked herself for sounding so nervous. She had no idea how to behave. Confidence might make her seem cruel; diffidence might make her pathetic. What had David told Marie about her? Had they discussed her at all?

Marie retook her seat, but she perched on the edge like a wild bird. 'David said you were visiting your mother? Are you close?'

Right now, thinking of her mother only made Hannah more anxious. 'Yes. I'm lucky; she's only twenty minutes away by car.'

Marie smiled. 'No, I mean do you see a lot of each other? Do you get on well?'

'Oh, yes. I'm an only child. So we were all close. The three of us. Mum, Dad and me.' This was torture. Worrying about her mum had brought all the emotions of losing her dad to the surface. It would take the merest scratch for it all to come out. But it wasn't Marie's fault that she didn't know this.

'David said you lost your dad a few years ago?'

Hannah sucked hard on her bottom lip to prevent the tears that threatened. 'Yes. Cancer. It was all quite sudden.'

'It's hard when it's sudden, isn't it? You don't get time to prepare yourself.'

Of course. Hannah wasn't the only person here to have lost someone they loved. This woman had lost her daughter. 'It is.'

'In some ways, it was easier when I lost my husband. I don't know if David has told you but my husband, Katherine's father, had a catastrophic stroke. It left him in a terrible way. It was hard on him. And Katherine. She was only a teenager at the time. Selfishly, though, the two years I cared for him meant I got to say everything I needed to before we lost him. To make sure that he knew how much I loved him. With Katherine...'

She didn't need to finish that sentence. The poor woman had lost her husband and her daughter. What could Hannah possibly say?

As always, David came to the rescue. Perhaps he'd had to

reroute Marie away from this conversational thread before. 'Have you decided what you're going to do for your holiday, Marie? You were looking at brochures last time I saw you.'

'No. I might go and visit my cousin in Edinburgh. She's been on at me to come and stay. I'd like to do a cruise, but I can't find anyone else who wants to go.'

David grinned at her. 'You could always try a singles cruise. Get chatted up at the bar by a silver fox.'

Hannah had had no idea that he had such an easy relationship with his former mother-in-law. Marie clearly enjoyed being teased by him. 'Get away with you. Those days are long gone. All the men of my age are miserable buggers anyway.'

Hannah had heard this before. 'My mum used to say that, but then she met Tony a couple of years ago at a quiz night and he's lovely.'

'Good luck to your mum, but I'm fine on my own.' Marie picked up the mug in front of her and held it out to David. 'Would you mind if I had another cup of tea, David? Mine's gone cold.'

'Of course.' He jumped up. 'Do you want anything, Han?'

Was David being sent out of the room for another reason than just a cup of tea? 'No, I'm fine, thanks.'

Sure enough, as soon as he was in the kitchen, Marie lowered her voice and leaned in closer. 'David told me about your plans. To use the embryos.'

Hannah shuffled around in her seat. What had David said to her? If she said that she categorically did not want them to use her daughter's embryos, would David still be prepared to go through with it? 'Did he?'

She nodded. There was a light in her eyes that hadn't been there before. 'I think it's a wonderful idea.'

That was surprising. 'Do you?'

When Marie smiled, her face lifted. 'Of course I do. I never thought I'd get to hold Katherine's baby. It's such a generous thing for you to do.'

Ouch. 'Generous' was uncomfortable. The way Marie spoke, it made Hannah feel like a surrogate mother. 'Well, it would be our baby. Mine and David's.'

Marie fluttered her hands to wave away Hannah's comment. 'Oh, of course. Of course it would. But to see some of Katherine again...' She held a hand to her chest. 'I can't tell you how much it would mean to me.'

'Well, we can't guarantee who the baby will look most like. David and his brothers have a very strong likeness.' Hannah didn't want to be unkind, but nor did she want to encourage Marie to think she would be giving birth to a mini-Katherine.

'Oh, I know. The three of them were like peas in a pod. They used to come at Christmas – Katherine was such a talented cook – and the way they used to tease one another.' She looked at the corner of the room as if picturing a festive scene. 'Good memories.'

Hannah liked David's brothers but, apart from at their wedding, she hadn't ever seen the three of them together. The elder lived two hours away, and the younger had three children under five.

David stuck his head around the door. 'Kettle is on. Can I get you anything to eat, Marie?'

'No, I'm fine. We're getting to know each other. You take your time.'

As soon as he'd gone, she turned back to Hannah. 'My Katherine was so clever and kind and beautiful. Have you seen her picture?'

'Yes, I've seen pictures at—'

Before she could finish, Marie had plucked an album from her bag and brought it out to show her. 'I carry this with me all the time. Look, here she is at her graduation. She got a first – did David tell you?'

Hannah couldn't believe this was happening. She felt very sorry for this woman who had lost her daughter, but she could surely see that Hannah wasn't the right audience for this?

But she clearly couldn't. 'Here she was on her wedding day. Look how happy they both look.' Finally, she had a moment of self-realisation. 'Oh, I don't mean that you and David aren't, dear. I know he loves you too. I just meant... well, actually I wanted to show you this.'

As she watched her flick to the beginning of the album, Hannah had a sickening realisation of what might be about to happen. 'It's okay, let's just—'

But again, Marie cut her off. 'This is it.' She turned the album and thrust it towards Hannah. 'This is Katherine as a baby. Look how beautiful she is. That's how beautiful your baby will be. Just like that, with a bit of David too, of course.'

Marie turned the photo back to herself and stroked her daughter's infant face.

Yes, 'a little bit of David' of course. But none of her. Hannah swallowed. 'Well, we haven't actually decided what we're going to do yet. I don't want to get your hopes up if we decide to go another way.'

Marie clutched at her hand. 'But it would be wonderful. Don't you see? I can tell you anything you want to know about Katherine. Anything at all. Wouldn't that be a good thing?'

The door opened and David entered with two cups of tea. 'Here you go, Marie.' He glanced at the photo album in front of her. His face was stricken as he mouthed 'sorry' at Hannah.

'I was just telling Hannah about Katherine. Showing her some baby pictures.'

David looked mortified. 'I can see. Maybe we should...'

Marie clearly couldn't read the room. Or perhaps she just didn't get the opportunity to talk about her daughter very often. 'She was desperate to be a mother, you know. Obviously you know what she and David were going through to have a baby.

When she died, I couldn't get it out of my head for a while that she might have been pregnant. That I hadn't only lost my daughter, but my grandchild too.'

This was too much. Hannah looked to David to stop this and saw his face darken. 'Well, you don't need to think that, Marie. She wasn't. It wouldn't have been possible.'

His tone of voice seemed to make Marie come to her senses. 'Sorry. I'm sorry. I know this doesn't help anyone. I just miss her so much. She would have made a beautiful mother.'

David's derisive cough startled Hannah. It was so unlike him. He covered it over with the smile he reserved for airport check-in desks and traffic wardens. He reached forwards and shut the photograph album, passing it back to Marie. 'I don't want you to forget this. I know how precious it is to you.'

Finally, she seemed to realise how tactless she'd been. 'Of course.'

For the remaining half hour she was there, Marie twittered on about family members that David hadn't seen in a while. The names meant nothing to Hannah of course, but served as a reminder that David had had this whole other life before her. A life she knew very little about.

She'd hoped to learn more about Katherine from her mother, but she was only going to get another list of her perfections. What if there was something else she should know? And how was David so absolutely sure that Katherine hadn't been pregnant when she died, when they'd been in the middle of fertility treatment?

NINE

KATHERINE

Some days being a producer was the best job in the world; others it was like herding cats.

Home to Home involved two sets of – ideally best – friends, swapping their homes for two weeks. In that time, the families had free reign to change the decor, move the furniture around, change the bedroom to a library – whatever they felt like. The trick was to find two families – or couples – who were very different from one another. If one was a minimalist neat freak who lived for sushi and the other was a cat-collecting, knick-knack-loving traditionalist who ate stew every night, they were on to a winner. Unfortunately, this was easier said than done. People tend to gravitate towards people who were like them on some level, which made for less interesting TV.

Today, they were a week into the shoot and the two families were just being far too nice. Other than tidying up and finding a surprising amount of dust behind the sofa, no one was being critical at all. And no one was making any changes.

Jeremy – as usual – was being no help whatsoever.

'You need to tell them to do something crazy.' Katherine had said this to him countless times. 'Paint a wall black, restock the fridge with fermenting bean sprouts, turn the baby's room into a gym – just something!'

'I've tried,' Jeremy whined. 'They don't want to.'

Was she the only one willing to do the hard work around here? 'For goodness' sake. I'll speak to them.'

Sure enough, when she knocked on the door to the Williams family, the mother opened the door to her with a wide smile and the smell of baking. 'Come in! We're just doing a trial run of the cookies we're planning to give them on reveal day.'

Katherine followed her through to the kitchen – country-style, neat, clean – and took the seat she was offered at the table. A small child with her front two teeth missing was elbow deep in a beige mixing bowl. 'We're making chocolate biscuits. They're not going to be ready for a while, but would you like a cup of tea?'

Katherine smiled. 'Thank you, but I've just finished a coffee. Actually, Mrs Williams, can I have a chat with you in another room?'

'Cheryl, please. And of course.' She turned to her daughter. 'Keep mixing, Verity.'

As soon as they were in the lounge, Katherine cut to the chase. 'The thing is, you and your friend Pippa are so lovely that, well, the show is going to be a bit...' *Boring? Rubbish?* 'Tame.'

Cheryl clearly wasn't the sharpest tool in the box. 'What do you mean?'

'The thing is, people tune into the show for the arguments and the tears.' Surely Cheryl must know this? She had applied to go on the show after all. Katherine was going to need to work out who had booked them – she'd designed a questionnaire to avoid just this kind of situation. They were basically hoping for borderline psychopaths.

Finally, Cheryl seemed to understand. 'I see. You want me to do something more... controversial?'

Hallelujah! 'Yes. Exactly that. Come on, the two of you have been friends for fifteen years. There must be something that's always bugged you. Something of hers you hate. Or her husband? Is he in love with his lawn perhaps?'

A marginally more wicked expression started to move across Cheryl's face. This looked promising. 'Well...'

'Yes?' Katherine knew how eager she sounded, but she needed to get something today.

Cheryl leaned towards her as if her friend – in Cheryl's own house three streets away – might be able to hear her. 'Pippa does have way too many cushions and candles.'

'Bingo! Let's start with that.' It wasn't much, but it was better than the bloody biscuits.

Her head was aching when she came out of the house. Maybe she should have accepted that cup of tea.

Jeremy came hurrying up to her. 'How did it go?'

'We're moving in the right direction. But you might need to visit the other house and knock a bottle of red wine onto the white carpet.'

Jeremy laughed. He thought she was joking.

She glanced at her watch. 'Look, I'm going to pop back to the hotel. I need to make some calls to the office and it'll be easier from there. Make sure there's a camera rolling in the house. But don't bother filming Delia Smith in the kitchen.'

The Premier Inn they were staying in was only ten minutes away. Since they'd started the damn fertility treatment, David had got into the habit of calling her during the day. So when her personal phone started to buzz with a FaceTime call, she assumed it was him, only registering that it was Lauren after she'd swiped to accept it.

'Hey, stranger! How are you?' Lauren's smile filled the screen; she looked like she might be in her kitchen.

Damn. Katherine had hoped to take a painkiller and close her eyes for ten minutes before she had to make those calls; now she was going to have to try and get Lauren off the phone. 'I'm good. Just dashing in and out of my hotel room. Shall I call you later when I've got more time to catch up?'

'But will you though?' Lauren tilted her head as if she was telling her off. 'I called you on Wednesday and you said the same. Plus I've left you two messages since then.'

Katherine sank down onto the edge of the double bed. She had been avoiding Lauren. Mostly because she didn't want a recount of Maisie's Marvellous Moments from that week. 'I'm so sorry. Work has been crazy and I've not known which way is up. I will call you tonight, I promise.' She glanced at the clock on the wall.

Lauren's face softened. 'Are you feeling tired?'

She was. But there was something about Lauren's expression that made her suspicious. 'Yes. Like I said, work is hectic at the moment.'

Sympathy was practically emanating from her now. 'I'm your friend, Katherine. Is there anything you need support with? Anything I can do?'

Katherine could feel her face flush. 'What do you mean?'

'Oh, Kat. I'm not supposed to say, but I *know*. About the IVF. David told Ben. Why haven't you said anything?'

Oh no. What the hell was David doing, telling Ben? She'd expressly told him that she didn't want Lauren and Priya to know. 'Oh. That. Well, we weren't planning on saying anything until we were further down the line with it all.'

'That's crazy. What are your friends for if not to support you when you're going through something like this? David told Ben that the first round wasn't successful. I know you must be worried about trying again, but I'm sure it'll happen next time.'

She couldn't bear this. 'Look, I'm so sorry, Lauren, but I've got an important call coming through in about two minutes. I will call you later, I promise.'

'Okay. As long as you—'

She cut her off before she could finish.

For the next four minutes – she checked the clock – she paced the floor. She was so angry with David. What the hell was he thinking?

She scooped up her phone from the bed and punched the buttons to bring up David's name. He answered in two rings. 'Hi, sweetheart, I was just thinking about calling you.'

'Well, Lauren beat you to it.'

He clearly wasn't picking up on the bitterness of her tone. 'That's nice. How's she?'

She ignored the question. 'Apparently a little birdy, who looks a lot like Ben, had heard it from another little birdy, who looks a lot like you, that we are having fertility treatment.'

There was a three-second silence on the other end of the phone, followed by, 'Ah.'

'Ah, indeed. I asked you, David. I told you. I don't want them knowing. I don't want anyone knowing.'

David sighed. 'I'm sorry. I really am. I told him to keep it to himself. I just needed... I wanted to talk to someone about it.'

Why the heck did he need to talk to someone about it? It was her who was having to go through the poking and prodding and pricking with needles. 'Couldn't you have chosen someone else? Anyone else? You know that Ben can't keep anything from Lauren. She can practically read his tiny mind.'

'I'm sorry, love. I really am.'

Sorry wasn't good enough. 'You keep going on about rescheduling that appointment at the clinic and then you do this. It makes me want to just give the whole thing up, David.'

There was quiet again. 'Don't do that. I know you're cross, but this isn't about anyone else. It's about us. I *am* sorry, and I'll never tell Ben anything again. You're home tomorrow, aren't you? I'll make it up to you then. Shall I book a restaurant?'

'Don't bother about dinner. I won't be home till late. Really late.'

She added the last to almost dare him to complain again about hardly seeing her, but he clearly knew he was already in her bad books. 'Okay, well maybe later in the week. What time will you be driving home? I meant to tell you, the tracker app seems to have been disabled on your phone. I can't see where you are.'

Damn. She'd hoped he wouldn't notice that she'd switched it off. Months and months ago, they'd both downloaded the app so that he could see how close she was to home when she was travelling back late from a shoot. Back then, it had been a comfort to know that he liked to make sure she was safe. 'Oh? Has it? I'll have to have a look at that.'

Hopefully, he'd forget that he'd mentioned it by the time she got back tomorrow. Because the last thing she wanted was him knowing where she'd been.

TEN

HANNAH

The Fairfield Clinic was actually closer than the clinic they'd been under previously. The waiting room was safely beige and white. Another couple sat on the other side of the room, her hand clasped in his. Then they were called in, and Hannah and David were alone.

David turned in his seat so that his body was angled towards her. 'How are you feeling?'

'I'm okay. You?'

The last time he was in this waiting room, he would have been here with Katherine, but neither of them had mentioned that. 'Yeah, I'm okay too. A bit nervous. It feels a little strange to be asking this question. I mean, it makes sense, but it can't be the sort of thing they do every day.'

She was nervous about that too, even though the consultant they were booked to see, Dr Nash, already knew what they were coming to discuss. Hannah wondered what she'd thought about their request. Not David so much. But her. What must Dr Nash think of the woman who was prepared to carry the child of her husband's first wife? Would she think her strange? Or desperate?

David had called last week and spoken to Dr Nash before making the appointment for today. The joys of private healthcare. 'We can afford all this, can't we?'

She knew the answer. As well as David having a lucrative job, his mortgage had been paid off by a life insurance policy after Katherine's death. It wasn't a pleasant thought, but that, combined with the fact he'd barely been anywhere except to work or Lauren and Ben's for a year after Katherine had died, meant that he – now they – were very comfortable financially.

He reached for her hand. 'Yes, we can afford it. Stop worrying about that.'

It was hard not to worry. Not about the money, but the whole idea of what they were thinking of doing. Today was only about asking the question; there was no point tying themselves in knots about whether to do it if they were going to be met with a flat 'no' anyway.

'Mr and Mrs Maguire?' They looked up to the smiling face of the receptionist who had booked them in. 'Dr Nash is ready for you.'

As they entered her consulting room, Dr Nash stood to welcome them both. 'Great to see you, Mr and Mrs Maguire. Are you both well?'

Given that she was there because her body wasn't working the way that she wanted it to, Hannah wasn't sure that was the most tactful of questions, but she nodded along with David. 'Yes, thank you. And it's Hannah and David, please.'

'Well...' Dr Nash slid behind her desk after waiting for them to take a seat. 'My colleague has passed your file on to me, so we have all the original documentation with regard to the storage of your embryos, David.' Dr Nash was clearly trying to be as sensitive as possible in the way she spoke. 'It seems that you and Katherine both signed a document giving the other person full custody of the embryos in the event of death.'

That word hung in the air for a few moments. Maybe it was easier to say for someone in the medical profession. David and Hannah only ever referred to Katherine's 'accident'; the word 'death' was never used.

Dr Nash had slipped a document out of a folder on her desk and now she pushed it across the table to the two of them. Hannah only skim-read the titles, but it read like a will, and there, at the bottom of the page, were two signatures: David's and Katherine's. Beneath Katherine's – in very neat print – her full name: *Mrs Katherine Anne Maguire.*

It had taken Hannah a while to decide whether to take David's surname. She'd been Hannah Hughes for forty years – it felt like a lot to give up. They'd considered whether to double-barrel it – Hughes-Maguire or Maguire-Hughes – but in the end, she'd decided to go down the traditional route. She still didn't really know why. In the last year, she'd enjoyed being a 'Mrs' more than she'd realised she would. It made her feel as if they belonged together.

Now, looking at 'Mrs Katherine Anne Maguire' in black and white felt very strange.

Dr Nash's voice was professional and non-judgemental. 'It's clear from the paperwork that you are legally able to use the embryos.'

Hannah's stomach flipped over. David had told her about this document, but she hadn't imagined it would be that straightforward. Did this mean they had the green light to go ahead?

David cleared his throat. How had he felt, looking at his and Katherine's names side by side? 'So what happens now?'

Dr Nash slid the document back into its folder, then clasped her hands. 'Even with this in place, we as a clinic still need to follow all our usual protocols. Although you have been

through this process before, David, we will need to proceed as if
you are a new patient, as Hannah is going through the process
for the first time.'

Despite Dr Nash's reassuring smile in her direction,
Hannah couldn't help but feel that she was going to have to pass
more tests in order to be approved. Thank goodness she'd asked
Dr Nash to call her by her first name at least. Right now, two
Mrs Maguires would be very confusing. 'So what is the
process?'

'Well, firstly I would like you both to see our in-house
counsellor.'

Something about the way she said this made Hannah
uneasy. 'Together or separately?'

'Initially together, but she might want to see you on your
own, too. It will be her call as to how many sessions you might
need with her.'

Sessions? Plural? Clearly this was not going to be straightforward at all. 'How long does all of this usually take?'

Dr Nash smiled. 'We don't want to rush it, Hannah. This is
a big step you're both making.'

Hannah dug her nails into the underside of the chair. Of
course it was a big step. But anyone else could get pregnant on a
one-night stand with a stranger. She was asking to have a baby
with the man she loved. Her husband. 'I understand. I'm just
trying to get an idea in my head of when everything happens.'

Again, that professional smile. 'Of course. Well, once the
counsellor makes her recommendation to me, I will consult with
the rest of the medical team and we will make a decision about
whether to proceed.'

It all felt so clinical, so cold. David leaned forwards. 'I don't
really understand. We are legally allowed to use the embryos
because of the paperwork you have here. But you could still
refuse to let us have them?'

'The thing is, David, we have a moral and legal obligation to the unborn child. We have to follow procedure.'

An obligation to ensure that she would be a fit mother? Hannah felt a little sick. If Katherine had already been through one round of IVF, she'd obviously passed the test. What if Hannah didn't?

Dr Nash leaned her forearms on the desk, her face a picture of kindness and support. 'I understand that this must feel frustrating. But this process is there to protect everybody. And this situation makes it even more important that we dot every "I" and cross every "T".'

'We understand.' David reached for Hannah's hand, but it was still gripping the sides of her seat so he settled for rubbing her arm instead.

She wanted to know everything. Before she – they – could make a decision, they needed to know about every step. 'And if we are accepted?'

Dr Nash steered the language in a different direction. 'If we proceed, we would take you on as a patient and use hormone therapy to ensure that, once we transfer the embryo, it has as much chance as possible.'

Chance was not a word that Hannah was keen on. 'And how does it all work? Do you only use one embryo?'

'On the day of the transfer, one of the embryologists in our lab will remove the agreed number of embryos from the cold storage. Whichever progresses the best will be the one we recommend for implantation.'

That didn't quite answer the question. 'So only one is implanted?'

'Yes. The law was changed so that we can only transfer one embryo at a time. A single embryo has better chances of survival. Unless there are exceptional circumstances.'

Hannah almost laughed. What were their circumstances if not exceptional? 'I know that I'm probably getting ahead of myself here, but if we are successful in having a child, those other embryos are their only possibility of having a full sibling. Would those circumstances be exceptional enough?'

Dr Nash held out her hands. 'We could definitely explore that if it's important to you?'

Hannah looked to David for support, but he seemed less certain, so she kept going. 'What happens after the embryos are transferred?'

'You would continue with the hormone injections until we are sure that the embryo is thriving. Once that has happened, the pregnancy will continue just like any other pregnancy. We'll discharge you and you will go to your GP as any other mother-to-be would do.'

She smiled at them both, but just that phrase made a lump rise in Hannah's throat. Mother-to-be. Would that ever be her? Would she be the happy woman circling her stomach with her arms, complaining about her legs aching and smiling all the while?

'So.' Dr Nash was looking at them both. 'Why don't you both take some time to think things through and then let me know if and when you're ready to proceed? Then I'll make an appointment with our in-house counsellor and book in all the other appointments for tests.'

David stood and smoothed the front of his trousers. 'Great, well, we'll be in touch. Thank you.'

Was that it? Shouldn't there be more questions, more information? Although the biggest questions that Hannah had were not ones that could be answered by a doctor. David seemed so calm and clinical about the whole thing. Was he not as confused as she was?

On the way back to the car, Hannah couldn't shake off the feeling that she was the only one of them completely bamboozled by all of this. Of course, she knew it wasn't new ground for David, but it still felt strange. 'Did you see a counsellor before? With Katherine?'

He avoided her eyes. 'Yes. But I don't remember it being a big deal. From memory, the counsellor just wanted to make sure that we'd discussed everything and knew what we were getting into.'

Something else occurred to her. They'd reached the car and she paused with her hand on the door handle. 'What about after Katherine's accident? Did you ever have any counselling then?'

David's answer was short. 'No.'

Once they were driving home, she ran through all the new questions the appointment had raised. 'It was interesting what she said about the number of embryos to be transferred. I mean, if we can, it might make sense to ask if we can have two.'

Again, he looked uncomfortable, as he had in the office. 'I don't know, Han. She also said that only transferring one gives it a better chance.'

'I know that, but we don't have the luxury of putting this off. I'm already forty. Time is running out.'

As soon as the words were out of her mouth, she realised how tactless they were. Before she could apologise, David reached for the car stereo and turned it on. 'I think we need to slow down a bit. One step at a time, Hannah.'

She bit her lip to prevent herself from saying that she didn't want to slow down. Time felt as if it was marching past them. With Dr Nash's assurance that she could have a normal pregnancy, give birth like anyone else, she'd allowed herself, just for a moment, to imagine how that would feel. This was all she wanted to talk about, think about, until they'd made a decision. Surely he could understand that?

She turned the volume down on the radio. 'What the doctor told us about the process. Was that the same for you and Katherine? Is that what you did?'

A flash of something – pain? guilt? – shot across David's face. 'Yes. The same, I think.'

It must have been tough for him to be in there, remembering

going through all of this before. She wanted him to know that she understood. That he didn't need to hide his feelings from her. She reached across and laid her hand on his leg. 'I know this must be bringing up a lot of things for you. Katherine's mother said how much Katherine had wanted to have children.'

Again, that gruff derisive cough. 'Well, maybe Marie remembers things a little differently.'

When he didn't continue, she couldn't help but ask, 'What do you mean?'

He kept his eyes on the road in front, but his expression tightened. 'We'd stopped the fertility treatment. Before her accident, Katherine had decided she no longer wanted to go through with it. The first round of IVF wasn't successful and she didn't want to try again.'

Hannah was so surprised that for a few moments she didn't say anything, not sure how to phrase her next question. Eventually, she went for the obvious. 'Do you know why?'

David's knuckles were white on the steering wheel. 'No. No I don't. Things were... difficult between us.' He let his left hand drop from the steering wheel so that he could lay it on hers. He gave the back of her hand a squeeze. 'I'm sorry, Hannah. I don't want to talk about it. It's just... it's too weird. This is different. Separate. We both want a baby and it's going to work out. I know it is.'

Hannah didn't want to upset him by pressing him further. Even when she didn't understand it, she'd always accepted his reluctance to discuss Katherine with her. Why open up an old wound? But now she wanted to find out more. Seeing 'Mrs Katherine Anne Maguire' on that form, knowing they were seriously considering using her fertilised eggs, that their child would have her DNA – it all made her want to find out more about what Katherine had been like. And if David didn't want to talk about her, she knew exactly who would.

ELEVEN

KATHERINE

Around twenty white plastic sunbeds circled the pool, standing on dark blue mosaic tiles. The air was warm and damp. The spa at Kentley Hall was small and, this morning, the three of them had it to themselves. Maybe it would do her good to just chill out for a couple of hours.

She was trying her best to shake off the prickly feeling from this morning. Awake at 5 a.m., she'd tried to slip out of bed before David woke up, but he'd reached for her hand as he came to semi-consciousness.

'Hey, beautiful. Where are you going?'

Hoping he'd slip back into dreamland, she kept her voice to a low whisper. 'Got to get ready for the spa day. Lauren's birthday, remember?'

David rolled his head to the side so that he could squint at the alarm clock but didn't let go of her hand. 'You've got hours yet. Come here and keep me warm.'

She resisted his gentle tug. 'No, I need to get up. I don't want to sleep late.'

He raised an eyebrow. 'I wasn't suggesting that we sleep.'

Even the thought of lying next to him naked made her skin

itch right now. She wanted to take a shower and get today over with. 'Not now. I'm not in the mood.'

Even if she hadn't heard how snippy she sounded, David's deep sigh of irritation confirmed it. 'When was the last time we spent the morning in bed together? Breakfast, the papers, a tumble in the sheets.'

She barked a laugh and wrenched her hand free. 'You make it sound like a montage from a cheesy eighties movie.'

Pushing himself up onto an elbow, he watched her. 'I'm serious, Kat. I know it's been difficult, but we haven't been... together for weeks.'

How many more euphemisms for sex was he going to use? 'I'm just tired, David. Work. The fertility treatment. It's been a lot.'

She pulled open the bottom drawer for her underwear, hoping he would go back to sleep. But he was awake now and wanted to talk. 'We don't have to do this, Kat. The IVF. If it's too much, we can stop.'

Hadn't he realised that they *had* stopped? How many times did she have to put off making an appointment at the clinic before he got the message? 'Go back to sleep, David. I'll see you tonight.'

She'd heard him punch the pillow in frustration as she'd left the bedroom.

Standing at the shallow end of the pool, Priya held out her hands. She was so tiny that the thick robe they'd been given at reception almost swallowed her. 'Where shall we sit, ladies?'

'Let's stay on this side.' Lauren was still tying her hair up in a messy bun on the top of her head, the belt of her white towelling robe hanging loose. 'I don't want to sit too near to the sauna and steam room in case it gets busier later.'

'Good idea.' Katherine led the way, her robe tightly fastened over her swimsuit and her arms full of magazines. If she could nab the bed on the end of the row, she could pretend to be asleep and not get in the way of their conversation. That was, if she could sleep. The acrid atmosphere between her and David on her way out of the house had left her feeling antsy and annoyed. Maybe she could work it off? A nice swim might do it. 'Actually, I can't wait to get in that pool. Do a few lengths.'

'You do realise this is supposed to be relaxing, don't you?' Priya spread a thick navy towel onto the sunbed before lowering herself onto it.

Katherine had brought enough magazines for all of them – there were always lots of lifestyle and celebrity magazines at the office. Lauren held out her hands for one, and Katherine piled the others onto the two tables between their three sunbeds.

Priya already had her eyes closed, a smile of contentment on her face. 'This is wonderful. Thank goodness Ben had no idea what to get you for your birthday, Lauren.'

Lauren had finished fiddling with her hair, and she stretched her arms above her head and yawned. 'Yep. This definitely beats the soup maker he bought me last year. I'm just pleased we could get *you* here, Katherine. Trying to get you to commit to a date was impossible. I was beginning to think you were keeping your diary open for a better offer.'

Lauren was joking, but the quicker Katherine could get her off that train of thought, the better. 'I can still hear Ben's poor confused voice when you yelled at him about the soup maker.' She mimicked Ben's accent. '*But you like soup?*'

Lauren laughed along with her and Priya. 'Well, we can't all have a David. What did he get you last year, Kat? Wasn't it a special edition of the book you did for A level?'

She used to like it when they hero-worshipped her husband. Not any longer. 'Yes. *The Go-Between*. Do either of you fancy the jacuzzi? I'd rather go in now than later, when other people's bodies have turned it to human soup.'

'Good idea, as you phrased it so eloquently.' Lauren swung her legs off the edge of the bed and sat up. 'Coming, Pri?'

Priya pressed her lips together before answering. 'No, I don't fancy it today.'

'What?' Katherine was amazed. When Lauren had hired a hot tub for a weekend last summer, they hadn't been able to prise Priya out of it for hours. 'What's happened to you?'

Lauren's gasp made her turn; her hand was up to her mouth and her eyes were wide. 'You're not?'

Priya opened her eyes and a smile spread across her mouth like jam. 'It's your birthday weekend. I don't want to—'

Lauren squealed and reached out for Priya's hand. 'That doesn't matter. I'm so excited for you.'

What the hell were they talking about? 'Priya? What's going on? And what does it have to do with the jacuzzi?'

Priya blushed. 'You're not supposed to use a jacuzzi when you're pregnant.'

It took a moment for Katherine to realise what she was saying. *Fantastic.* As if it wasn't difficult enough for her to avoid talk about babies. 'Pregnant? That's great – congratulations.'

Even to her ears, the words sounded hollow. She was pleased for Priya, but she could really do without this today.

She could also do without Priya's sympathetic expression. 'It'll happen for you soon, Kat. I know it will. And David will make such a great dad.'

Katherine loosened her robe. This further adoration of her husband made her even more irritated. And had someone turned the heating up in here? What had been comfortably warm now felt oppressive. 'No, it won't. We've having a break from it all.'

That wasn't the only thing they would be having a break from, but she wasn't about to get into that with them. Especially seeing their disappointment that she wouldn't be joining the cult of motherhood anytime soon. Though they'd been her friends for years, Lauren and Priya had changed since marriage and moving to the suburbs.

Lauren was the first to recover herself. 'Well, I'm sure it's a lot to go through. Maybe it's a good idea to give yourself a break.'

Priya took her lead. 'Someone at work stopped their fertility treatment and spent the money on a trip to Thailand. Came back pregnant. She says it's because she stopped being anxious about it.'

Katherine squeezed her hands into fists in her lap. A combination of their sympathy and the damp heat was making her nauseous. She should have got in the pool at the start. 'Yeah. Cheers. Anyway, I'm going to go for a swim.'

Thankfully, neither of them followed her. She could almost feel their eyes on her back, knew that they were waiting for her to be out of earshot before they whispered their embarrassment, sympathy and surprise to one another.

When she slipped into the pool, the cool water was a relief and, within a couple of lengths, a calm settled on her shoulders. She resisted the urge to look at either of the others as she passed them on her third length. At least with her safely in the pool, they could get all the baby gushing out of the way. How long did she have to stay before she could make her excuses and leave?

Because there was somewhere else she needed to be while David wasn't expecting her home.

TWELVE

HANNAH

For most of their relationship, Hannah had accepted that David didn't like to talk about Katherine. Occasionally, after an evening with his friends, something would come up in conversation and he would answer any question she had. Now, though, the conversation with Katherine's mother, plus seeing Katherine's name on the form at the clinic, had brought David's late wife into focus for Hannah as a living, breathing woman. A woman who had not only been married to the same man as her, but who had been through many of the same experiences. Maybe she did need to find out more about Katherine. Speaking to the clinic about the embryos was one thing; what about the woman who had helped produce them?

Although David had offered to tell her anything she wanted to know, it hadn't helped. 'What do you want me to tell you? She was fit and healthy. And you know what she looks like because you've seen the photographs.'

She needed more than that, a picture of the whole woman, but didn't even know the questions to ask. There was something he wasn't telling her; she was sure of it. First, he hadn't told her about the fertility treatment. Then he'd kept back the fact that

Katherine had wanted to stop trying for a baby. It wasn't that she thought he was being deceitful, more that he didn't want to speak ill of his late first wife. In the end, she'd decided that the only way she was going to find out what she needed was to ask Katherine's friends.

She got the perfect opportunity that weekend. Luke had been given corporate tickets to a rugby match and invited David and Ben along. Lauren had called to invite Hannah to join her and Priya for afternoon tea. For once, Hannah hadn't invented a prior engagement. 'That would be lovely. Let me know if I can bring anything.'

Judging by the tone of surprise in Lauren's voice, she clearly hadn't been expecting Hannah to accept either. 'Oh, great. Yes, great. Will be lovely to see you on your own for once. And no, you don't need to bring anything. I'm planning to order in an afternoon tea from a new cafe that's just opened. Everyone's raving about their scones.'

In the event, Hannah arrived at about the same time as the food delivery. The afternoon was warm and, when she arrived, Priya was already sitting in the back garden, a glass of Pimm's in her hand. The children were in their swimsuits, playing in the paddling pool. Priya held up a jug. 'Would you like one? I can only have one because of the kids, so there's plenty here if you're not driving.'

'Yes, thanks. I am driving but I can have one. I might have to leave to collect David from the station after the match.'

Priya laughed. 'Good luck with that. The corporate hospitality often goes on a while after.'

Lauren appeared holding a fancy cake stand where she'd arranged the tiny sandwiches and cakes. Two small pairs of feet came running over, and the little girls hovered close to the table like bees around jam. 'Hold on, you two, this is for the mummies. I'm bringing yours out in one minute. Go back to the pool.'

As they ran off, she turned to Hannah. 'Sorry to refer to you like that. Slip of the tongue.'

Hannah was never quite sure just how much David shared with his friends, but this seemed as good a time as any. 'Actually, David and I are having fertility treatment.'

She could see by the look on their faces that he hadn't told them. Priya was the first to recover. 'David wants children?'

Having seen the way he was with theirs, she was surprised that this came as such a shock to them both. 'Yes. For as long as I've known him he's wanted a child. He's great with kids.'

They knew this; didn't Lauren always make a big show of Uncle David every time they turned up at hers? Now she was shaking her head in that patronising way that made Hannah want to throw something at her. 'He's great at playing with kids. Being a father is a different thing. And – without being rude – you haven't actually known him that long.'

Without being rude? Hannah dug her nails into the centre of her palms. 'We are married.'

'Yes. We know.'

Those three words were heavy with so much disapproval that Hannah wasn't quite sure which angle to start with. 'I know you think we moved too quickly. But once we knew we wanted children, there didn't seem any point in waiting.'

Priya smiled tightly. 'You can't rush into something like this. Having a baby can put a terrible strain on a relationship, you know.'

She was the same age as both of them, yet Hannah felt like a small child, the way that they were speaking. 'I know that. David has told me how things were with him and Katherine. I know how difficult things got between them.'

Lauren narrowed her eyes. 'He said what? There were no problems between them.'

Priya was shaking her head too. 'Katherine and David were the happiest couple you could meet. It was a standing joke with everyone how perfect they were.'

Was it Hannah's imagination or had they moved closer to one another; presenting a united front? 'I wasn't suggesting that they weren't. David just said that it had got difficult between the two of them.'

Priya tilted her head. 'Maybe he was trying to make you feel better?'

Better? About what? 'Look, forget I said anything. We're just starting out with all this. We don't even know if they'll let us use the embryos.'

'What embryos?'

Oh crikey. She'd really put her foot in it now. 'There are some embryos. From Katherine and David's treatment. There's a possibility that we might use them.'

For a few moments there was absolute silence around the table. Then, 'Is this your idea or David's?'

Lauren's icy tone made Hannah uncomfortable. 'Well, obviously he was the one to tell me about their existence, but we are making the decision together.'

'Making? So you haven't fully decided to do it?'

The children ran back to the table; Maisie got there first. 'Mummy! You said we could have cake!'

'Okay, okay, I'm going to get your lunch. But you all need to have a sandwich first.'

Priya sipped slowly on her Pimm's while Lauren disappeared inside to get the children's lunch. The silence between them was so awkward that Hannah had to fill it with something. 'Anya is very sweet. She looks just like you.'

Priya smiled over in her daughter's direction. 'I know. She has my temperament too. It's funny arguing with a small version of yourself.'

They watched as the girls descended like tiny savages on the plate of sandwiches that Lauren had brought out for them.

Priya turned to Hannah and lowered her voice. 'Have you thought about that? That the baby will look like Katherine. Doesn't that worry you at all?'

Wow. She really wasn't pulling her punches. Hannah took a deep breath. 'Of course I've thought about it. That's why I want to ask you both about her. You were her closest friends. You knew her better than anyone.'

Lauren took her seat back at the table, pushing her sunglasses down from the top of her head so that her eyes were covered. 'You want to know what she was like? She was wonderful. Funny, clever, beautiful. She had a great career. Did David tell you that she'd won awards for her TV shows?'

Hannah didn't want to admit that David rarely spoke about his wife. 'Actually, I think you might have mentioned it.'

Lauren was impossible to read with those huge sunglasses on, but the wobble in her voice suggested she was either really upset or really angry. 'She was at the top of her game. All she wanted was a baby.'

Priya nodded. 'And David was the one who stopped that from happening.'

This didn't make sense. David? Her David, who loved kids, hadn't wanted children with Katherine? This was not the version of the story she'd been told. 'I don't understand.'

Priya shrugged and reached for a sandwich. 'Neither did we, to be honest. One minute they were having fertility treatment, the next it was all off.'

This, at least, tied up with what David had told her. But not the part about whose decision it had been. She didn't trust either of these women enough to say that though. 'What made you think it was David's decision to stop?'

Lauren folded her arms. 'Because Katherine told us. She tried to be loyal at first – that's what she was like, she loved him so much. But eventually she admitted it. David didn't want children and he hadn't given her an explanation for it.'

'I felt terrible for her. I was pregnant with Anya at the time.' Priya's hands settled on her stomach as if she was feeling the memory there. 'I didn't know where to put myself when we met up. It was so obvious that she wanted a baby and there I was with this huge bump.'

All of this was so different from the little that David had told her that Hannah didn't know what to say. But these were Katherine's closest friends. Surely they would know if this was true?

As if she'd suddenly remembered the afternoon tea, Lauren leaned forwards to hand them both small china plates. 'We were quite angry with David for a while, but Katherine wouldn't let us say anything. She was so loyal to him.'

'And then, of course, after she died, he needed us. He was a complete mess. Kept blaming himself.' Priya helped herself to a couple of sandwiches, and Lauren did the same. Hannah's throat was so tight, she didn't think she'd be able to eat a thing for the rest of the afternoon.

Blaming himself? For a car accident that he wasn't even party to? None of this was making sense. Was there any way that both sides could hold an element of the truth? 'David told me that their first round of IVF had failed. Could it be that they just hadn't had time for another round before Katherine's accident?'

Lauren picked up the tray of sandwiches and held it out to her. 'That was months before she died. They could easily have had at least another cycle in that time. If not two.'

Priya waited for Hannah to take a sandwich before continuing the story. 'It was David who said no. And when he lost her, we couldn't help but think that if they'd started earlier, if things had been different, at least he would have had a child to comfort him. A piece of Katherine that he could keep forever.'

They stopped talking, and those words just hung in the air, before the silence was broken by Anya and Maisie, hand in hand, coming to demand that it was their turn for cake.

Both mothers busied themselves, collecting plates and handing out juice and cake. Hannah just stared at the untouched finger sandwich on her plate. Was this true? Was David not as keen to become a father as she'd always believed? And was he asking her to carry Katherine's baby because – now she was gone – he felt guilty that he hadn't granted her one wish? Or, worse than that, was it because he wanted to regain a part of the wife that he'd lost?

When Lauren sat down again, she slid a photograph album across the table towards Hannah. 'You wanted to know what Katherine was like? This is a photo album she made for me for my birthday. That was the kind of thing she loved to do. It's pictures of all of us on girls' nights out.'

Hannah wasn't sure that she wanted to see more pictures of David's beautiful wife, but she'd come here to find out more. Inside, there was picture after picture of them in beautiful clothes at glamorous venues, brightly coloured cocktails in their hands. There were pictures of Lauren with Katherine, and of her with Priya. Some of all three of them together, but also several with another woman who Hannah had never seen before. 'Who's this?'

Priya leaned forwards. 'That's Hayley.'

Her tone suggested that Hannah would know who she was referring to, but she'd never heard the name before. 'Who's Hayley?'

Lauren looked surprised. 'Has David never mentioned her? Hayley was Katherine's best friend. They'd known each other since university.'

Hannah looked again at the laughing woman in the photographs. She featured in enough of them to suggest that she'd been a firm fixture in their group. 'Do you not see her anymore?'

Priya shook her head. 'She moved to the States almost immediately after Katherine's accident. We don't really hear from her.'

This didn't add up either. Surely Katherine's best friend would have stayed in touch with her husband? Would have called him now and again to check how he was?

And why had David never even mentioned her name?

THIRTEEN

KATHERINE

Gianni's was on a side street from the High Street. It wasn't the trendiest of bars, but – as Hayley had said – 'If we're going for a catch-up, we want to be able to actually hear one another.'

Hayley had arrived back from America the week before. After a six-month secondment to the New York office, she said she was happy to be home, but Katherine was interested to hear all about it tonight. She'd hoped to see Hayley on her own, but somehow, Lauren and Priya had ended up inviting themselves along.

Bonded by a shared loved of Dostoevsky and Disaronno on the rocks since Freshers' Week at Loughborough University, Hayley had always been the kind of friend Katherine could see every day or once every six months and nothing would change. God, she'd missed her. Though she was close with Lauren and Priya, their husbands were just as tight with David. How could she expect them to keep anything she told them to themselves?

Although she'd been the one to choose the bar, Hayley was running late, but Lauren and Priya were already there when Katherine arrived, seated towards the back around a square table for four. There were so many mirrors, it was impossible to miss Priya's burgeoning bump. She kissed her and held her at arm's length. 'Look at you. You look fantastic.'

Priya shuffled back onto her stool and glanced at Lauren. 'Yeah, I'm fine. All good. What about you? How's work been this week? Manic again?'

Katherine almost blushed. She'd cancelled on Lauren and Priya at the last minute at least three times in the last month. Little did they know, they'd been providing her with a cover story. 'Work's fine. We got two really good families this week, so that might be our first show of the new series sorted.'

Work had been great. So busy that she'd been able to throw herself into that and not think about anything else.

Lauren tilted her head and looked at Katherine through one eye, as if she was appraising a work of art. 'You're looking pretty good yourself. Have you been on that clean eating regime everyone's doing? I don't think I've ever seen you so slim.'

'Maybe she just looks skinny because I've got so fat.' Priya blew out her cheeks then winked at Katherine. 'You do look positively gamine. David better up his game or you might get whisked away on the arm of a passing supermodel.'

She could only hope that the blush creeping up her face would be hidden by the low lighting and not give her away. 'Oh, you know. Just trying to keep up with the youngsters I'm working with these days.'

Thankfully, Hayley chose that moment to arrive. 'Sorry I'm late! I'll get a round in.' She motioned towards the girls' glasses. 'Mojitos all round, is it?'

'I probably shouldn't have a third, but yes please.' From the colour of Lauren's cheeks, the first two were hitting the spot.

Priya raised a hand. 'Mine's a virgin one, please. No alcohol.'

'Of course.' Hayley winked at Katherine. 'I'm assuming you're not a virgin?'

Katherine shook her head. 'Nope. In fact, if the bartender wants to double up on the alcohol, he can go right ahead.'

The bar must have been empty or Hayley had put in some good flirting with the barman, because she was back with their drinks by the time Katherine had told Priya and Lauren about the couples she was working with at the moment. Ever the organiser, Hayley had remembered to ask the barman to put a different-coloured straw in the alcohol-free drink and she passed that to Priya first. 'There's the boring one.'

For the next twenty minutes, Hayley regaled them with her exploits stateside, Priya laid out her possibly naïve plans for maternity leave and Lauren – predictably – recounted something terribly funny that Maisie had done that afternoon. Then the attention turned to Katherine and it was Lauren who took the plunge. 'So what's new with you, Katherine?'

Obviously, they wanted to know about the IVF. Lauren was bound to have quizzed David when he'd collected Ben for a game of squash on Tuesday, but Katherine was going to make them work for it. 'Not much.'

Lauren's third drink did nothing for her tact. 'What about the fertility treatment? Any plans?

Katherine sipped at her mojito; the sharpness of the lime almost made her eyes water. Handy, really. 'No change there. We're still putting it on hold for a while. Just not the right time.'

Priya and Lauren made sympathetic noises; Hayley sucked at her straw in silence.

Lauren waved her drink around. 'But you've come so far, put yourself through so much. I know it must be disappointing, but you just need to get back on the horse.'

She'd known this was how they'd be, which was why she hadn't wanted to talk about it. 'We're not saying never. We're just saying not now.'

Priya's bump was clearly visible now that Katherine knew she was pregnant. She tried not to look at it when Priya spoke.

'What about the embryos you have in storage? What will happen to those?'

That was an easier answer. 'They just stay in storage until we're ready to use them.'

Hayley still hadn't spoken. Of course, she knew all of this already, but Katherine would have appreciated a little back-up.

Lauren had that look on her face. She was about to give what Ben called 'one of her opinions'. Well meant, but less than tactful. 'I think this is a mistake, Katherine. If you wait too long, it'll be like starting all over again. Now the drugs are in your system, you—'

'It's not me. It's David.' She hadn't meant to blurt that out, but it seemed like the only way to stop Lauren from talking. She lowered her voice. 'David is the one who doesn't want to go through it all again.'

There was a sharp intake of breath from Priya. Lauren just looked confused. 'David? I don't understand.'

Now she'd started, she had to follow through. 'Well, he isn't even a hundred per cent sure that he wants children. He said he did, but now I think all this has given him time to start doubting it again.'

She could almost feel the weight of Hayley's frown as the lies rolled out of her mouth. She willed her not to say anything. *Please just wait and let me explain.*

Lauren was shaking her head. 'I can't believe it. He makes such a fuss of Maisie. The first time you visited us after she was born, Ben and I were having bets after that you two would be the next to announce you were having one.' Her eyes widened as she realised how tactless that had been and she smacked her hand to her lips. 'I am so, so sorry I just said that.'

Katherine waved away her apology; there was no need to make this more dramatic than it needed to be. 'Don't worry. Honestly. Yes, that's what I thought too. But I guess there's a big difference between liking babies and wanting one.'

She could almost feel the bile forming in her stomach talking about David in this way, but what choice did she have? If she told them it was her decision, they wouldn't let up all night.

Priya was ever the optimist. 'Maybe he just needs some time to process everything. I'm sure this hasn't been easy for either of you.'

Finally, Hayley joined in. 'Well, let's just leave that for now and work on operation cheer up instead. I think the barman fancies me, so you lot had better up your game or I'm off.'

It was clunky, but it worked. The conversation moved on.

Half an hour later, Katherine was washing her hands in the ladies' toilet, speaking to Hayley through the cubicle door. Though she knew she was being unfair, she felt irritable. 'You could have helped me out a bit earlier back there.'

Hayley's voice echoed in the cubicle. 'What? When you were telling complete lies about poor David not wanting kids?'

The joy of a good friend is also the pain of one: they could be honest without holding back. 'Even so. You're usually the first person to complain when women are presumed to be desperate to have children. You could have supported me.'

The toilet flushed and Hayley came out laughing. 'Really? The one woman without children telling you not to bother with IVF? I can imagine how that would have gone down. And why did you tell them it was David? That doesn't seem very fair. Next time she sees him, Lauren will go for him.'

Katherine had to raise her voice over the sound of the hand dryer. 'No she won't. I told her not to.'

Hayley washed her hands and waited for the dryer to stop blasting air into the room. 'But why didn't you just tell them it was you? Crikey, Kat. The injections, the hormones, the internal scans – anyone would understand why you wanted a break from all of that.'

Katherine leaned against the wall with her arms crossed. 'Anyone except the two most recent members of the "motherhood is life" club. Surely it must get on your nerves too?'

'Of course it does. I think the month we had to hear about Lauren's extensive research into teething rings was a particular low for me, but this is different.' Hayley dropped her bag onto the counter next to the basins and started to rummage around in it.

'Tell me what's been happening with you. Was it amazing, living in New York?'

They'd spoken about it over the phone, but Katherine got a surge of envy at the smile that came over Hayley's face. 'It was incredible, Kat. You'd love it there.'

Katherine knew it was true. She'd only ever been to New York for a long weekend but even then, she'd known it was the kind of city that would make her feel twice as alive. 'What were the people like? Who did you hang out with?'

Applying her lipstick in the mirror, Hayley didn't reply immediately. Then she paused and looked Katherine's reflection in the eye. 'Actually, I met someone. A guy who worked on the floor below. He's called Gerard.'

There was a twinkle in her eye that suggested that she wasn't talking about a brief encounter. 'Really? That's so exciting. Is it serious?'

Hayley had gone back to her lipstick. Six months in New York hadn't changed her; the lipstick brand she'd bought for years cost more than a pair of shoes, so she always used it right down to the nub. 'Maybe. He's applying for a secondment to the UK office.'

There was something different here though. Hayley had always been very easy-come, easy-go about relationships, but

Katherine could almost see the excitement coming off her friend in waves.

Katherine, of course, knew exactly how she felt. The pop of attraction, the fizz of a brushed hand or a long kiss: nothing was more thrilling than beginning a new relationship. There was no history, no resentment, no expectation. Turning a fresh page on a story with no idea how it was going to end. Who wouldn't want to be caught up in the bubble of a love affair? 'That's so brilliant, Hayls. I'm so happy for you.'

Turning around and slipping her lipstick back into her bag, Hayley pulled a face. 'Don't get too excited yet. Who knows whether it will develop into anything. We can't all be you and David, you know?'

She was clearly joking, but a crack of guilt fractured Katherine's chest. 'Yeah, well. Maybe me and David aren't quite the couple you left six months ago.'

Hayley frowned. 'What's the matter? What's happened?'

How was she going to start this? 'Nothing. That's the problem.'

Hayley adored David. In a more inebriated moment, she'd been known to call him 'the perfect husband'. They all talked about him like that: Lauren and Priya too. *David is so good-looking. David takes you to all the best places. David is so in love with you.*

Now Hayley looked genuinely worried. 'Is it the fertility treatment? I'm so sorry that I haven't been more in the loop with all of that. I know it's no excuse, but the time difference and the job and—'

'The sexy American?' Katherine nudged her and smiled. 'Don't apologise, you loon. I've been busy too. Now that I'm an award-winning producer, everyone wants a piece of me.'

She'd meant it as a joke, but she almost winced at how true it was.

It wasn't enough to throw Hayley off the scent. 'What are you not telling me? I know you. You're hiding something.'

This wasn't the time or the place for this kind of revelation. Especially with Lauren and Priya back in the bar waiting for them. 'It's nothing. Just an argument. We're fine.'

Hannah narrowed her eyes as if she was trying to read Katherine's mind. 'I'm your best friend, Kat. You can tell me anything – you know that. I'm back now. What can I do?'

There was nothing Hayley could do, except not judge her or make her change her mind. Was it too much to ask? 'Right now, you can help me work my way through the cocktail menu and fend off any questions about babies, husbands or fertility treatment from the fecund two in there.'

'Of course.' Hayley smiled. 'Tonight, we'll drink, but tomorrow we'll talk.'

Tomorrow we'll talk. Katherine would trust Hayley with her life, but could she trust her with the secret that was going to blow apart her and David's marriage?

FOURTEEN

HANNAH

Priya had been right about the men wringing every last drop from their corporate box at the rugby. After that, they'd continued the party at a Walkabout with some Aussies they'd befriended, so it was pretty late when David had got home and he'd been in no condition for a heart-to-heart about his first wife.

The next morning, Hannah was awake at seven; her mind a hive of thoughts and concerns. After pouring David a large glass of water and leaving it on his bedside table with a packet of Alka-Seltzer, she left him in bed sleeping off his hangover and took a walk around the block. She needed to get these buzzing thoughts out of her head.

Lauren and Priya had taken everything she'd thought about her husband and turned it on its head. Of course they were going to idealise their friend now she was gone, but David was their friend too. Why would they have said that it had been him who stopped the treatment if it wasn't true? And if it was, then why had he told Hannah that he wanted children when they first met?

Round and round she went, her thoughts circling her head

in time with her feet pounding the streets. When David got up this morning, she was going to need to talk to him. But what would she say?

The only other person she knew who would be up at this time was Tessa. She was the kind of person who had her first load of laundry on by 5.30 a.m. Talking it through with her would really help. She sent her a text. *Are you up? Fancy getting breakfast at the cafe?*

The reply pinged before she'd even put her seat belt on. *Yes! But Gareth needs the car to take Josh to training. Can you pick me up?*

Tessa's front door was opened by her ten-year-old daughter, Daisy. In the last six months, she'd changed from a giggly little girl who ran around in old T-shirts and shorts, to being more reserved and concerned about how she looked and what she wore.

'Hi, Hannah. Mum is finding Josh's rugby shorts because apparently he has lost them.' She rolled her eyes at Hannah as if she was one of the grown-ups, exasperated at her brother's ineptitude. It made Hannah smile.

'No problem. I'm not in a rush.'

'You can come and sit in the kitchen with me? I'm leaving to hang out with my friend Luna in a minute, but I can't go until Mum has found Josh's stupid shorts.'

Hannah stifled another smile. 'That would be great. Thanks.'

Tessa's kitchen was a sunny yellow and spotless. The breakfast bar smelled faintly of lemon; clearly Tessa had already been on a cleaning binge this morning. Hannah took a stool. She'd sat here many times over the years, chatting, crying, consoling, cackling with laughter. All the friendship stuff.

Daisy leaned against the kitchen cupboard opposite. 'I hate my brother.'

Hannah shook her head. 'You can't hate him. And you're lucky to have a brother, you know. I always wanted to have a brother or sister when I was growing up.'

Daisy frowned. 'You wouldn't if you knew how annoying they are.'

Hannah leaned her elbows on the breakfast bar. It was still a little damp from Tessa's efforts. 'Do you know what my dad used to say to me? He used to say that your family were the only thing in your life you couldn't replace.'

It was the first time she'd spoken this aloud in many years and, for the first time, it sounded different. Because wasn't that exactly what she was? A replacement wife?

She could remember her dad saying that to her many times when she was small. Once, she'd asked him outright why she didn't have any brothers or sisters, but he'd looked so sad when he'd told her it 'just didn't happen' that she hadn't asked again. To this day, she still wasn't sure whether her parents hadn't been able to have another child or whether her mum just hadn't wanted another.

Maybe it had been worse for her dad because he was an only child too. She would imagine that there were many children who were happy to be the only one in their family, but it wasn't true for her and, she could tell, it hadn't been true for her dad either.

Daisy wasn't believing a word. 'Maybe if I had a sister. But a brother? No. I'd much rather be with Luna.'

'Your friend?'

Daisy nodded. 'My best friend. She's like a sister anyway. Ask Mum. She said she might as well adopt her because she's at our house so much.'

Hannah knew that feeling; of course she did. Hadn't she felt the same about her friend, Viv? They'd been inseparable at

Daisy's age too. Every other weekend they would sleep over together at Hannah's or at Viv's. Their mothers had become friends; their fathers had gone fishing together. They were better than sisters – they used to say – because they'd chosen one another. But she and Viv had lost touch after they went to university. Even a best friend wasn't the same as family.

'Friends are important, of course they are. Look at me and your mum.' Hannah nodded towards the door, where they could hear Tessa telling her son to, 'Open your eyes and actually *look*, Josh.'

Daisy grinned. 'Yeah, Mum always says that about you and Charlotte being her best friends.'

Hannah tried not to look surprised. She counted Charlotte and Tessa as her closest friends, but Charlotte and Tessa had known each other longer. It had seemed obvious to her that they were closer. It was nice to think that they saw her like that. 'Yes, well, exactly that. It's really important to have that. But look at your mum and her sister.'

Daisy raised an eyebrow. 'Auntie Cheryl?'

'Yes. They are even closer, aren't they? I mean, they've known each other their whole lives.'

That was it. Family knew you forever. From your earliest moments. There was something deep in that. Something that couldn't be supplanted by anyone else. You could lose a friend and gain another – she certainly had. But family? Like her dad had said, that was forever.

Her mobile rang in her bag and she mouthed an apology to Daisy as she accepted the call. 'Hello?'

'Hannah? It's Tony. I got your number from your mum's address book. I hope that's okay?'

Was her mother the last remaining person who wrote telephone numbers down in her little address book? 'Of course it's okay. Is everything all right with Mum?'

'Yes. She's fine. I was wondering if you had some time in the next couple of days to meet up. I wanted to have a chat with you about something. Without your mother there.'

Hannah's could feel her heart rate quicken. 'There is something wrong, isn't there? What is it?'

'No. No. Nothing like that.' She heard him sigh deeply at the other end. 'I wanted to ask you this in person, but... well... I wondered if I could have your permission to ask your mother to marry me?'

Relief that he wasn't about to tell her that her mother's condition had worsened was quickly supplanted with an uneasy feeling. Marriage? Did they really need to do that? 'Oh, I see. Well, it's not really up to me, Tony. You need to ask Mum.'

'I know that. But there's no way she'll even consider it if you're not happy about it. So I wanted to run it past you first. Are you okay with me asking? About us getting married, if your mum agrees.' He paused. 'I will look after her, you know.'

Hannah softened. She knew that Tony would look after her mother. Wasn't he doing a great job of that already? However strange it was to think of her father being replaced at home, she would have to be the biggest of hypocrites to stand in their way. Because, however unpleasant the thought, wasn't she a replacement too? 'Of course I'm happy, Tony. And I know how happy you make Mum. Good luck with your proposal.'

She could almost hear him smile at the other end. 'Thanks, love. After three years, it's about time I made an honest woman of her. Fingers crossed, eh?'

As she'd said goodbye to Tony, the kitchen door opened and Tessa appeared. 'Sorry about that. Apparently, the best place to leave your rugby shorts is stuffed under your bed. Who knew?'

Daisy pulled a face at Hannah as if this confirmed everything she'd been saying. 'Is Dad ready to take me to Luna's now?'

'I think so. Go and find him.'

Daisy bolted for the door with a wave. 'Bye!'

Tessa held out her hands to Hannah. 'Take me away from all this.'

Dunes cafe had been their regular haunt since their early twenties, when it had been the place to break their hangover with a Breakfast Baguette and rake over the events of the night before. Now, they came at a more civilised time of day and drank lattes and ate mozzarella and basil sandwiches.

It was still early enough for there to be several empty tables. They sat in the far corner with their coffee and pastries. Hannah told Tessa what Priya and Lauren had said about David. She didn't give away the real concern she had, but Tessa was her friend: she didn't have to.

'Please tell me you're not thinking that David only wants you to use Katherine's embryo because of some guilt he's carrying from her death?'

That was exactly what she was worried about. But when Tessa spelled it out like that, it did sound kind of crazy. 'I'm being ridiculous, right?'

Tessa put down her cup and reached across to squeeze Hannah's arm. 'Oh, Hannah. Why do you always think the worst? David loves you. We can all see that.'

It was more complicated than being in love though. 'But you and Charlotte were concerned about me using Katherine's embryos. Why was that?'

'Because we're your friends and we're looking out for you. The same as when you told us you were dating a man who'd lost his wife nine months before, and we were worried you were going to get hurt. Or when you announced you were marrying him three months after you started dating and we worried you were going too fast. We worry about you because we love you, and we want your life to be as easy as it can be because you deserve it.'

Hannah's eyes filled at these protestations of her friends' love. 'It's not though, is it? Life, I mean. It's not easy.'

Tessa shook her head. 'Sadly no. But too much easy is boring.'

Hannah smiled. 'I'd take an easy pregnancy. Or at least conception.'

'I know, love. It sucks that you have to go through all this.' Tessa winked at her. 'I wish I could tell you it'll all be worth it.'

Of course this was a joke; the smile of pride on Tessa's face whenever she talked about Josh or Daisy was clear to anyone. That's what Hannah wanted. Her own child. Someone who belonged to her.

This was something else that had been on her mind. 'When you had your two, did you feel like a mother straight away? After you gave birth, I mean.'

Tessa frowned, taking a few moments to consider her answer. 'Well, it was quite difficult with Josh because of the general anaesthetic. The first couple of days, I felt a little detached. But with Daisy, yes, it was pretty instant.'

'And do you think it was the giving birth that made that happen? Or do you think it's a genetic thing – you instinctively knew she was yours?'

Tessa shrugged. 'That's impossible to say. But you don't have to give birth to have a child. Look at Charlotte. I can barely remember her without a small boy either side of her.'

It wasn't an exaggeration. Charlotte was such a natural mother that it was hard to recall what she'd been like before she'd adopted the boys. 'I know. Oh, this is all so difficult to get my head around.'

'You need to talk to David. Tell him how you're feeling. There's no rush for you to make this decision, is there?'

'No. And we have to go and see a counsellor before they'll agree to it anyway. Our first appointment is this Tuesday.'

'There you are then. You're a speech therapist – surely talking is your thing?'

Of course Tessa was right. And maybe it would be easier to go through all of this with the counsellor; she would know the right questions to ask, wouldn't she?

If it didn't come up during their session, Hannah would *definitely* bring it up with David herself. It wasn't that she couldn't talk to him about it all; it was that she was worried what his answer might be. Would she still want to have a baby with him if it turned out he was doing it for all the wrong reasons?

FIFTEEN

HANNAH

The day of their first counselling session didn't get off to the greatest of starts.

Hannah didn't like to let any of the children down, so she'd made the appointment for 4 p.m. when the school day was over. Her *Paw Patrol*-loving student Ethan had had a breakthrough today. His communication skills were getting better every week. Hopefully, Hannah could follow his lead.

David had left his office earlier and collected her from school so that they could travel to the session together. As soon as he'd pulled away, she'd known there was something on his mind. 'Are you nervous?'

He shook his head and glanced at her. 'I don't think so. This first appointment is just a getting to know you, isn't it? I don't think she'll have us lying on a couch talking about our childhoods.'

He smiled, but it didn't reach his eyes. Hannah let the silence settle. She felt as if she was on her way to an exam. One that she hadn't prepared for.

As they got closer to the clinic, David began to tap on the

steering wheel. Hannah had worked with enough anxious children to recognise the signs. 'Are you sure you're okay?'

He took a deep breath. 'I've just been thinking about it all, and the thing is...' He was hesitating, and it made her heart thump as she wondered what he was about to say. 'If we're going to do this, we need to do it. I mean, I don't want to get all the way through it and then you change your mind and it's all been for nothing.'

His voice was calm and kind, but his words stung. Where had this come from? 'It's a big thing, David. That's why we're seeing the counsellor today. To talk it all through. I want a baby; you know how much I want that. But we have to make sure this is right. For both of us.'

He held up his left hand, his right still on the wheel. 'I know that of course. It's just that I don't want to get my hopes up and then it all be for nothing.'

Did he mean getting his hopes up about having a child or about using Katherine's embryos? She didn't actually want to know the answer to that question. 'I understand that. But I'm not going to do something as massive as this out of fear that you'll be disappointed.'

He looked horrified. 'No, I'm not saying that, I'm just... being an idiot. Ignore me. Please. I'm sorry.'

It was so out of character that it was pretty difficult to ignore. David was usually so laid-back – it was strange to see him so tense. At least he was talking about it though. The same couldn't be said for everything she'd tried to discuss with him lately. 'It's okay. It's important we say how we're feeling. I'm nervous too.'

There were so many other things she wanted him to talk to her about, but she was still hoping that they would come up naturally when they were talking to the counsellor today. After they'd pulled into the car park and got out of the car, David took her hand, and she was grateful for its reassuring warmth. 'Let's do this.'

The waiting room at the clinic was beginning to feel very familiar. When their counsellor, Anita, came out to collect them, she took them further into the building than they'd been before. Her office was slightly smaller than Dr Nash's, but that might have been because there were three armchairs taking up room as well as her own desk and office chair. In many ways, the layout reminded Hannah of her own Speech and Language Therapy classroom: designed to put people at ease.

Anita looked a little younger than the two of them. Hannah wondered if she was a mother herself and how that affected her work with the people who came through here, desperate for a child of their own. Professionally, it shouldn't make a difference; personally, did she go home each night and hug her own children close? Or worry that she needed to start a family as soon as she could?

Anita held her hands out to indicate the armchairs. 'Take whichever seat you like. Can I get either of you a drink?'

Hannah nodded. 'I'd love a glass of water, thanks.'

David shook his head. 'I'm fine.'

Anita stepped outside the office to get Hannah's drink and they hovered near the chairs. Then David looked at her. 'Do you think she can tell something about us according to which chair we choose?'

Nervous laughter bubbled up from nowhere and Hannah covered her mouth. 'She's not a psychiatrist.'

David raised an eyebrow. 'How do you know? I mean, if I take the one looking out the window, she might think I'm trying to distract myself from the seriousness of having a baby, but if I take the one at the door—'

As he motioned towards it, the door opened and they both jumped to sit down as quickly as possible.

Anita placed the glass of water in front of Hannah, picked

up a file from her desk and took the third seat. 'It's great to meet you both. I've been through all of the notes from your consultant, so I am aware of the situation. My job is just to make sure that you've fully considered everything associated with using the embryos and that you are both ready to take that step.'

Her voice was soft and calm. Clearly she wasn't here to judge their decision, but it was difficult for Hannah not to let her mind run ahead of her. Had she imagined Anita's emphasis on 'both'?

David reached out and took Hannah's hand, giving it a squeeze as he spoke. 'We're ready when you are.'

'Okay, great. Well, today we'll go through everything that needs to be covered, but it is very likely that we'll want to meet at least one more time. As I'm sure Dr Nash said to you, we want you to take your time and be really sure that you are making the right decision for you both.'

That word again. Hannah was starting to feel paranoid. What had Dr Nash said in her notes? 'We understand. I'm sure this seems a little strange. Wanting to use embryos from David's first wife.'

Anita shook her head. 'Not at all. It's what works for the both of you. Can I ask why you wish to use these embryos rather than use eggs from an anonymous donor?'

She looked from one to the other, so Hannah was unsure which of them was expected to answer. Rather than let it appear to be David's idea, she went first. 'We want to have a baby as soon as we can. And, I suppose, it's also because we know the heritage of these embryos. Your notes must tell you that David lost his first wife in an accident, so...'

She trailed off, not sure where she was going with that statement. *Damn.* She wasn't starting well.

David came to her rescue. 'Yes, like Hannah says. I – we – know that Katherine was intelligent and sporty and generally a very successful human being, so the baby would be getting good genes.'

That sounded even worse. The room felt stuffy and warm and she couldn't shake off the feeling that the counsellor was giving them enough rope to hang themselves with.

But she seemed nice as she smiled at them. 'That's all very clear. Have you discussed any issues that might arise from using these embryos?'

David shifted in his seat. 'Such as?'

'Such as the child looking like' – she glanced down at her notes – 'Katherine? It's possible that that might affect each of you in different ways.'

Of course Hannah had thought about that. 'I'm not a jealous person by nature. I think it will be okay.'

David put a finger inside the collar of his shirt and ran it around as if to loosen it. 'For my part, I've considered that and I don't feel it will be a problem for me.'

He hadn't really answered the question. Up until now, Hannah had only really examined how *she'd* feel if they had a little girl who looked exactly like Katherine. But how was David going to feel if that happened? He barely ever talked about his first wife. What if Katherine's biological daughter triggered another wave of grief for him?

'We will also need to discuss your desire to implant more than one of the embryos. Obviously, this will be dependent on how many are suitable for transfer. And, of course, I want to talk you through the process itself: what to expect, how to manage those expectations.'

Hannah fought the urge to close her eyes and block this all out. On the one hand, she understood the need for it; on the other, wasn't it obvious to everyone what great parents she and David would make? Thousands of couples all around the world were having babies without anyone else's permission. Wasn't it bad enough that they had to go through the medical side of all of this without also feeling that they were being judged in some way?

Anita changed position so that she was angled towards Hannah. 'Hannah, I understand that Dr Nash has been through the procedures with you in terms of what will happen physically. Is there anything that you would like me to explain further?'

'No, I'm pretty clear about everything.'

'Good. Well, if anything occurs to you, you can call me anytime and we can talk it through. As you know, the hormones can sometimes bring side effects similar to those you might get around the time of your period, but stronger. So it's good to be prepared for the fact that you might feel more emotional or low than you usually do. All of that is very normal and usually doesn't last very long.'

That side of things Hannah was prepared for. She didn't look at David, but she knew he'd been through this already.

He still had hold of her hand and he squeezed it again. 'You just said about managing our expectations. How likely is it that we will be successful?'

'Well, there are some decisions that you will need to make with your consultant. You have four embryos available. It's not certain that all four will progress as we would want them to. On the morning of the embryo transfer, the embryologist will call you regularly to update you on whether the embryos have survived the thawing process. Often, they will thaw two or three at a time. But as this is a more complex situation, your consultant might suggest that they only thaw one at a time, leaving the others for a subsequent cycle.' Anita pulled a leaflet from her sheaf of paperwork and passed it to them. 'This goes through our current success rates, as well as any extra treatments you can add on for peace of mind, such as having the eggs under constant video surveillance after the embryologist takes them out of storage.'

Hannah glanced at the sheet, which seemed to have the same information that she'd already memorised from the website. 'We understand that it's not a guaranteed success.'

The counsellor nodded kindly. 'It's important to remember that this journey is full of ups and downs. You both need to feel able to be honest with each other about how you're feeling.'

Was this the moment that she should ask David why he hadn't wanted to go through a second round of IVF with Katherine? To ask him if he'd been really honest with her about how he was feeling?

But David smiled at Hannah and then the counsellor. 'We are.'

The entire session with Anita lasted around fifty minutes, but it seemed a lot quicker than that. Anita encouraged them to open up about their feelings, and Hannah hoped that David might say something about his previous experiences. But Hannah did most of the talking, unable to bear the silence each time after Anita asked them a question.

When the session came to an end, Anita smiled at them. 'It was great to meet you both. Thanks for sharing your journey with me.'

Hannah smiled and shook her hand, but inside she was screaming. She might have shared her feelings, but David hadn't said anything personal that she hadn't heard before.

If Hannah wanted answers to her questions, she was going to have to be the one who brought it up with him. And she needed to do it today before she lost her nerve again.

Back in the car, they sat for a few moments, catching their breath.

'Well, that was intense.' David smiled at her.

Hannah had the itchy feeling in her fingers that she used to get before an exam. 'Yeah. Lots to think about.'

David shifted around in his seat and looked at her. 'I'm sorry about before. I was just a bit tense, thinking about it all.'

'It all' was a phrase he seemed to be using a lot. She had no idea what it encompassed. 'Because of us, or because you've been here before?'

That wary look came over him again. She hated that this was coming between them, but they needed to be able to talk about it; wasn't that what the counsellor had said? Be honest with each other about how you're feeling. Well, she was feeling like she'd just been turned around wearing a blindfold and was dizzily trying to work out what direction she was going in.

'This doesn't have anything to do with Katherine, Hannah. This is about us. I wish you wouldn't keep bringing her into it.' That dark frown was back. His handsome, open face became shrouded and unreadable. She couldn't recall him ever looking at her like this before they'd started on this journey.

But she couldn't keep letting him slip away from her questions. 'These embryos are half her, David. She has everything to do with it. Our child will have her blood in its veins. It will be half her. I just want to know what that might be like. I just want to know a bit more what she was like. You told the counsellor she was sporty. I've never heard you say that before. What sports did she play?'

It was like she was picking at the ends of several threads and he was holding so tightly to the other end of them that she couldn't pull them towards her. His face had darkened further with the effort it seemed to be taking him to speak. 'I meant she was sporty as a child. By the time I knew her, it was mainly running and the gym. I just meant that she was fit and healthy. That must be a good thing for the child's genes, I'm guessing?'

The child. Suddenly articles and pronouns had become weighted with meaning. The child, her child, my child, their child. Which was it really? 'Yes, that is a good thing. A definite bonus on him or her getting my preference for couch over 5K.'

She'd meant to lighten the mood, but even she could hear the wobble in her voice.

David reached out for her. 'Oh, Hannah, please don't focus on all of that. Genes are a small part of what makes a person. Their nature is formed far more by the environment they grow up in. The environment we will provide. You are going to be such a wonderful mother. A natural mother. If you really want to know about Katherine, I know that being a mother wasn't anywhere near as important to her as it is to you. That has to mean something, surely?'

Even though he'd told her that Katherine had wanted to pause their fertility treatment, she couldn't help thinking that Lauren had said almost the exact same thing about him. So which was it? 'And you want it too? To be a father, I mean?'

'Of course! I really want it, but what I want most is for you to be happy. I want us to be happy. A baby would be a wonderful addition, but if it doesn't happen, I'm just glad that I found you.'

It was a beautiful thing to say, but it just made her feel more uncertain. She wanted him to want this as much as she did. With a desire that bordered on desperation. 'The thing is, I spoke to Lauren and Priya, and some things came out.'

He sat up straighter. 'What things? What did you ask?'

His behaviour wasn't quite what she'd expected. He was so defensive. To be fair to him, she could see how this might sound as if she was going behind his back. 'I wasn't exactly prying. It was the day you were at the rugby and I was at Lauren's. I just mentioned about the embryos and they acted really strangely.'

She could feel him relax a little next to her. 'Well, I'm sure it sounded strange to them. I mean, it's not an everyday occurrence, is it? And Katherine was their friend.'

'Yes. I know. But they said something that confused me.' She needed to get going now, get it all out there; she was tired of skirting around the conversation. 'They said Katherine told them that it was *you* who had wanted to stop the fertility treatment. They also said that she was desperate to have a child.' Something else occurred to her. 'Which is what her mum said too.'

She hadn't accused him of anything, but that's how he looked at her. His tone was cold. 'And now you don't believe me?'

She'd really hoped that this conversation would go better. 'I didn't say that. I just don't understand how they could have got it wrong.'

'Well, I don't know either. To be honest, we didn't tell them much about what was going on. Katherine wanted to be private about it. She didn't even want them to know that we were having treatment.'

It was strange that he thought Katherine wouldn't confide in her closest friends. 'But they did know.'

'Because I let it slip. She was angry about it, to be honest. But I don't know how much she told them after that. Maybe they just joined the dots and assumed it was me who stopped the treatment.'

Even this didn't make much sense. Lauren and Priya hadn't sounded as if they'd made assumptions. They'd sounded certain. Lauren had even seemed bitter towards David. 'So you did definitely want children? You do want a child now?'

'Yes. Of course.' He slipped an arm around her back. 'I don't know what they've said to rattle you, but I want a child. One hundred per cent.'

It was impossible to get to the bottom of this without outright calling him a liar. And maybe Lauren and Priya had got the wrong idea from Katherine. 'I'm sorry. But surely you can see how confusing all this is for me? Especially when you refuse to talk about her.'

He closed his eyes and nodded. 'Okay. You're right. I have been holding back a bit on telling you much about Katherine.

And the reason is that I find it difficult. Because it's quite complicated.'

Hannah was beginning to feel as if complicated was her middle name. 'I can understand that. I'm sure it's difficult to talk to me about her, but it's not like I'm jealous. I understand that you loved her. She was your wife.'

She couldn't quite read his expression. 'That's not what I mean. Yes, she was my wife and, yes, I loved her. Very much. You asked me what she was like? Well, she was full of life. Bigger than life even. Everything she did was at a fast pace and full steam ahead, and I loved to follow in her wake. But that could be quite exhausting too.'

Maybe he'd been right that it wasn't best to have this conversation in her current tired state, but she couldn't help but ask, 'So you went for a slower, less exciting wife?'

David looked horrified. 'No. Not at all. That's not what I meant. I think our marriage is so good because we're alike in so many ways. We enjoy – and want – the same things.'

It had been petty of her to make that jibe. 'I'm sorry. Go on.'

David looked down at his hands, twisting his wedding ring around his finger. For the first time, Hannah wondered what had happened to his first ring. He hadn't been wearing it when they met – she knew that because she'd always checked – but it had never crossed her mind to ask. Like many things.

'Katherine was a lot of fun, and she was interesting and very kind to her friends. But in the year before her accident – well, pretty much from when we started fertility treatment – she changed. There was a distance between us that just seemed to grow wider. We argued all the time. She was away with work more and more.' He looked up at Hannah and the pain in his eyes almost made her gasp. 'She really stopped being a nice person. To me, at least.'

Hannah tried not to react with the shock she was feeling. 'Is that what you wanted to tell me? What made you so upset with me earlier?'

He looked down at his hands again. 'Kind of. I told you that the reason we didn't continue with the IVF treatment was that Katherine changed her mind. And I told you that I didn't really understand why.'

Hannah's heart thumped in her chest. What was he about to tell her? 'Yes.'

He took a deep breath. 'Well, that's not quite true.'

So Lauren and Priya had been telling the truth? It was David who had wanted to pull out of the treatment? 'Why did you lie to me?'

He shook his head. 'Because I was embarrassed? Ashamed? Maybe because Katherine is gone and I felt... disloyal telling anyone about it. Even you.'

This didn't make sense. 'Why were you ashamed that you didn't want children?'

He frowned. 'I did want children. Very much. The reason that Katherine didn't want children was because she was planning to leave me. Katherine was having an affair.'

SIXTEEN

KATHERINE

Hayley's office was on a side road at the bottom of Victoria Street. Busy and loud, the fumes from the traffic crawling past the Houses of Parliament made Katherine cough more than the hurry to get there on time. She'd tried to call ahead, but Hayley hadn't answered her mobile which probably meant she was in a meeting. Now Katherine was dashing across London to catch her before she left work.

It had been stupid to tell David she was out with Hayley tonight. But when he'd told her his plans for a romantic dinner, she'd just panicked.

He'd met her in the hall and helped her off with her coat. Then pulled her towards him and kissed her; she'd tried not to freeze in his arms.

'How was filming in Gateshead?'

Her mind raced to remember the story she'd told him. Best to keep it vague. 'Yeah, you know. The usual.'

He laughed. 'I remember when you first got that job. You said every day is an adventure, or something like that. Maybe you're ready for a new adventure?'

She almost laughed at that. She was. But not in the way he thought. 'No, it was fine. Just busy.'

'Well, how about I cheer you up with a reservation at Minelli's? I called them this afternoon and used my effortless charm to get them to squeeze us in.'

She was glad she'd turned to go upstairs; he wouldn't be able to see the expression on her face. 'No can do. I'm meeting Hayley tonight. Just going to run upstairs and put my jeans on.'

She managed another three steps before he spoke. 'Katherine?'

She looked over her shoulder at his frowning face. 'Yes?'

'We've hardly seen each other this week. You've been up in Gateshead for the last three days. I just assumed that we'd have a night together.'

She hadn't been in Gateshead at all; in fact, she'd been in a hotel in Central London. It was more than fortunate that she had a job where he didn't question long absences. 'You should have called me. How was I to know?'

His expression hardened. 'With everything that's gone on in the last few weeks, I thought we could do with a night out. No fertility conversations, no one else to please. Just us. I thought it might be a nice surprise.'

In another life, it would have been. Right now, she couldn't face being locked into a conversation she couldn't escape from and, even more importantly, where it would inevitably lead to. 'We can go there another time.'

He wasn't letting this one go; it was almost as if he knew that something was amiss. 'Can't you meet Hayley another time?'

One lie led quickly to another. 'She's already arranged to leave work early. It's too late to reschedule.' Fortunately for Katherine, Hayley was still working on projects with the New York office, so she usually stayed at work until around 8 p.m.

As she'd hurried up the stairs, she'd heard him mutter, 'Sorry might have been nice.'

Katherine made it to Hayley's building just in time to see her leave, laptop case strung across her body like a college student, and her face lit up when she saw Katherine waiting outside. 'This is a nice surprise. What have I done to deserve this?'

Katherine thought of the surprise David had tried to give her and guilt sliced through her. Thank goodness for Hayley and her powerful hug; Katherine held on for a few more seconds than she would normally. 'You might not be so pleased with me when I ask you to fib for me. Do you fancy getting some dinner?'

'Yes. Great. What about the Pizza Express around the corner from the station?'

'Perfect.' Actually, Katherine's stomach was churning so much, she wasn't sure that she could manage a plate of pizza, but she wanted to go to a bar even less.

Hayley put her arm through Katherine's and they started to walk up the street towards the station. 'So what great crime have you committed that you need absolving from? Have you been maxing out the joint account again?'

'Yes, but I can always get around David on that one.' Katherine tried to keep her voice light. If she made nothing of it, hopefully Hayley wouldn't be concerned. 'I told him you were leaving work early so that we could go out together.'

'Okay, but why did you need a cover story in the first place? Don't tell me David has turned into some kind of psycho husband, because I won't believe you.'

She'd had the Tube journey here to think about this. She hated lying to Hayley, but there was nothing else for it right now. 'Because I'd already arranged to go and look at a couple of venues. I want to plan a birthday celebration for him and you know what he's like at seeing through me. I want it to be a surprise.'

Another surprise. This much at least was true. She'd never been able to keep a secret from David. Until now, that was.

'Of course. It's his fortieth, isn't it? That's what you get for marrying an older man. Well, let me know if I can help. You know how much I like to organise a party. Do you remember that fancy dress one I had at the flat in Earls Court?'

'When you were living with all of those Australians? How could I forget?'

They were opposite the Pizza Express when a taxi screeched to a halt in the road beside them, sounding its horn at the apologetic pedestrian who had stepped from the kerb without looking. Hayley put her hand to her chest. 'Crikey. That made me jump. Let's get inside. I need a glass of wine to settle my nerves. Then we can start to make a list of the things you'll need to organise for the party.' She clapped her hands. 'I can't wait. Although I wish you'd told me a bit sooner. It's going to be tricky to book somewhere decent now.'

Katherine followed her into the restaurant. It would have been difficult to tell her about the party before now, when she'd only come up with the idea on the way over here.

The air in the restaurant was thick with garlic and conversation. When the waiter appeared to take their order, Hayley ordered a Penne Pesto, but even the thought of a large bowl of pasta made Katherine feel queasy. 'Could I just get a salad? Maybe a little chicken?'

The waited nodded his approval and took their menus. Hayley filled their glasses from the carafe of water he'd left. 'You're not on a diet, are you? Surely the advantage to being married is that you can let everything go?'

If only. 'No. Just not in the mood for anything heavy.'

Hayley folded her arms. 'Okay, so now I know there's something up. You always stop eating when you're worried about something. You were like it at university every time you met a new man or had an essay deadline. I'd be pushing down my stress with the nearest biscuit and you'd get more waif-like by the minute. What's going on with you and David? Talk to me.'

Katherine still couldn't make up her mind whether it was fair to involve Hayley in all of this yet. What if it turned into nothing? She would have asked her friend to lie to her husband for no reason.

She had that horrible bubbling feeling in her stomach, her heart thrumming with her indecision. There was no way she could untell Hayley: once it was out, it was out. But was this the right time? Small steps. 'I've decided I don't want to go through the fertility treatment again. I don't want to use the embryos we have stored.'

Hayley looked relieved. 'I thought it might be that. It's totally understandable, Kat. Has David taken it badly? Is that why you're upset?'

'I haven't told him yet. I can't face it.'

Hayley tilted her head to the side. 'I get it. I do. But you need to be honest with him, Katherine. He's a good man.'

She nodded. 'I'll tell him soon. Maybe a birthday bash will put me back in his good books.'

Hayley knew Katherine well enough not to push her point. 'Then let's start planning. I can do as much of it as you want me to do.'

Using the back of a paper napkin and an eyebrow pencil, Hayley made a list of things they needed to consider. There were a lot of things Katherine needed her to do, but it was a question of asking in a way that wouldn't arouse suspicion. 'Actually, I wondered if you would do me another favour? I'm going to need an address to use to have some things delivered. For his birthday. Can I use yours?'

Hayley held out her hands and shrugged. 'Of course. But I'm not at home during the day. So the postman usually leaves any packages in the communal hall. It's pretty safe, but I'm not sure about anything valuable.'

'It'll be mainly letters.'

'Letters?' Hayley's eyebrows came together. 'What are you getting him that needs a lot of letters?'

For the first time in the litany of lies that had been the last few weeks, Katherine's mind went blank. She looked at the beautiful face of her dear, dear friend, the face that had made her laugh so many times, that had made her cry when she'd left her for the US all those months ago. She'd missed her so much, and yet now she had her back again, she was lying to her. Yes, Hayley loved David, but she was Katherine's friend first. Surely she would stand by her and support her decision?

She took a deep breath. 'There's something I need to tell you, but you have to promise not to tell anyone. Not even David.'

Hayley raised an eyebrow. 'That's intriguing. Is it to do with the party?'

If only. 'No. It's nothing to do with David. It's me. And it's pretty big news.'

The smile dropped from Hayley's face. 'What is it, Katherine? You're scaring me.'

Katherine swallowed. This was it. 'The thing is. I've been lying to everyone.'

SEVENTEEN

HANNAH

An affair? Saint Katherine who never put a foot wrong?

Any momentary feelings of vindication were wiped from Hannah by David's expression: pain was written across it in indelible ink.

She reached across the handbrake to take his hand. It would have been easier to talk about this at home, but she didn't want to risk him clamming up again by suggesting it. 'Oh, David. I'm so sorry. Are you sure?'

He let out a long breath, though whether it was the release of long-held pressure or the deflation of revealed disappointment, Hannah didn't know. 'Completely sure. It took me a while to get up the courage to ask her, but when I did, she admitted it.' He flashed a brave smile at her which took her back to their first meeting in the bar, when his air of sadness had made her want to hug him.

If they hadn't still been sitting in the front of his car, that's what she would have done now. 'What made you suspect?'

He shrugged. 'Lots of little differences. Small and gradual to begin with, then faster and bigger. When I look back, I think that things started to change about the time she won her big producer award. The night of the ceremony was actually the first time I'd met any of her colleagues. Weird, isn't it? It had never occurred to me before that night how much she kept the two sides of her life – work and home – completely separate. Even that night, she barely introduced me to anyone. It was almost as if she was a little embarrassed about me. I'd never felt that before. With anyone.'

Hannah bet he hadn't. He was the kind of man women would be proud to be seen with, and that wasn't just her looking at him through the rose-coloured lens of love. She was always aware how other women looked at him, reacted to him. It was only the fact that he never, ever gave her cause to feel jealous that prevented it. 'And you think it was one of them?'

David looked down at his hands. The way he twisted his wedding band twisted something in Hannah too. Was he remembering a different band on his finger? The one Katherine had placed there? 'I don't know. Later, once she'd admitted the affair, I started to run the faces of those colleagues through my mind. Was it one of them? A cameraman, perhaps, or one of the presenters? It was agony.'

It was painful watching him relive this, but now he was speaking, she wanted to know everything. 'She didn't tell you who it was?'

He shook his head. 'No. Although I didn't actually ask her. I didn't want to know. Because if I knew who he was, I'd have to accept that he existed, that it was real. And then...'

He looked at her as if to check whether he was sharing too much. She could finish the sentence for him though. 'Then, if you worked through it and stayed together, you'd have to picture him forever.'

She knew how that felt. The photographs of Katherine on Lauren's walls were tattooed on her brain. 'So what were the other changes? What made you think she was having an affair?'

He stared forwards, through the light patter of rain which

obscured the windscreen. Was he picturing Katherine out there, in front of his headlights? 'She was working away more and more frequently. I mean, she'd always had to stay over on location – that was the nature of the show she worked on. But it happened more and more. She was hardly ever home. And when she was, she was just... not there. It's difficult to explain.'

He didn't need to. 'I think I understand. Was this after you'd started the fertility treatment?'

He kept his gaze straight ahead. 'Yes. It was after the first round had failed. Even her reaction to that wasn't what I'd expected. We were disappointed obviously, but I'd really expected her to launch herself into trying again. That's what she was like usually. Ambitious, a go-getter, a ball-buster, whatever you want to call it. She was someone who met every challenge head-on until she'd beaten it.'

There was something in his tone that made this sound as if he wasn't complimenting her. 'But she didn't?'

He turned to face her. 'No. She kept putting it off, avoiding talking about it. I assumed that she was worried about starting the hormone treatment again. Just shows how much you can kid yourself if you want to, right?'

Hannah shuddered. 'And you think it was because she was having an affair?'

'I'm certain. The night of my fortieth birthday, she threw a surprise dinner with all of our friends. It really was a surprise; she'd hardly spoken to me for the week before. When we first got to the restaurant and everyone was there, I was annoyed because I'd been hoping we could talk. But then she'd been her old self, laughing and joking with everyone, and I started to relax, taking it as a sign that we were going to be okay.' He coughed out a dry laugh. 'What a fool.'

'What happened?'

'I remember someone talking to the whole table. It might have been Ben, telling one of his "live TV fails" stories. And she kind of froze and went pale. She was staring straight at this tall young man at the bar. He looked just as you would expect someone who worked in TV to look, if you know what I mean.'

She did know. Impossibly attractive. Like Lauren. And Katherine. 'You think it was him?'

'All I know is that she really didn't want him to spot her. She wriggled around in her seat, shaded her face with her hand, kept her voice low or didn't speak at all until he left shortly afterwards, and then she went back to normal.'

This didn't sound like an open and shut case. In fact, David seemed more like a jealous partner. 'I don't mean to speak out of turn, but are you sure you weren't just imagining it?'

'Don't worry, that's what I told myself too. I asked when we got home whether she was seeing someone and she told me I was being ridiculous. So I just believed her. Again. You see what you want to see, right?'

Hannah was getting confused. 'But you said that she admitted it.'

'That came later. Things just kept getting worse between us. She could barely bear for me to touch her. She'd come home and go straight out again. Even Lauren called me because she was worried about her. Apparently, she was cancelling on them all the time too.' He shifted around in his seat and looked at her. 'Are you sure you want to hear all of this?'

To be honest, she wasn't sure. Wanting to know was pretty different from actually knowing. But she'd started now. 'Yes. Keep going.'

The rain on the windscreen was hard enough now that David needed to raise his voice to talk over it. 'That's it really. We argued more and more, and then I asked her again whether she was seeing someone. And this time she said yes.'

'Oh, David. How long was that before the accident?'

His expression didn't change. 'Two weeks.'

. . .

They couldn't sit in the car park all afternoon. David seemed wrung out with his revelations and needed to send some business emails before dinner, so, as soon as they got home, Hannah left him to it and disappeared upstairs to take off her make-up and change out of her work clothes.

When she'd first moved into the house, David had given her free rein to decorate their bedroom however she wanted. Soft grey walls, a white bedstead and navy scatter cushions – which he professed to be totally bemused by – had made for a beautiful restful space that she loved. But it was still the same room he'd slept in with Katherine.

For so long, she'd felt as if she was fighting to emerge from his first wife's shadow. That she was lesser than her somehow. The replacement wife, who had never lived up to the original in everyone else's eyes.

She found an Alice band in the top drawer of the dressing table and used it to push her hair away from her face. The whole of their relationship, she'd seen David as a grieving widower. But now she had to reimagine the last weeks of his marriage. Katherine's affair cast everything in a different light. How did he actually feel about her? Was he upset? Angry?

And if his feelings for Katherine were clouded by her treatment of him, how much more complex must his feelings be about the embryos they'd created together? Hannah had got answers to some of her questions, but they'd only sprouted more.

She stared at her face in the mirror as she dragged the make-up remover across her face with cotton wool. Wiping off her 'work face' took seconds. David had said that Katherine had kept her work and home lives completely separate. Was it possible for someone to live two lives like that and not be discovered? How long had her affair been going on? And why did it make Hannah feel so uncomfortable to know that David had discovered the affair only two weeks before Katherine died?

The door to the bedroom opened so slowly that she was almost expecting a ghost, but it was only David whose face appeared around the door. He smiled at her in the reflection of the dressing-table mirror. 'You look so different with your hair pushed back like that.' He waved her mobile phone at her. 'You left this downstairs and it keeps dinging with messages so I thought it might be important.'

'Thanks.'

He passed over the phone and left her to it. There were three messages, but they were all from Tony.

Just to let you know that your mum turned down my proposal.
I thought you should know.
Thanks, Tony.

Despite her discomfort at the idea of her mum being married to someone other than her dad, Hannah felt a pang of disappointment on Tony's behalf. She could imagine how crushed he would feel at being turned down.

I'm sorry, Tony. Hope you're okay.

Why *had* her mum turned him down? They were a married couple in all but name and postcode, so it wasn't a huge step to make it official.

With everything going on in the last week or so, Hannah was overdue a visit to see her mum. She'd go over there tomorrow evening and see what she had to say. And maybe it was time for her to tell her mum about Katherine's embryos too.

EIGHTEEN

HANNAH

When Hannah arrived at her mother's house straight from school on Wednesday, it was Tony who answered the door. As she followed him out to the kitchen, where – judging by the rainbow display of vegetables on the counter – he'd clearly been preparing a complicated dinner, she tried to offer her condolences about the refused proposal. She didn't get very far before he waved her words away with the potato peeler and a shake of his head. Instead, she had to listen for ten minutes about all the research he'd done around the best foods to keep her mum's heart healthy and which foods she should avoid. While he was speaking, Hannah hid the box of biscuits she'd brought behind her back. Eventually, he'd pointed upwards. 'Your mum is sorting stuff in the junk room if you want to go up?'

Since Hannah's childhood bedroom had been turned into a boutique-hotel-worthy guest room, the third bedroom at her mum's house had become a storage area for all the boxes she was going to 'sort out' someday. When she pushed the door open, there was resistance behind it – a combination of the carpet that had hardly ever been walked on and, it turned out, a large, heavy cardboard box – and she found her mum sitting on the floor surrounded by photographs. When she turned to face her, she looked as if she'd been crying. 'Oh hello, love. I didn't realise the time. I'll sort these out later.'

Hannah perched on the single bed that was pushed against the wall and leaned down to pick up a pile of photos of herself as a baby. 'Crikey, I was a chubby kid. What did you feed me on?'

Her mum snatched them back out of her hands. 'Don't you dare say that about my beautiful baby. You were well covered. Healthy.'

Hannah laughed as she picked up some more. 'Is that what you call it? There's three rings of fat around each wrist. And what am I wearing? Was that Nana Boothby's evil crocheting hook at work again?'

Now her mum laughed. 'God bless her. There wasn't an item of clothing she wouldn't crochet for you. If I'd let her, you'd probably have been wearing crocheted knickers to school.'

'Because that wouldn't have got me bullied at all.' Hannah flicked through more pictures until she came to one of her dad holding her. He was wearing a patterned tank top and the collar of his shirt pointed halfway down his chest. As she stroked his kind face, she allowed the familiar ache to settle in her chest. His loss never got easier.

Her mum leaned forwards to see what she was looking at. Her voice thickened. 'I love that one. Look how proud he was.'

In the photo, he was holding a tiny Hannah – this must have been before she drank milk by the gallon – in the crook of his arm, and was gazing down at her as if he couldn't believe she was his. 'He was a good dad.'

'Yes. And a good husband.' Her mum's voice wobbled and she pulled a crumpled tissue from her pocket and blew her nose – that explained the red eyes.

Hannah continued to flick through photo after photo. She'd

had no idea there were so many of them. 'Tony told me about the proposal. Well, actually he asked my permission.'

That made her mum smile. 'Did he? The silly sod.'

'He said he wanted to make an honest woman of you after all this time. I didn't realise it's been three years since you got together.'

Was her mum blushing? 'You make it sound like we met on one of those dating sites on the internet. We were just on the same quiz team. We were friends.'

She *was* blushing. 'But you're more than friends now though. I mean, he practically lives here. It's only your council tax discount keeping you apart, isn't it?'

Her mum shrugged and didn't meet her eye. 'Yes. I know. And he's very good to me. You know he's cooking up all these recipes of "heart-healthy foods" as he calls them?'

'Yes, I've just had the full run-down on your menu for the next week. So why did you turn him down?'

Her mother sighed. 'I don't know why it's important to him. We're fine as we are. We don't need to be married.'

Hannah understood; she'd felt weird about it at first too. But the more she'd thought about it, the more she saw it from his point of view. 'I get that. But Tony has never been married before, Mum. Maybe it's important to him.'

Finally, her mum let her hands, and the photos she'd been pretending to look at, drop into her lap. 'The thing is... I still feel as if I'm married to your dad. When we said our vows, it was forever. I was only twenty when we met. He was twenty-five but still as daft as a brush. We kind of grew up together. Our first house was together, there was you. It just doesn't feel right.'

Though it was difficult, Hannah tried to separate her mum's words from thoughts of David and Katherine. 'Oh, Mum. It's okay. Either way is okay. Tony loves you. He's not going anywhere.'

'I know. But, like you said, he's never been married before. I think he likes the idea of it. Having a wife.' She rolled her eyes. She might mock him, but it was obvious how much Tony meant to her.

It was a strange feeling, being the one to give her mum advice. All Hannah wanted was for her to be happy. 'I love Tony. But you can't just do it because he wants to. It has to be what you want too.'

'It's not that I don't want to, it's just... oh, it's a complicated feeling.'

Hannah reached down and squeezed her mum's hand. 'Well, there's no need to rush, is there? But if it's Dad you're worried about, you know that he would just want you to be happy, don't you?'

Her mum returned the squeeze. 'Yes, love, I do. I do know that. Now let's get these tidied away and go downstairs before Tony's kale starts to curl. Or flatten. Or whatever it's not supposed to do.'

Hannah didn't want to go just yet; she wanted to tell her mum about the fertility clinic before they joined Tony again. After she'd pulled her up from the floor, she nodded towards the bed. 'Actually, can I just talk to you for a minute before we go?'

'Of course.' Her mum sat down beside her on the bed. 'What can I do you for?'

There was something about sitting like this on the bed together that made Hannah feel like a child again. How many times had they sat like this through her teenage years, when Hannah was upset about a failed test or a mean boy or an argument with her best friend? If only her problems were teenage-sized right now. 'I want to tell you what's happening with the fertility treatment.'

As she explained about Katherine's embryos, her mother reached out to hold Hannah's hand. 'Oh, love. That's a lot for you to be thinking about. Do you know what you want to do?'

'No. That's the problem.' The feel of her mum's hand, the smell of this house, the pictures of her dad; it brought everything to the surface and her eyes blurred. 'I just wanted a baby. My baby. A baby that would have you and Dad in it. I know this is stupid, but I had a really clear picture of having a little boy or girl one day and being able to see Dad in them. You know? Almost like getting him back a little bit.'

'Oh, love. That's not stupid. It's lovely. But you will be able to share all the things with your child that your dad shared with you. You can sing them Beatles songs and take them fishing and teach them that ridiculous card game the two of you invented that I never understood.'

Hannah wiped tears away with the back of her hand. 'It didn't have any rules, Mum. We were winding you up.'

Her mum nudged her. 'You think I didn't know that? But they are all the things that made your dad your dad. And you can share all of those with your little girl or boy.'

She knew that, but there was more to it than that. 'I wanted my baby to be mine. Completely mine. I'm just scared that if I use these embryos, or a donor egg, or even adopt, that that child won't be completely mine. I know that is totally wrong, but that's what I feel.'

'It's not wrong. I was fiercely possessive over you when you were tiny. Every time someone else was holding you, I would hover like a mother hen. But the thing is, love – and it took me a while to learn this – your child doesn't really ever belong to you. You get to borrow them for a while. You get to guide them a little. But one day they will leave and become their own person and, if you're lucky, you get to watch them spread their wings and fly. And sometimes, if you've done it right, they fly home and sit in your spare room and you get to hold them again for a little while.'

'Oh, Mum.' Hannah turned and let her mum pull her close

for a hug. Maybe she was right. Maybe Hannah was looking for something that no one had.

Once she sat up, her mum looked her in the eye, as if she was making a decision. 'I want to show you something.'

She leaned forwards and scooped up a pile of shiny photos with white borders. One dropped out of her fingers and fluttered onto Hannah's lap. In the picture, her dad looked to be about eight – his distinctive smile made him recognisable at any age – and he had his hands around another boy who looked similar to him but was a few inches shorter. 'Who is this with Dad?'

Her mum took the picture Hannah was holding out to her. 'That's your dad's brother.'

To begin with, Hannah thought she'd misheard. 'But Dad was an only child. Like you. Like me.' She didn't add that he'd told her, more than once, when they were at his allotment together, that he wished they'd been able to give her brothers and sisters so that she would 'never be alone'.

Her mum shook her head. 'No. He had a brother. But they fell out in their early twenties, before I met your dad. I never met Ronnie, his brother.'

She couldn't believe that her mum was only telling her this now. 'But why didn't I know this? Why did he never mention it?'

'Your dad didn't like to talk about him. He said his brother was dead to him. He only told me about him once, and he wouldn't speak about him again. To be honest, it was like he didn't exist.'

'But why didn't you at least tell me?' This didn't make any sense. They were a close family – they didn't have secrets from one another. Or so she'd thought. All those afternoons at the allotment with her dad. When he used to tell her how important family was, and how she could always come to him whatever happened in her life. *Family is everything, Hannah Spanner.*

'I know it sounds unbelievable. But it was your dad's business. He was adamant that he wouldn't have his brother mentioned in this house and it wasn't for me to tell you. To be honest, because I'd never met his brother and knew nothing about him, it was easy to do that.'

Hannah stared at the photo. Two little boys in shorts and caps. Wide smiles for the camera. What could have happened that had made them break all contact? And where was this brother now? 'So I have more family out there? An uncle? Cousins?'

Her mum shook her head. 'He died before your dad did. An old friend of your dad who still lives that way let him know. He didn't have any children.'

Knowing her dad, Hannah assumed that whatever his brother had done to upset him must have been pretty bad. That would explain why he didn't want to know him, but it didn't excuse him never telling her about him. 'What happened between them?'

'I don't really know all the details. It was something to do with money. He'd either stolen from their parents or had borrowed a lot of money and never repaid it. I only know that because your grandmother – Dad's mum – whispered it to me once in the kitchen, because even his father wouldn't have his name mentioned in the house. Either way, he wasn't a very nice man.'

Hannah stared at the photograph. 'I just can't believe that Dad had a brother out there all those years. When he used to go on to me so much about family and how important it was.'

'Don't tie yourself up in knots about it, sweetheart. Your dad loved us. We were his family. Family is about more than where you come from. You are given one family, but you can also make yourself one. And that's what your dad did. We were everything to him. Come on – let's go and have a ridiculously healthy dinner.'

Hannah needed time to let this information settle. It was as if the picture of her family had been picked up and shaken around like a snow globe with moving parts. Maybe her mum didn't think it important, but she wasn't so sure. 'I'm just going to go to the bathroom to wash my face. I'll follow you down.'

Her mum kissed her cheek. 'I'll see you down there. I love you.'

'I love you too.'

In the bathroom, Hannah splashed cold water on her face and looked at herself in her dad's shaving mirror, which still sat in front of the window. The last ten minutes had blown apart everything she'd thought about her family. All she'd ever heard from her dad was how important family was, and all the time he'd cut himself off from his last surviving relative. 'Oh, Dad. Why didn't you tell me?'

There was more that troubled her about all this though. If her dad had managed to keep this huge secret for decades, what might David be keeping from her? How had it taken him so long to tell her about Katherine's affair?

Also, had Lauren and Priya known about Katherine's affair? She could only assume not. Otherwise, their constant deification of her in front of David would have been in extremely poor taste. How had he been able to endure their constant references to how kind and good she was, while he'd known all along that she'd betrayed him?

All this time, Hannah had thought that David idolised Katherine like they did. Had assumed that that was why he wouldn't talk about her. She'd become this mythical creature to whom Hannah felt she could never measure up. That was why she'd never tried to push him to tell her more. Who would want to volunteer themselves for more battering of their self-esteem?

But maybe she'd been wrong all along. What if the reason

David never spoke about Katherine was that he'd actually hated her? And if that was the case, was he doing all of this just for Hannah's sake? Because he knew how desperate she was to carry a child?

She picked up the picture from where she'd left it beside the mirror. Looked again at her dad, his brother. Maybe David was right. Maybe a blood connection was less important than being the parent who brought up a child? Was it irrelevant whether a baby was biologically hers, born from her body, or whether she welcomed a child born to someone else? She thought again of Charlotte and her boys. Had she been too rash to rule out adoption?

Her dad and his brother looked very alike. She'd have the same eyebrows as them both if she didn't pay a beauty therapist to tame them into submission every six weeks. But their physical similarities hadn't been enough to keep them connected. What if she'd been looking at this all wrong?

Even with the photographic evidence in front of her, it was still impossible to believe that her dad had kept such a huge secret. And David had been keeping the truth about Katherine's affair to himself for years.

She shuddered. What other secrets might she not yet know?

NINETEEN

KATHERINE

As one of four in a Victorian house in North Islington, Hayley's flat was all about location over size. Technically a two bedroom, she'd joked when she bought it that she would have to find a three-year-old flatmate to actually be able to rent the room to someone. Since she'd moved in, the second bedroom had become an extended wardrobe, stroke office, stroke store cupboard. For friends staying over, she'd bought a sofa bed for the living room.

Dressed in borrowed pyjamas, Katherine sat with her feet under the spare duvet while Hannah stared at her from a small armchair opposite. Back at the restaurant, she'd finally told Hayley the secret she'd been hiding for what felt like forever.

To begin with, Hayley had just been confused. 'What do you mean you've been lying to everyone? About what?'

It was like holding a hand grenade and deciding which moment to pull the pin. 'Shall we go back to yours? We can talk about it there.'

'No.' Hayley paled. 'You're scaring me, Kat. Tell me now. Whatever it is, I'm on your side. Is it a man? Have you met someone?'

That was almost funny. 'No. It's not that. There's no one else.'

She'd assumed that Hayley would guess then. But maybe she just didn't want to believe it. 'Then what is it? I don't understand. What have you lied about?'

Here it was. The moment. No going back after this. 'The truth is... And my God, I can't believe I'm saying this out loud at last. I can't believe any of it really. But... well. Here goes. I'm ill, Hayls. Really ill.'

After the briefest of explanations, they'd finished their meal quickly and she'd called David to say she was staying over with Hayley. Thankfully, despite his annoyance earlier, she'd done this enough in the past for it to not raise any suspicion. They'd got soaked to the skin walking from the Tube to Hayley's apartment.

'How long have you known?'

Between her fingers, Katherine twisted the towel that Hayley had given her to dry her hair. 'I knew there was something wrong a few weeks ago. I'd been feeling sick and having headaches. To start with, I just blamed it on the hormone treatment. It was one of the reasons I knew I couldn't just do it all again straight away. But when the symptoms didn't go away, I went to see my doctor.'

'And he said?'

'To begin with, the same as me. He thought it was the hormones. He also asked if there was any chance I could be pregnant. I had to do another pregnancy test.'

Hayley winced. 'I'm so sorry.'

Katherine shrugged. That paled into insignificance with all the rest. 'Anyway, when the symptoms didn't go away, he sent me for further tests. I've had scans and blood tests. That's where I've been the last couple of days, when David thought I was in

Gateshead. This morning they told me for sure. They've found a tumour on my brain.'

Hayley shook her head slowly, as if she was trying to take it all in. 'Why didn't you tell me? I could have been there for you. I'm your best friend, Kat.'

How could she explain that, up until this morning, she'd been holding on to the vain hope that it was something easily fixed with a packet of painkillers? 'Well, I need you to be there for me now. I have to have a biopsy so that they can ascertain what kind of tumour it is.'

A tiny flash of possibility lit up Hayley's face. Had hers looked the same this morning? 'So there's a chance that it's not malignant? That it's not cancer?'

All she could do was echo the words of the consultant she'd spoken with. 'Yes, there's a chance.'

Actually, she'd held back on some of the details. The consultant's summary of the situation had sounded far bleaker. *There's a possibility it's benign, yes. But it's a very small possibility. About two per cent.* When she'd asked what the chances were of a cure, he'd been professionally evasive.

A dry sob erupted from Hayley. 'Oh, Katherine. I just can't believe it's true. Are they sure? I mean, you don't even look ill. How did David react?'

Hadn't she made it obvious? Clearly the shock of her diagnosis had thrown Hayley off. 'I haven't told him.'

Hayley's face twitched through a range of emotions from confusion to disbelief. 'What do you mean?'

Again, she thought she'd been obvious. Although Hayley's confusion as to why was understandable. 'I mean that I haven't told him about the tests. Or the tumour.'

'But why?'

The headache which had been at the edges of her brain for the last hour was now spreading and getting worse. Katherine closed her eyes and massaged the top of her head with firm fingertips. 'Because things haven't been great between us and, to be honest, I can't face it right now. I can't face telling him or seeing his reaction or even having him there for the appointments.'

It sounded irrational – she knew that. But she also knew that she was doing the right thing.

But Hayley clearly didn't agree. 'You have to tell him. He has to know, Katherine.'

Surely Hayley knew her well enough that she knew not to tell her what to do? 'Not yet. I'll tell him when I'm ready.'

'This is crazy. He's your husband. I know the last few weeks have been hard, but he loves you. I know that you don't want to hurt him, but surely it's better to be honest?'

Was it? She'd been honest with him when she'd asked him not to tell anyone about the IVF, and look where that had got her. Within days of her telling him, everyone would know. David wouldn't accept the way she wanted to handle this. It was better that she deal with it at her own pace. 'I know what I'm doing, Hayley. You have to trust me. You just told me that you wanted to be there for me. This is what I need. As my best friend, I need you to do this for me. I don't want him to know yet.'

Hayley brought her fingers up to her mouth. They were trembling. 'Okay. Okay. Let's calm down a minute. Just on a practical level. How are you going to keep this from him? You'll have appointments to attend. Drugs to take. Treatment to go through. How are you going to manage to keep it all from David? Isn't he going to wonder where you keep disappearing to?'

Katherine shook her head. 'The joys of a job that takes me away from home all the time. He's used to me being away. He won't even question it.'

'But what about work then? How will you actually be able

to be all over the country when you're going through this treatment?'

She'd already been thinking about all this. Lying awake last night, going over every possible outcome. 'Well, my boss knows about the fertility treatment. And she's been telling me for months that I need to delegate more of the filming. She foolishly believes that Jeremy is ready for more responsibility, so I can easily hand a chunk of the location filming to him. Plus, most of the creative work gets done in the editing suite anyway, and that's in London, so I can do that.'

Hayley looked as if she was trying to come up with another reason why Katherine needed to tell David, but she settled for repeating herself. 'I just don't see how you're going to keep it from him, Katherine. The man adores you. He notices every time you've done your hair differently; you only need to raise an eyebrow for him to know you want to leave a bar; his eyes follow you around the room at parties. He will know, Katherine. He will.'

The strain in Hayley's throat as she begged her to listen pulled at Katherine's chest, but it wasn't enough to make her change her mind. 'I can do this if you help me.'

Hayley's eyes spilled the tears that had threatened since they'd arrived home. 'Oh, Kat, I can't believe this is really happening. But yes, of course I'll help you. I'll do anything. Whatever you need.'

Dealing with the practicalities was much easier. 'Well, to begin with, I want to give the hospital your address as my contact. That way, I won't risk David seeing letters stamped with a hospital logo on the envelope.'

Hayley sniffed loudly and wiped at her eyes with the heels of her hands. 'Well, that's no problem obviously.'

The next part was harder. 'And I was hoping you would come with me for the biopsy. I'm a little bit scared at the thought of them sticking a needle into my brain.' Katherine's voice wobbled and she bit down hard on her lip to try to keep it under control. There was no point getting upset until she knew exactly what she was dealing with.

Hayley got up from her armchair and perched on the bed by Katherine's knees. She took her hand. 'Try and stop me from coming. I'll be with you for as long as they'll let me stay, and I'll wait so that I'm there as soon as it's done. It's going to be okay, Katherine. I know it is. They'll do the biopsy and it'll be benign and everything will be okay again.'

Katherine tried to smile, but she didn't have the same optimism. Nor would Hayley have if she'd seen the expression on the consultant's face when he'd shown her the results of her scans. But she couldn't afford to let the fear drag her under. Not yet. 'There's something else. I might need to stay over sometimes. If the treatment makes me look unwell, or I feel really bad. It'll be easier to come and recover here.'

'Of course. Of course. Anytime. Whenever you need it. And you can stay in my room. I'll take the sofa bed. Or I'll just make myself up a bed in the other room now, so that my bedroom can be yours whenever you need it.'

Katherine smiled. 'In your tiny second bedroom? Are you going to put up a bunk bed or something?'

Hayley squeezed her hands. 'For you, I'd sleep on the roof. We'll get through this, Katherine. We will. When is the biopsy? I'll book a couple of days off work.'

Katherine barely wanted to think about it. The idea of a doctor, however skilful, that close to her brain... She swallowed. 'It's the day after tomorrow.'

TWENTY

HANNAH

A wall of noise hit them as they entered Jungle Kingdom. Bright primary-coloured furniture and climbing frames were a similar assault on the senses. Hannah had never seen anywhere like it. 'Well, this place is all kinds of hell, isn't it?'

Charlotte nodded. 'Oh yes. I think Dante had play centres at the third level. But at least the boys can run off some energy and we can talk.'

Sure enough, Jamie and Ben couldn't get their shoes off fast enough and were throwing themselves onto something inflatable in seconds. Jamie face-first, Ben more tentative but just as happy. Each of them were never more than an arm's length away from their brother. 'It's lovely that they have each other.'

Charlotte watched them too. 'Yes it is. Like Jim always says, if we find it too much, we can always pretend that there's only one and we've got double vision.'

She winked and smiled, knowing they were both clear that Jim had been keen from the minute they'd found out about the twins. Charlotte had been a little more tentative, not knowing if she was up to the job of taking on two children at once. Looking at her now, it was clear that they were the best thing that had ever happened to her.

'How was the centre yesterday?' Alongside her work at the speech and language resource base at school, Charlotte volunteered at a centre for stroke survivors one evening a week.

'It was good, yeah. Had a big success this week with one of my patients, who was able to speak on the phone to his daughter in Canada for the first time since his stroke. He told me about five times that she'd understood every word he said. He was so chuffed about it.'

Days like that, their job was the best in the world. Being able to communicate with the outside world was something everyone took for granted, until they couldn't do it any longer.

They found a table close enough to the climbing frames that they could keep an eye on the boys. Charlotte called out to them and waved so that they knew where to find her. Then she sat opposite Hannah. 'And how about you? You haven't updated me on your last clinic appointment. Did it go okay?'

'Yes, it was fine. One of the things we talked about was the number of embryos. They only transfer one normally, but we've asked if they'd consider implanting two.'

Charlotte raised an eyebrow. 'So you might end up with twins too?'

'I guess so, yes. If we go ahead with it, and if it all works and progresses. What do you think? Are we being mad?' It was horrible to think that all these conversations were still so hypothetical. There were still so many wires they could trip over at any point and it would have all been for nothing.

'Well, I won't lie to you, twins are a lot of work, and I didn't have the newborn stage when they're basically tag-teaming to keep you awake. But I wouldn't have it any other way now.'

Hannah knew that was how she felt, but it was good to hear it out loud. 'And it'll be nice for the boys to have each other when they're growing up. Family for each other.'

Charlotte raised an eyebrow. 'As opposed to me and Jim who are just, what? Their carers?'

Hannah's cheeks burned. 'No. I didn't mean that. I'm so sorry. You know how great I think you are as parents.'

Charlotte laughed. 'Relax. And stop beating around the bush. We're mates, Hannah. You don't have to censor what you say to me, and if there's ever anything you want to know about adoption, you can ask me whatever you want. I won't be offended.'

Hannah didn't feel as if she'd relaxed in the last year. It was all very well Charlotte saying that she could ask her anything, but the things that Hannah wanted to know were possibly really offensive.

'It's just, now we're getting close to making a decision about using the embryos, I'm worried about whether we're making the right decision. I mean, at the beginning, David was quite keen on adoption.'

'And you weren't?'

'I don't know. I mean, obviously it's a great thing to do, giving a child a home, but I'm not sure it's for me.'

Charlotte laughed. 'Well that's fair enough. But I'm interested that you put it like that. "Giving a child a home", as if it's an act of charity.'

They were moving into uncomfortable territory. But Charlotte did say she should be honest about how she felt. 'Well, didn't you? I mean, the boys had a tough time of it before they came to live with you, didn't they?'

Hannah didn't know the ins and outs of the boys' background, but Charlotte had alluded a few times to the fact that their case file had broken her heart. To know that she'd saved them from a life like that and given them so much must feel wonderful.

'Yes, they did. They weren't cared for as babies, which does, as you know, still make me want to wrap them up in more love and protection than is probably healthy, but that wasn't why we adopted them. We wanted a family, Jim and I; we wanted children. We adopted them for our sake, not theirs. We wanted them desperately. Does anyone have children for the sake of the child? Surely it's always something you do because you want it?'

When she put it like that, it almost sounded selfish. But she was right: Hannah definitely wanted a baby for herself. 'I suppose so.'

'Look, I'm not going to sell adoption to you as an option – it has to be something that feels right for you. You miss out on a lot. I never got to have the scan picture to pass around to my work colleagues and joke about whether it's a leg or something else in the picture. I didn't have the growing belly or the feeling of my child moving inside me. I never got to have that "It's a girl!" or "It's a boy!" moment that you see on TV. I don't get to look at my children and see parts of myself or of Jim. And I'd be lying if I said that I didn't mourn that a little. It's the picture you have in your head, and it hurts to let it go and know that it won't happen.'

They'd never really spoken like this about it. Once she'd made up her mind that they were going to adopt, Charlotte had been so positive, so determined; it was strange to hear her sound so vulnerable. It was also a little worrying; these were exactly the things that Hannah had played over and over in her mind as soon as she and David had started to discuss having children. Actually, a lot longer than that. 'Oh, Charlotte. Why have you never said?'

'Because once we got the boys, all of that became less important. There were these two beautiful toddlers who needed us to love them and, Hannah, when we met them, when they climbed all over Jim and he was throwing them in the air, I knew. I just knew that they were our boys.'

Hannah couldn't help the tears falling at the memory of the first time she'd been to Charlotte's house and seen the room they'd decorated, ready for the two boys to arrive. 'It was beautiful seeing you all together.'

'And it was beautiful being together. But that doesn't mean it was easy. Adoption takes such a long time. You have to be prepared to ask yourself some really difficult questions about the child that you think you're looking for. And they ask you difficult questions about yourself. You must remember; you were one of the people they interviewed about us.'

She did remember. It had been the easiest thing in the world to recommend the two of them as parents.

'And then, once they were with us, I worried all the time that I was getting it wrong. I know from Tessa that it's hard to look after a newborn, but at least you can put them down on a play mat so that you can go to the toilet, and they'll still be there when you come back. And you get a chance to do each stage as it comes. With adoption, you go straight in at the deep end. Two-year-old twins do not stay where you put them, believe me.'

Her smile made Hannah do the same. 'I remember the time you lost Jamie and then found him in the laundry bin.'

Charlotte laughed. 'Yes! I remember that too. That boy could hide better than a marine on special ops. Still can. Jim often jokes that he'll either be a top-level spy or a master criminal.'

Both of them looked across to the inflatable area, where Jamie was currently upside down in a huge pit of plastic balls. 'You're such great parents though, you and Jim. You make it look easy.'

'Well, appearances can be deceptive. Sometimes the children would get really upset about something and I wouldn't be able to console them. In the back of my mind, I would always worry that it was because they needed more than me. I mean, rationally I know that every parent finds it difficult and gets things wrong. But in the moment, I would think it was a problem caused by me. Has Tessa not told you how many times I called her up in a panic about something?'

Hannah felt a stab of envy. No, Tessa had not told her. Probably out of loyalty to Charlotte, but maybe because she didn't want to talk about children in front of her childless friend. She knew that they both kept 'kid chat' to a minimum around her. Though she knew it was out of love, it actually made her feel a little excluded from that part of their friendship.

'Do you not worry about them going to look for their birth mother? When they're older, I mean.'

'Yes. I do think about it sometimes, although I try not to. They do ask sometimes and it's difficult, because I know that they're going to have to face some tough truths about their beginnings someday.'

Their conversation was interrupted by the twins appearing beside them. Although they were identical, Hannah was just beginning to be able to tell them apart. Jamie was a little bit plumper in the face and, usually, his hair was far more dishevelled than that of his more meticulous brother. He was also the one who took the lead in most things. Like now, when he was holding Ben's hand and leading him back to the table with a determined expression. Meanwhile, Ben's face was screwed up and wet with tears.

Charlotte reached out her arms to him. 'Hey, you. What happened?'

Jamie relinquished his charge and crossed his arms. 'He fell off the turning thing. His knee hurts.'

Charlotte had pulled Ben onto her lap and was talking to him soothingly in between kissing the top of his head. 'Oh, baby boy. Does it hurt?'

He nodded vigorously. 'It really stings, Mummy.'

She held him close to her with one hand whilst she rummaged around in her handbag. 'Let's give it a wipe and then we'll have a little cuddle to make it better, shall we?'

Jamie was glancing back in the direction of the inflatables and hopping from foot to foot. 'Can I go back and play now?'

'Yes, you can. Thanks for looking after your brother.'

Jamie was out of sight before Ben whispered, 'He was pushing it too fast, Mummy. That's why I fell off.'

Charlotte rolled her eyes at Hannah. 'Your brother, eh, Ben? What are we going to do with him?'

It was so lovely to see Charlotte with the boys; Hannah was envious of her easy way with them, that a five-minute cuddle with their mum was all it took to make everything okay again. Charlotte tore open a sachet with her teeth, then used the anti-septic wipe inside to dab at the graze on Ben's knee.

'It's bleeding, Mummy.'

'I know, sweetheart, but it's only a little bit.'

His bottom lip started to wobble again. 'I don't like blood.'

'But blood is good, Ben; it's the stuff that keeps us alive. You have lots of lovely blood pumping around your body to keep you strong and healthy.'

Satisfied with that explanation, a kiss and a plaster, Ben ran off to join his brother.

Once he was out of earshot, Charlotte turned back to Hannah. 'And that's its only job. Blood doesn't connect us to anyone, Hannah. Family does that. And you can make a family in any way you want. I've told the boys everything we had to get through to have them. How much they were wanted. How long I had to search to find them. I didn't need to give birth to them to know that they are my sons.'

Hannah leaned over and hugged her beautiful friend. 'I'm so glad you all found each other.'

'It'll happen for you too. Whether you go with these embryos or donor eggs or adoption. You'll find your child too, Hannah. I know it.'

If only someone could tell her which of those paths was the right one to take. She hadn't told Charlotte about Katherine's affair because it felt disloyal to David somehow. But she was going to have to ask him some difficult questions before they could make this decision together. How did he really feel about using the embryos? How did he really feel about his unfaithful first wife being biologically related to their baby? How would he cope if he or she looked exactly like the wife who had rejected him, gone behind his back? And, she couldn't help thinking, what else was there that she might need to know?

Tonight she was going to sit down with David and talk it all through. Cards on the table.

TWENTY-ONE

KATHERINE

Crashing thunder had woken Katherine at 3 a.m. and she'd pulled the curtains apart to watch the sky illuminated by the lightning that preceded each tumbling roar. Even when the storm had passed, to be replaced by heavy rain, she hadn't been able to sleep. Getting back into bed, she pulled the quilt up to her chin and lay on her side, watching the shadows of the rain as they moved across David's face. Maybe she'd managed some snatches of sleep, but she'd seen the clock at 4 and 5 and 6 a.m.

Hayley had pleaded a family emergency to be able to take the day off work at such short notice. Katherine's biopsy was booked for 10 a.m. and it was possible that she'd be allowed home later that day. Not knowing how she was going to be afterwards, she'd told David that she was working in Lancashire; far enough away that he wouldn't expect her home tonight.

Though the chances were slim, she'd be lying if she wasn't hoping, like Hayley, that the tumour would be benign. Since the consultant had given her the news, she'd kept herself as busy as she could: at work, shopping for food, catching up on emails, anything except thinking about today. But now it was here and there was nothing left to do except face it.

At 6.30, she sent Hayley a text to see if she was awake. When Hayley didn't reply, Katherine gave up trying to sleep. As she was slipping out of bed to make tea, David stirred beside her and rubbed at his eyes. 'Are you okay? What time is it?'

He was whispering, so she did the same. Not that they had anyone they were in danger of waking. 'It's early. Go back to sleep.'

But he yawned and pushed himself up. 'I'm sorry about last night. I was so determined not to mention it. I really am sorry.'

She didn't want to get into this now. Dinner had been strained; she'd been preoccupied with the biopsy today and David had been so focused on not mentioning the IVF that he'd looked physically uncomfortable. It was eating him up inside, she could tell. He'd become fixated on the embryos they had in storage and what was going to happen to them if they didn't use them.

'It's okay, David. I know how you feel. I get it.'

He reached across the bed and took her hand. 'But I shouldn't have said anything about it. You need time and I want to give it to you. It's just, I'd had a few glasses of wine and... that's no excuse. I'm sorry. I won't bring it up again. I'll wait until you're ready to discuss it.'

In the half light of the bedroom, his eyes beseeching her forgiveness, she felt a rush of love for him like she hadn't allowed herself in weeks. He must have sensed her pulling away from him, but it was the only way she could get through this without telling him. Right then, though, it would have been so easy to let him tug her back into bed, to tuck herself under his arm, to tell him everything that was going on. It would be such an unbelievable relief to put down this load she'd been carrying alone and ask him to help. Her throat was so tight, she was grateful they'd been whispering because that was all she could manage. 'Okay. Thanks.'

He turned her hand and kissed her open palm. 'I do love you, Katherine.'

Before she could respond, the screen of her mobile lit up the bedside table and buzzed with a message. Hayley. Katherine pulled her hand from David's and snatched up the mobile before David could see anything incriminating. She couldn't even look him in the eye. 'I need to jump in the shower. I'll speak to you later.'

David left for work at 8 a.m., so he was long gone by the time Hayley collected Katherine thirty minutes later in her trusty Citroën. She took Katherine's overnight bag from her and threw it onto the back seat, then smiled. 'Ready?'

'As I'll ever be.'

The ride to the hospital took fifteen minutes. Hayley chattered about work and about Gerard's application for a six-month work visa, so that he could come to England and they could spend time together. Katherine was grateful that she was trying to keep her mind from what was about to happen but couldn't shift the feeling of dread from the pit of her stomach.

Hayley insisted on carrying her bag into the hospital reception as if she was incapable of carrying it herself.

'I'm not an invalid.'

Hayley was already three steps in front of her and showed no signs of handing it over. 'And I'm not arguing with you. I'm carrying it and that's that. Come on.'

The small reception area was quiet apart from two men and a woman who sat at three corners, all wearing their coats and reading newspapers with an intensity that suggested they needed to keep their minds away from whatever was happening on the other side of those double doors.

Katherine leaned over to whisper to Hayley, 'You really

don't need to wait here, you know. They'll call you when it's time to collect me.'

Hayley winked at her. 'As soon as you go in, I'm going to treat myself to a cheese sandwich and a packet of Quavers in the canteen. I've been looking forward to those.'

There was only one person ahead of them in the queue to check in – was that even the right expression? – and then they only had to wait another ten minutes before a tall nurse in a pale blue tabard came out to meet them.

'Hi, I'm Patrick. Sorry, we had some staffing issues this morning, so we are a little behind. But we'll get you settled in a room and then I'll come to prep you as soon as I can. Are you coming too?'

The second question was directed at Hayley and she nodded effusively, reaching out for Katherine's hand and squeezing it. 'Yes please. If I can.'

They followed Patrick down a short corridor and into a small room on the left-hand side. On the bed, a hospital gown was folded into a neat square. 'I'll leave you to get changed into the super stylish outfit we have ready for you and I'll be back shortly to go through the paperwork.'

'Thanks.'

As soon as the door closed, Hayley pretended to fan herself. 'Well, your nurse is easy on the eye.'

Katherine had to laugh. 'I don't think he's my private nurse. And what about your six-month-visa-applying American?'

Hayley shrugged. 'He's not here yet. It's good to keep your options open.'

They both stared at the gown on the bed. The print on it – interlocking yellow squares – wouldn't be seen on anything else except in a hospital. Even Hayley, with her relentless positivity, was taking a pause.

Quickly, she recovered and nudged. 'Come on then. Let's get your clothes off.'

Katherine smiled. 'I bet you say that to all the girls.'

Again, she was grateful for Hayley keeping her amused as she slipped off her clothes and pushed her arms into the loose, gaping gown.

'So tell me more about the American. Is he very sexy and worldly-wise?'

'Actually, he's pretty quiet and – I know this is unbelievable – but this will be the first time he's been out of the States.' She paused. 'I actually really like him.'

Katherine stopped tying her gown at the neck and stared at her. 'What, *like* like? As in, you could see yourself in it for the long-term?'

Hayley walked around the other side of the bed so that she could tie the gown at the waist. 'Maybe. He makes me laugh and he's clever. And kind.'

'Well, that's the perfect trio.' She remembered speaking to Hayley about David like this. After years of dating men in the industry, she'd taken a chance on a quiet accountant and had never looked back. 'How much longer until he gets here?'

'A couple of months. Although he did say he might take some of his annual leave and come a little earlier. So we'll see.'

The way Hayley blushed made Katherine realise that she really did like this guy. She'd never seen her look like this before. 'I'm pleased for you, Hayley. I really am.'

'Well, it might all come to nothing, so we'll see.'

There was a knock on the door. 'Are you okay for me to come in?'

'Yes. I'm decent.'

It was Patrick, bearing a tray of medical paraphernalia. 'I just need to fit your cannula and then I'll come back to take you down to theatre.'

Generally, she was fine with injections, but there was something about the thin skin on the back of her hands that made her hate even the idea of having a needle in it. 'I'm going to look the other way, if you don't mind.'

Again, Hayley stepped up. 'Okay, let's talk about something else. David's birthday. Have you had any more thoughts about what we should do?'

She kept her eyes fixed firmly on Hayley, not looking at whatever Patrick was doing on her left. 'Not really. I don't even know who to invite. Apart from your American if he makes it over in time, of course, so that I can give him the once-over. And we'll definitely have to do a party at home now because it's too late to book a venue.'

Hayley wrinkled her nose. 'A party sounds like a world of pain. Why don't you just have a meal out somewhere swish with all the usual crowd? I can organise it, and then all you have to do is turn up with David.'

She felt a pinch in her hand but kept her face focused on Hayley's. 'Okay. That sounds good.'

There was a ripping sound and then she felt Patrick press down on the surgical tape. 'All done. And a good friend of mine has just opened a fabulous restaurant not far from here. If you give him my name, he'll definitely find you a table.'

Cannula safely in, she let herself turn to look at him. 'That sounds great. You can give my party planner here the details.'

'Will do. I need to show you out now anyway, Hayley.' He turned to Katherine. 'I'll be back for you in about ten minutes.'

Hayley's face was a study in being brave. 'I'll be waiting for you as soon as it's over.'

When she pulled her into a hug, Katherine had to focus on a spot on the opposite wall to stop herself from crying. 'Save me some of your Quavers.'

Once they'd gone, the room was oppressively silent. She'd stood to hug Hayley, but now Katherine perched on the bed and waited for Patrick to come back. As well as her clothes, her mobile was in her bag and she pulled it out to distract her.

There was a message from David. *Sorry I was grumpy before you left. How's your day going?*

She'd spent most of the morning trying not to give in to her fear, but seeing his face on the tiny circle next to his name was enough to make her want to call him right now, tell him everything and beg him to leave work and come to her. In the whole time she'd been with him, David had been the person who made everything in her life work, from issues with her car, to black holes in her credit card, he would take it all in his capable stride.

But she was determined not to lay this one on him. At least until she knew what she was dealing with. By the time of his birthday party, she'd have all the facts about what the doctors were going to do and then, once she knew what the treatment was going to be, maybe, on her own terms, she would tell him.

TWENTY-TWO

HANNAH

The Garden Room at the Clarence Hotel exuded understated elegance and sophistication. Silk-covered walls and thick blue carpet absorbed all but the merest murmur of conversation as Hannah and David followed the waitress to their table in the far corner. Georgian glazed doors on either side gave views of the eponymous gardens and their lush green grass.

This afternoon tea had been an anniversary gift from her mother weeks ago, but it was such a popular venue that – when Hannah had called to redeem the voucher – she'd had to book it for weeks in the future. Until she'd turned the page on her diary on Monday, she'd actually forgotten all about it.

David reached for her hand across the crisp white linen and silver cutlery. 'Well, this is nice.'

It was, but Hannah couldn't really enjoy it with everything swimming around her head right now. 'Yes. It's so quiet.'

Most of the tables were full of couples or groups of women. On the table nearest to theirs, three chairs and a high chair held what looked like four generations of the same family. Hannah couldn't take her eyes from the happy toddler smearing herself greedily in the clotted cream from a decimated scone on the tray in front of her. Her mother, a slim blonde woman around ten years younger than Hannah, looked ready to swoop in with a napkin when a white-haired woman the other side of the child waved her away, added a strawberry to the mulched mixture and laughed.

The familiar yearning in Hannah was so strong she almost gasped.

David must have followed her gaze because he squeezed her hand. 'Speaking of quiet, you've hardly said a word since we got up this morning. Is everything okay?'

Speaking to Charlotte about adoption yesterday had made everything clearer and yet more confused. What remained clear was that they had three paths to choose from: Katherine's embryos, donor eggs from a stranger, or adoption. What was confused was that she still didn't know which path was the right one for her and David.

Obviously, she needed to talk to him about it, but her stomach was churning at the thought of what he might say. Which was ridiculous. He was her husband; why had she started to feel as if she was walking on eggshells around him?

This wasn't the place though, so she returned the squeeze of his hand and smiled. 'Just thinking about everything. Like how lucky I am to have such a handsome husband.'

David leaned back with a swagger and flicked a thick white napkin onto his lap with a nod. 'Yes, you are a very lucky woman.'

She laughed. This was David, her lovely David, who was funny and kind and still made her stomach flip over when he walked into the room. If she couldn't talk to him about how she was feeling, who could she talk to?

Before she could start though, a waitress brought a wooden box to their table and opened it to reveal a display of brightly coloured sachets. 'Good afternoon. Would you like to select your choice of tea?'

David peered into the box, then up at the waitress. 'What would you recommend?'

The girl looked to be only about twenty and she blushed under his gaze. He always had that effect on women; hadn't she been the same the first night they'd met? The waitress glanced at Hannah and then back at David before she answered. Was she wondering how a man that good-looking was with a woman so ordinary? 'I don't know. To be honest, most people just go for the English breakfast tea.'

Hannah often wondered if David knew the effect that he had on women. It wasn't as if he was flirtatious, he just had a way of looking at people – men too – as if he were genuinely interested in what they had to say. 'Then I'll go for that too. What are you going to choose, Hannah?'

For a moment, she wanted to surprise him. Go for a lapsang souchong or masala chai. But she stuck with the predictable. 'I'll have the same. Thank you.'

The waitress backed away with a smile and David reached for Hannah's hand. 'There is something wrong, I know it. What is it, Han?'

Maybe it was okay to talk about this here. Somewhere anonymous, where there were no memories floating around like a third unwelcome guest. 'I've been thinking about the clinic. And our plans. I'm feeling... worried about it all.'

That wasn't the right word, but she couldn't phrase the unsettled feeling that had been growing for the last few days.

David frowned with concern. 'Of course you are. It's a lot to go through. Is it the treatment? The injections? What's troubling you?'

Actually, the treatment itself was the last thing she had on her mind. 'Well, I'm a little bit concerned about doing those, but it's not that.'

As he leaned closer towards her, she could smell the fresh cologne he wore that she liked so much. How could Katherine have wanted anyone else other than him? He rested his free hand on the back of her chair, his deep blue eyes full of concern. 'What is it? You can talk to me about anything – you know that.'

That was the crux of the problem. If he'd have said that a couple of months ago, she would have believed him. But there had been so many revelations in the last few weeks – the fertility treatment, the stored embryos, Katherine's affair – and she still didn't feel as if she knew the whole story. She couldn't help but feel frustrated and uncertain. 'Can I? Because I feel like I've been trying to talk to you, and you just keep closing me down.'

David started as if she'd just slapped his face. 'What do you mean?'

She sighed. Where to start? 'Well, with Katherine. You've never talked about her properly. Apart from a few details, specific answers to specific questions, I know nothing about her at all.'

He covered his eyes with his hands and took a deep breath. 'I'm sorry, Hannah. I understand why you're curious, especially now with the embryos. But it is really hard. Katherine, our marriage, it was another life. And now you know about the affair, you must know why it's so painful for me. This is my life now, you and me.'

Aside from the affair, this was what he'd said any time she'd asked about his wife since they'd met. Before, she'd chosen to respect his way of dealing with his loss. Now, after learning that he'd never even had counselling after the accident, and knowing about the affair, she wondered if that had been wise. 'I understand, and I don't want to put you through any pain, but I need to know. If we're going to go through with this—'

'If?' he cut her off.

'I've been thinking about it a lot the last few days. Since we saw the counsellor.' It was more to do with the conversations she'd had with her mother and friends, but she didn't want to bring them into it.

'Yes?'

'Maybe I got fixated on the whole thing without really considering using anonymous donor eggs or adoption. I mean, we didn't even discuss it really, did we?'

David had frozen next to her. 'Are you changing your mind again?'

Again? When had she changed her mind before? 'No. I'm not changing anything. I'm just thinking that we need to slow down a little bit. I need to slow down a little bit. I know it's been me pushing everything forwards, but...'

They were interrupted by the waitress bearing a tiered cake stand laden with sandwiches, scones and cakes. She slid it onto their table before giving them a guided tour of the levels. 'The sandwiches are ham and mustard, cucumber, egg and cress, and smoked salmon. The macarons are strawberry and vanilla, coffee and—'

David cut her off. 'It's fine, thank you. We'll work it out.'

His curt voice and tight-lipped expression were so different from the careless charm five minutes earlier that the waitress couldn't hide her surprise. 'Of course. I'll leave you to it.'

Once she was out of earshot, David spoke without looking at Hannah. 'If you don't want to do it, I understand.'

Why was he being so cold about this? 'That's not what I'm saying. I just want to talk about it, David. When we went for the first appointment, we were just looking into it all, and now the whole thing seems to be rolling on at a pace. Plus, you're not talking to me about any of the things that happened before with Katherine and I feel like you're shutting me out.'

'Because Katherine is not relevant to our lives!' It was the first time he'd ever raised his voice to her and she could feel the women at the next table looking in their direction. Why was he behaving like this?

The volume of his voice seemed to have shocked him too. 'I'm sorry. I'm really sorry that I shouted, but we're talking about a really painful time in my life. It's difficult for me, Hannah. Even talking about her is difficult.'

She felt sympathy for him, but she couldn't give up now. 'I get it. I do. But this is a huge thing that we're about to do, and I need to know that we're choosing to use the embryos for the right reasons. I'm not even sure that *I'm* doing it for the right reasons. And I have no idea how you're feeling about it because you won't tell me.'

At least now he was looking at her directly. 'I don't understand why you're even questioning how I feel about it. I was the one to suggest using the embryos in the first place. Surely that tells you that I'm okay with it?'

That wasn't quite the way that she remembered it. He'd brought up the embryos – revealed their existence actually felt more accurate – but it had felt more like a confession than a suggestion. She'd been the one to drive it, and yet she hadn't had all the facts. 'I don't think you've been completely honest with me, David. At any point. I'm your wife, and yet I know so little about these big things that happened in your life.'

He closed his eyes and took a deep breath as if he was trying to compose himself. How did he get to be the one who was angry?

'You knew about Katherine and the accident. I told you about that the first time we met. After that, I just wanted to move on. Be here, in the present, not the past.'

The present? When their friends were people he'd met through Katherine? When they were living in the house he and Katherine had shared together? Even the paint on the kitchen walls had been chosen by the two of them. She'd never felt it so strongly before, but Katherine was everywhere in their home. How many of David's shirts had she chosen? How many of the utensils in the kitchen had she bought? Which of the photos in frames had she taken? When Hannah had thought that David's first marriage had been happy, she'd found it in herself to accept that this home had happy memories that he'd wanted to privately preserve. But now? If Katherine had left him before she died, it gave everything a different filter and she wasn't sure she could make it out.

'All the secrets you've kept, it feels as if you've lied to me.'

David shook his head. 'It wasn't like that. I just didn't want to taint this with any of that.'

He looked so pained that she didn't want to push him any further, but she needed to know. 'But what about the embryos? Won't they feel tainted, as you put it? Do you really want to use them rather than have an anonymous donor egg?'

He sighed deeply. 'What do you want, Hannah? I can't help feeling that you're bringing all this up now because you're having second thoughts. That you want to put the brakes on this, but you're too scared to tell me. You said that you might be doing this for the wrong reasons. What do you mean?'

How could she put it all into words? She'd told David about her dad's brother. But she hadn't really been able to explain how it had made her feel. He was right though. If she wanted him to be honest, she had to be too. 'I think I've been searching for something that doesn't exist. Or maybe it does exist, but it's not important. Using Katherine's – your – embryos seemed like it was a safer option than someone anonymous because... because she was gone. She wasn't coming back to claim my child for herself.'

David frowned. Clearly this wasn't something he'd ever considered. '*That's* why you wanted to use the embryos? Because Katherine is *dead*?'

It sounded so terrible when he said it like that; she had to make him understand. 'It terrifies me, David. I want to be a mother so much that it almost physically hurts. The thought that my child might one day decide to search for another mother... I can't bear to even think about how that would feel. I know that you're supposed to support your child whatever they want to do, but I don't know that I have that in me. Adoption or egg donation – either way, there could come a day when my child, our child, could go looking for someone else.'

'Hannah, I—'

She held up a hand to stop him. 'But now, I'm not sure that's a valid reason for using Katherine's embryos. And ever since we made the decision to use them, I feel as if she's come back. As if she's coming into our lives.'

When he looked at her, his eyes were dark with something she couldn't recognise. 'Exactly. This is what I wanted to avoid. This is why I haven't spoken about her. Can't you see?'

It was him who couldn't see, or couldn't hear; couldn't understand what she was trying to say. 'But you *should* be able to talk about her. I *should* be able to handle it. And I can't help thinking that we need to sort that out before we go ahead and use those embryos.'

Before David could reply, Hannah's phone rang. She pulled it out of her bag quickly, planning to switch it off before the ringtone disturbed the peaceful atmosphere outside of their table. She would never have answered it if she hadn't seen Tony's name flash up on the display. Was this about the proposal again?

It wasn't. As soon as she picked up the call, Tony's breathless voice sent jagged fear straight to her heart. 'Hannah? Are you there? It's your mother. You have to come to the hospital now.'

TWENTY-THREE

KATHERINE

Although it was David's birthday – not hers – Katherine had taken the afternoon off work to get ready. Hair, nails and make-up. It was an extravagance she couldn't really afford, especially after their savings had been ransacked for fertility treatment, but working in TV meant she knew the magic of a good make-up artist. No one really looked as good naturally as they did after an hour in the beautician's chair. She was also hoping that it would cover up the fact that she was starting to lose weight and look pale.

Hayley had taken the recommendation of Katherine's handsome nurse, Patrick, and had organised the whole evening – invites, guest arrivals, timings – at his friend's new restaurant. They'd been to visit it together after work one evening. Everything was very industrial and modern; the menu was similarly stark: organic ingredients and simple but well-cooked dishes – exactly the kind of place that David liked. The plan was that Katherine could pretend to David that it would be just the two of them. She hoped that he would be as happy as she was that it wouldn't be.

He'd spent the whole taxi ride over there trying to put her

off. 'Are you sure you want to go out tonight? You look really tired.'

'Gee, thanks. Just what a girl wants to hear when she's spent the afternoon getting ready.'

David held his hands out in supplication. 'You know what I mean. You've been so busy lately, travelling here, there and everywhere, that I've barely seen you. Is work going to calm down soon?'

If only he knew she'd been travelling for work much less than normal. Jeremy had been thrilled that she was giving him more autonomy on location while she worked in the editing suite or, thanks to her boss's cost-saving hot-desk initiative, worked from home. More specifically, Hayley's tiny second bedroom.

The cab dropped them pretty much right outside the restaurant. David peered through the glass front and she crossed her fingers in her coat pocket that he wouldn't see their friends sitting there. 'It looks pretty nice. How did you find out about this place?'

She kept her fingers crossed. 'Someone at work recommended it.'

As it turned out, the table for eight was nowhere near the front of the restaurant; it was tucked away in the back left-hand corner. Clever Hayley.

The concierge had obviously been primed, as he obscured their view while walking them to the table, standing aside with a flourish to reveal a sea of outstretched hands. 'Surprise!'

Their closest friends were all right in front of her, broad smiles on their faces, beaming their warmth. If only she could freeze time, take a mental snapshot that she could keep close to her heart. They were here for David; she couldn't indulge herself by crying as much as the urge to do so was overwhelming her. Would this be the last time she would see them all together like this?

After his initial shock, David took it all in his stride. If he wasn't pleased that it wouldn't be just the two of them, he did a good job of hiding it. 'What are you all doing here?' He leaned to kiss Priya and then Lauren.

Hayley held out her hands to take in the table, which she'd sprinkled with tiny paper confetti shaped like the number forty. 'Celebrating your old age.'

David shook hands with Luke and Ben; the latter came in for a hug and David slapped him on the back. 'You didn't mention this when we played squash on Friday.'

'That's because I didn't know, mate.' Ben reached to kiss Katherine; she stood slightly out of reach in case he decided to hug her too: the last thing she needed was one of his tactless comments that she felt too thin to him.

Lauren laughed. 'I didn't trust him not to slip up and tell you. I actually only told him on the way here, so this is almost as much of a surprise for him.'

'Very wise.' Katherine kissed Hayley. 'Thanks for getting everyone here on time. Is the champagne coming?'

As if she'd conjured him, a waiter appeared with a bottle and glasses.

David raised his eyebrows. 'Champagne too? Have we won the lottery and you haven't told me?'

She hoped that was a joke and not a barb. 'You're worth it. Let's sit down and look at the menu.'

The evening was a success. Everyone was on top form and the conversation flowed as fast as the champagne. Ben was in the middle of telling a story when Hayley caught Katherine's eye and nodded to the right, her eyes wide with warning.

Slowly, Katherine turned to see who she was looking at. When she saw who it was, she wanted to slide down under the table.

Patrick the nurse was at the bar, laughing with the staff. Why hadn't she considered that possibility when she'd taken his recommendation for the restaurant? She was an idiot. What would happen if he came over to say hello?

Tilting her body and leaning forwards, she shielded her face with the hand she rested it in. Ben was almost at the punchline of his story. She joined in the roar of laughter without moving her head. Twenty excruciating minutes later, Patrick left the restaurant after blowing a kiss at the waitress who had just left their table. She'd got away with it. Or so she thought.

The cab ride home was quiet after the noise of the restaurant, and she lay her head on the back of the seat and dozed. The last couple of weeks had been exhausting and she couldn't wait to get into bed. She'd been back and forth to the hospital several times for more scans, tests and consultations. Her arm felt like a pin cushion, and she'd had to wear long sleeves whenever she was around other people to cover it. Four days ago, her consultant had made the decision to begin with a very targeted form of radiotherapy. 'You're very fortunate that we have the equipment to do it here. Not a lot of hospitals have.' She'd bitten back the temptation to tell him that fortunate was not a word she would use to describe herself right now.

The consultant had also explained that the type of radiation therapy she would have often resulted in fewer side effects than she'd read about. Still, she could expect to feel some sickness and tiredness. Two days ago, she'd been to have a mesh mask moulded to her face. Her first 'fraction' – or dose – was due for Monday. She would then have a second and third on Tuesday and Wednesday. Hayley had booked the week off work to be with her. She'd need to invent a location shoot for David before then.

David nudged her gently as the cab drew up outside their house. He held the door open for her, and she tried to keep her eyes half closed so that she could shut them again as soon as she climbed into bed.

But that didn't happen. As soon as they were through the front door, David was onto her. 'So who was that guy at the restaurant?'

Instead of going straight upstairs, she kept walking in the direction of the kitchen for a glass of water. How had he seen that? 'What guy?'

He raised his voice to call after her. 'The one that Hayley was looking at just before she gave you the death stare.'

Damn. He had seen. 'I have no idea what you're talking about, David. After that much champagne, I could barely see Hayley's face, let alone notice her giving me a look.'

That was a lie too. She'd merely sipped at the one glass that Ben had poured for her. But pretending to be drunk might be her only chance of escape. Hopefully, not being able to see her face meant David wouldn't see how clearly she was lying. He followed her into the kitchen and rested against the counter, watching her run the water tap until it was cold enough for the water she needed.

'Yes, the champagne. How much did that all cost tonight? I told you that I didn't want to celebrate. We don't have the money for that right now.' His tone was short, abrasive. Nothing like the way he usually spoke to her.

'Thanks for arranging a party, Katherine. You're very welcome, David.' She mimicked a pretend exchange, then gulped at the water in her hand.

He sighed deeply and ran a hand over his face. 'You don't get to turn this around like I'm the bad guy again, Katherine. You know we need to pull our belts in. We barely have enough savings for the next round of IVF and we already know that there's no guarantee that it'll happen second time. I just don't want to be splashing money around like that.'

With everything she had going on right now, even the

mention of the IVF made her want to collapse onto the floor and just lie there. This was what Hayley didn't see when she told her to speak to David about her diagnosis. He would be exactly the same with her treatment. Like a dog with a bone. She couldn't handle it.

Instead, she went on the offensive. 'You don't want to be splashing money around? What about what I want? All you want to talk about is having children. I do have other things in my life, David.'

'I have to keep bringing it up because you keep avoiding it. I'm forty, Katherine. I don't want to keep putting it off. I don't want to be an older dad. At this rate, I'll be retiring at the same time they go to university.'

She should have nipped this one in the bud before now. 'The thing is, since I got the Media Star Award, I've had a ton of offers, some of them really interesting. This is a good time for me, with my career. I just don't think it's the right time to be taking time off to have a baby.'

David's expression was as confused as his voice. 'And you were planning to tell me this when?'

He had a right to an explanation, but right now his words were like darts into her tired brain. 'I can't do this now. I have to be up early tomorrow.'

He frowned. 'But it's Sunday tomorrow. Where are you going?'

Anywhere but here. 'We've got a shoot in Wales next week. I'm going to get the train there tomorrow.'

'That's the other problem. You're never here. I never see you.'

'That's my job, David. You know that.'

'But you've never been away as much as you have these last few weeks. It feels as if you're doing it on purpose. That you're avoiding being here.'

She'd had enough of this now. 'And can you blame me?

When I'm here, all we do is argue. Or you want to talk about the damn IVF.'

He shook his head at her in disbelief. 'That's just not true. I haven't pushed once, and we never actually talk about it. I will do whatever you want, Kat. Just be honest with me. Is there something I should know? Is there... someone else?'

It was clear how much it was costing him to ask that question, but being honest was the one thing she couldn't do right now. She needed more time to work out what to do. 'You're being ridiculous. I don't want to talk about this any longer. I'm going to bed.'

As she climbed the stairs, she heard him sit heavily on the bottom step, but she didn't dare turn to look at him. Then he would see her trembling lip and the tears that were threatening to fall at any moment. Did he really think she was having an affair? Would that be easier for him to get over than the truth?

TWENTY-FOUR

HANNAH

As David drove them to the hospital, Hannah called Tony again and again, but there was no answer.

David glanced at her. 'What did he say when he called? Did she go in an ambulance or did he take her?'

Hannah knew nothing. At the first mention of the hospital, she'd grabbed her coat and David had followed. It wasn't until they were already in the car that she'd realised that they'd just left a full table of food without saying a thing. Thank goodness it was prepaid. 'He didn't make sense. He said she'd collapsed and he'd taken her in. But then someone wanted to talk to him and we got cut off.'

She tried his number again. Why wasn't he answering?

'If he's gone further into the hospital, it might be that he's not getting phone reception. Some of the A&E wards are on the lower level.'

That didn't make her any less frustrated with Tony. 'He must realise that I'd be trying to call.'

David's voice was soothing, calming. 'I know, but it's more important that he's with your mum. We'll be there really soon. I'm sure she's going to be okay.'

Of course he would try to make her feel better, but there was no way he knew what condition she was in. From the moment her mum had told her about her heart condition, Hannah had been terrified of getting a call like this. All the fertility stuff had taken her eye off the ball; she should have paid more attention to what was going on.

As they turned into the entrance for the hospital, Hannah barely waited for David to stop the car at the drop-off point. Before she closed the door, he called to her. 'I'll come and find you as soon as I've parked the car.'

She ran towards the main entrance. Hospitals were rabbit warrens and she walked into reception with no idea where she was supposed to go. She fumbled in her pocket for her phone, hands shaking, and called Tony again. This time he answered on the first ring. 'Tony. It's me. I'm here. Where are you?'

'She's been taken away for tests. I don't know where she is. I don't even know where I am right now.'

He barely sounded like himself; more like a confused old man. 'What happened?'

There were two beats of silence on the other end. 'They think she's had a heart attack.'

The phone slid from Hannah's hands and hit the floor.

Tony was at the end of a long corridor, bent forwards on a plastic seat that was fixed to the wall. Normally so busy and active, seeing him like this made Hannah realise that he was getting older. Her mother was getting older too, even though she hadn't wanted to accept it. She could have kicked herself for not insisting that Gwen visited her doctor sooner. Especially after losing her dad. How had she been so short-sighted?

Tony sat himself up as she drew closer. Looked at her with a smile. 'Hello, love. Did you get parked all right?'

Why did people do this at the worst of times? Ask about the

traffic or the weather, anything to distract from talking about the real reason they were there. 'David's parking now. He'll be here in a minute.'

Once she'd picked up her mobile from the floor and called Tony back, he'd told her that Gwen was on the medical assessment ward, but they couldn't go in to see her yet. Hannah had practically run there. Now she was standing in front of him, his lack of urgency was frightening her. 'Why can't we go in?'

He shrugged helplessly. 'I don't know.'

She pulled down the flapped-up seat beside him and sat down, lowering her voice. 'What happened exactly? Why did she collapse?'

Tony shook his head. 'I don't really know that either. She was out for lunch with her friends and she came over unwell, so she called me and asked me to pick her up early. When I got there, she looked really pale and she said that her chest was tight and she felt sick. She tried to pass it off as indigestion – you know what she's like – but then she came over faint, so I drove her straight to the emergency department. I didn't want to take any risks.'

Thank goodness for Tony and what her mum would call his 'fussing'. Hannah would never laugh at him again. 'And what happened when you got here?'

'As soon as I said she had chest pains and was feeling faint, they took us straight in to a doctor. He was checking her over when... when...'

He brought his hands up to his eyes, gulping for air as if he was drowning. Hannah rubbed his back. She wanted to say something comforting, but she didn't have anything to give.

Footsteps clipped towards them and she looked up to see David. Relief at his steady presence lifted her. 'Can you go to the ward door and ask if we can see her?'

He reached out and squeezed her shoulder. 'Of course.'

Tony sat himself back up. 'I'm sorry, love. I should be

looking out for you. Your mother would never forgive me for making all this fuss.'

He knew her mother so well. Hannah realised she'd never considered her own feelings for Tony. In that moment, she realised she loved him, too. For loving her mother, for looking after her, for just being there. She reached out and patted his hand. 'No, she'd tell us both to pull ourselves together, wouldn't she?'

David's footsteps echoed before they turned back around the corner. He shook his head. 'We still can't get in to see her. They said they'd let us know as soon as they can.'

Waiting, not knowing, was torture. 'Can they tell us anything?'

'The nurse I spoke to said he'd let us know as soon as he could.'

Tony stood up and stretched. 'I can't just sit here. I'm going to walk to the canteen and get some tea. What can I get you both?'

David had just sat down next to her, but now he stood again. 'You stay here. I'll go.'

But Tony waved his hand. 'No. I need to move. To do something. And you need to stay here with your wife.' He turned to Hannah. 'Call me if they say anything before I get back?'

She nodded. 'Of course. And I don't want a drink, thanks.'

David also shook his head at a drink, then sat back down and put an arm around Hannah. 'How are you doing?'

'I'm terrified. She's had a heart attack, David. This is serious.'

'I know. But there's a lot they can do now. Medication for heart conditions has come a long way.'

She knew he was right, but it didn't help. A heart attack was confirmation that, despite Hannah not wanting to face facts, her mum would not be around forever. Even if it wasn't now, one day she was going to lose her.

They sat quietly for a few moments before David spoke again. 'Look, I want to apologise for before. The way I spoke, it wasn't... well, it wasn't about you. It was me.'

Hannah screwed up her eyes. She didn't even want to think about this right now. 'David, I can't talk about this. Any of it. All I can think about right now is my mum and whether she's going to be okay.'

'Of course. We don't have to talk about anything now. I just wanted to say I'm sorry. And that, later, tomorrow, whenever... there's a few things I need to tell you. You deserve to know answers to the things you've been asking.'

There was a small part of her brain that was curious about what these answers were going to be. But it was no more than a buzz on the periphery of her worries about her mum. All this time, she'd been fretting about whether or not using Katherine's embryos was the right thing to do. She'd got herself so wrapped up in finding out about Katherine, and in working out if she could become a mother, that she hadn't spent enough time making sure that her own mother was getting the medical help she needed.

She didn't even bother to reply to David's comment. That was something for another time. 'If anything happens to her, I don't think I could cope.'

He brought his other arm up and around her so that he held her in an embrace. She let herself fall into his chest and allowed the tears to come. He lay his cheek on the top of her head. 'It's going to be okay.'

She let him rock her gently for few moments before sitting up to wipe her face. As they waited, they watched the people passing them in the corridor. A pregnant woman. A young man on crutches with his leg in a cast. An elderly couple walking slowly past, the woman with her hand in the crook of the man's arm. Hospitals saw so many of the highs and lows of human life.

Something occurred to her. 'Was this the hospital Katherine was taken to after her accident?'

David nodded. 'Yes. The police came to the house to tell me. And bring me here.'

The pain on his face was palpable. How awful must that have been? Had Katherine still been alive when he got there? Had he ever spoken about that night before to anyone else? 'Did they know? I guess you wouldn't have mentioned to them that you were breaking up?'

He shook his head. 'No one knew she was having an affair.'

So she was the only other person that David had told? How could they have kept that from everyone? 'No one?'

David swallowed; this was obviously uncomfortable territory. 'Maybe Hayley knew. She was Katherine's best friend – she told her everything.'

Hayley. Priya and Lauren had mentioned her too and she'd forgotten to ask David about her. 'You've never mentioned Hayley before.'

'I haven't seen or heard from her since Katherine's funeral. I don't know what Katherine had told her, but she didn't hang around to speak to me even then.'

None of this made sense. If Hayley really was Katherine's best friend, surely she'd known David well? Wouldn't she want to speak to him, comfort him? Lauren and Priya had been quite dismissive of her too. Even in the midst of everything going on right now, Hannah couldn't help but wonder why this woman had effectively disappeared without a trace. 'And no one else knew? That Katherine had left you.'

David took a deep breath and let it out slowly before answering. 'How could they? She left me on the same night that she had her accident.'

Just when she thought he'd told her everything, another revelation came to light. Hannah had a thousand more questions to ask, but before she could, a tall man in a pale blue uniform turned the corner and tilted his head to one side. 'Hi. Are you Gwen's daughter? She's asking for you.'

The relief washed over her as she stood on wobbly legs to follow the nurse through the double doors into the ward. If her mum was well enough to ask to see her, it meant that she was alive.

She threw her mobile onto David's lap as she left. 'Call Tony and let him know.'

She sent up a silent prayer of thanks that her mum wasn't going to die today.

TWENTY-FIVE

KATHERINE

With their disinfectant smell and general air of sadness, Katherine had always hated hospitals. In the past, she'd done her very best to avoid ever being in one. Considering that, it was surprising how quickly she'd grown used to it. Between the IVF and now this, she'd spent more time in hospital in the last six months than the rest of her life altogether.

The consultant's office was on the fourth floor. Katherine and Hayley rode the elevator in silence until the loud 'ding' heralded their arrival.

Possibly the only advantage to the fact that she'd come here so often was that she didn't need to check the names on the other doors. Still, it was a long walk down the echoing corridor.

'I'm going to hand in my notice at work.'

She'd tried to keep her voice neutral, but Hayley's head snapped around to look at her. 'Really? Why?'

Hayley's surprise was understandable; she knew how much Katherine loved working on that show. 'It's getting too difficult to explain away why I need time off. I can't keep lying that I'm having fertility treatment. It isn't fair on the rest of the team.'

'You could just tell them the truth. Then they'd give you some time off until you're well again.'

Hayley's relentless optimism that she was going to beat this tumour was starting to grate. It was better to change the subject. 'Thanks for coming with me today.'

Hayley took her hand as they walked. 'Of course. There's no way I was letting you come here on your own.'

They'd reached the door of the consultant's office. The receptionist on the ground floor had told them to go straight up. Behind that beige MDF door were the results that would determine the rest of her life.

Katherine knocked on the door with the hand that wasn't holding on to Hayley's. 'Here we go.'

Rather than call for them to enter, Dr Williams met them at the door. 'Hi, Katherine. How are you feeling?'

If she was casting a TV show and needed a character actor to play an experienced gruff-but-kind doctor who didn't mince his words, Dr Williams would be first on her call list. He always greeted her in the same way, and she was never sure whether this was a pleasantry or the beginning of his diagnostic questions. 'Okay. A bit tired.'

He nodded at Hayley in lieu of a greeting and motioned the two of them towards the chairs in front of his desk before taking his place behind it. 'Well, that's to be expected from the radiotherapy. Are you feeling sick at all? Because I can give you something for that.'

There were enough chemicals taking over her body; she didn't want more. 'No. That's okay.'

'Well, let me know if that changes. Sometimes symptoms can come on three or four weeks after the initial treatment.'

'Okay, I will.'

He paused. And in that moment, that very second, she knew. She just knew.

'I'm afraid it's not good news.'

Most of what he told them next sounded as if he was speaking from the other side of a window. She caught most of the words, knew that the radiotherapy had not been successful, that – in fact – the tumour had actually grown in size, but it was as if he were speaking about someone else. For all her dismissal of Hayley's positivity, her natural instinct to deal with the worst possible scenario, she hadn't actually ever believed that it would come to this.

Hayley was frozen beside her, until Dr Williams began to speak about courses of treatment, when she scrabbled in her bag for the notebook and pen that Katherine had told her she wouldn't need. When he used the phrase 'life-prolonging', Hayley's head shot up from where it was bent over her scribbled notes. 'What does that mean?'

Dr Williams glanced at Katherine before he spoke. 'It means a course of treatment to give Katherine as much time as we can.'

Katherine didn't even turn in her seat. 'It means there isn't a cure.'

Hayley's deathly pale face looked at Dr Williams. 'That's not what you mean, is it?'

He steepled his hands together, his elbows on the desk. 'I'm afraid it is.'

A cold numbness trickled down Katherine's spine like anaesthetic. She heard herself ask the question that she didn't want an answer to. 'How long have I got?'

They left the office less than five minutes later, Katherine promising she would make another appointment when she was ready to talk about her options from this point on.

As they retraced their steps back up the corridor, there wasn't so much a silence between her and Hayley as a vacuum. As if every word they could have spoken had been sucked out of them. When she pressed the button to call the lift, Hayley turned to her. 'We can get a second opinion. There are other doctors. Other options. We can speak to someone else.'

So much of the last few months had been spent in consulting rooms, hospitals and clinics. First the IVF and now this. Tests, scans, injections, extractions and insertions; it had all been too much and she was tired. So very tired. 'Can you just take me home?'

'You have to tell him now.'

When Katherine had asked to be taken home, Hayley had assumed she'd meant to her own house, to David. But she'd actually wanted to come back to Hayley's flat. They'd been home from the hospital for about two hours. Hayley had tried to persuade her to eat something, even a piece of toast, but she just couldn't stomach it. In the end, she'd accepted a weak tea just to stop her from asking.

'No. I've told you. I don't want him to know.'

Sitting at either end of the sofa in Hayley's lounge, they weren't far apart. Hayley's voice was gentle, almost as if she were speaking to a small child. 'But that was before. When you thought... when you didn't want him making a big deal about your treatment. This is different.'

Katherine stared at her friend. Had she believed that story because Katherine was a convincing liar or because she'd desperately wanted to? 'It was never just about that, Hayley. It wasn't just about him making a big deal of the treatment.'

Hayley frowned. 'What was it then? Why have you kept him in the dark?'

Katherine closed her eyes and rubbed at the crease at the top of her nose. How did she even begin to explain?

'Okay. First of all, it *was* about the treatment. David was so full-on with the whole IVF thing that I couldn't cope with him switching his attention to my hospital appointments and tests. I wanted to find out exactly what was going on and get my own head around it before I spoke to him.'

Hayley nodded. 'Yes. That's what you told me. I still don't know if that was the best idea, but I get it.'

The next bit was harder. 'But now I know that...' She paused; it was actually pretty difficult to say out loud. 'Now I know that I'm not going to get better, I just don't want to do that to him. I don't want him to know.'

It made perfect sense to her inside her head. But she didn't seem to be able to find the right words to explain it to Hayley.

Hayley reached out and placed a hand on her shoulder. 'But the doctor is still talking about treatment. He says the chemotherapy will give you more time.'

Katherine swallowed, looked straight ahead. 'I'm not having that either.'

She heard Hayley gasp. 'What do you mean? The doctor said—'

'I heard what the doctor said. All chemotherapy will give me is a few more months. A year at most. What's the point?'

She turned to face her once more. Now Hayley was the one who looked ill. And as if she was trying to follow a foreign language. 'What's the point? In staying alive?'

Finally, she seemed to understand. 'Exactly. What's the point in dragging it out? I already feel awful. Sick and tired and aching everywhere. I've seen what chemotherapy does. How ill it makes you.'

In the course of her radiation treatment, she'd passed many people who looked so frail that a breeze might blow them away. That wasn't how she wanted to go. That wasn't how she wanted to be remembered. By anyone.

Hayley wasn't giving up her argument for treatment. 'But then it makes you better again. You can't just give up. Doctors can be wrong. He said a few more months, but it could be years.

I read a case about a man who was told that he only had six months and—'

'Enough, Hayley. Please.' Listening to miracle cancer cures was almost as bad as miracle fertility stories. Everyone wanted to believe in life finding a way, but it was just another fairy story to ward off fear. She hated how sad her friend looked, how devastated. How much more would she hate to see this expression on David's face? The person she loved most in the world.

For a few moments they sat there, in silence, but Katherine could feel the heat of unsaid words coming from Hayley. It was clear she hadn't finished.

Sure enough, she tried again to make Katherine understand how much she believed that David had to be told. The tight whisper betraying just how much she was struggling. 'This is too much, Katherine. I know this is so awful, but keeping it from David isn't fair on him.'

She really didn't understand. Katherine tried to muster up what little energy she had. 'What's not fair is watching someone you love die. Seeing them get sicker and sicker in front of you. Not being able to do anything about it. I am protecting him, Hayley.'

'But he would want to know.'

'What he would want to do is turn heaven and earth over looking for a cure. He wouldn't rest until he'd persuaded me to try everything I can to stay here with him. He loves me, Hayley. I know that. And that's why I can't let him know, can't let him live through this and then leave him to deal with it. He loves me as I am. Confident, outgoing, attractive. I don't want him to see me like that. Ill and wasting away. I don't want it.'

'But what about what he wants? He'll want to look after you.'

Even the thought of that made her stomach churn. Being in bed, sick, with David having to watch her fade away. She screwed her eyes up tight, trying to block out the images there.

Her dad, lying in bed after his stroke, her mum living a half life of caring for someone who couldn't eat or wash or even go to the bathroom without help. With every ounce of her being, she knew that her dad would have rather died than live like that, and have her mum do the things she'd had to do. She wouldn't put her mum through that again either. Her dad hadn't had a choice. But she did. 'No.'

Tears were falling down Hayley's face as she reached for her hand. 'But if you go through with never telling him, how are you going to keep it from him? If you're not having the treatment, the symptoms are going to get worse and he's going to guess. If you stay here with me, he's just going to come and find you.'

Whatever she did had to be quick and final. Tear off the plaster quickly and cleanly. David was going to get hurt – there was no avoiding that. He loved her. But what if she could erode that love? Maybe he could recover fast enough that he could find happiness with someone else.

Maybe, one day, he could even have a baby with someone else. Because David deserved to be a dad. He was made for it.

TWENTY-SIX

HANNAH

As Hannah followed the nurse into the ward, she tried not to look left or right as they passed groups of hospital beds with patients. It felt like just a short while ago that she and her mum had been the visitors sitting around her father's bed. How cruel that, five years later, she was visiting a parent again, terrified of what she was going to find. Every inch of her prayed for a different outcome this time.

'Here you go.' The nurse smiled and held out his hand to direct Hannah to her mum's bed.

Lying in the hospital bed in one of those gowns which tie at the neck and gape at the back, her skin as pale as tissue, her mum looked smaller, frailer, more vulnerable than ever. It was all Hannah could do not to fall on her and sob. Instead, she hovered at the end of the bed, unsure whether her mum was strong enough to see the emotions Hannah had dammed up inside. 'Oh, Mum. How are you feeling?'

Her mum smoothed over the top of the sheet covering the lower half of her body. 'A little bit silly, to be honest. I've worried you all and I'm fine.'

It was just like her not to want to cause a fuss, but this was no time for trivialising. 'You had a heart attack, Mum. It's hardly silly.'

'Not a serious one. I'm okay. Come and give me a hug.'

She held out her arms; there was a wire trailing from the back of one hand. Hannah stepped into them, scared to squeeze too hard. Her whole life, her mum had comforted her in this exact way. Now, she felt frail and fragile between her arms. She could barely get her words out. 'I thought I'd lost you.'

'Hey, hey. None of that talk. The doctors are going to sort me out. I need to start looking after myself a bit better. Turns out Tony was right about all those foods he keeps trying to make me eat.'

Hannah released her mum and pulled up a blue plastic chair, not letting go of her hand: she never wanted to let go again. 'What else did they say? What do we need to do?'

Her mum laughed; it made her look a little more like herself. 'You don't need to do anything. You've got enough going on. Tell me what's happening with all that.'

That was the last thing she wanted to lay on her mother right now. On the way here, she'd been running through plans of getting her mother healthy as a way to ward off bad news. 'No, I want to talk about you. I've been looking online at all the things you can do to keep your heart healthy. Tony has the food covered, but I was thinking – as soon as you're up to it – maybe we could go for a walk together, three or four times a week? Just around the block to start with. We'll take it slow. And then there are—'

She stopped as her mum raised her hand and shook her head. 'Stop. I don't want you taking on responsibility for this. I know what I need to do. You don't need to be taking me on as another job you've got to add to your list.' She held up her hand a second time as Hannah started to interrupt. 'I know that you're worried, and I promise I will tell you everything the doctor says, but right now I want to talk about something else.

Tell me what's happening with your treatment. Have you got a date yet?'

Unable to lie to her mother's face, Hannah pulled at the thin hospital blanket, making sure it covered to the end of the bed. 'Not yet. We're just going through the final arrangements now.'

Met with silence, she looked up to see that her mum was shaking her head. 'Hannah, I'm your mother. You can straighten that blanket all you want, but don't try and pull the wool over my eyes. What's going on?'

Hannah had been determined to pretend that everything was fine, that her mind – and heart – wasn't being stretched to tearing point by the decision about whether or not to use Katherine's embryos. But this was her mum, and she couldn't help the truth that came tumbling from her mouth. 'Oh, Mum. It's all such a mess. I've made such a mess of everything.'

'What's happened?'

'I don't know if I can do it. Any of it. It's just all so hard.'

'Oh, darling, I know it is. But you can do the hard things. I know you can.'

This was a conversation they'd had many times when she was young. Her mum and dad had always taught her that she could be anything she wanted as long as she worked hard and never gave up. 'But I have worked hard, Mum. I've tried to do everything I can and I still can't be a mother. I've failed. I'm a failure.'

Tears rolled down Hannah's face faster than she could wipe them away with the flimsy tissues in the box by her mother's bed. Visitors at the opposite bed were glancing in her direction, but she couldn't stop the tears from coming.

Her mother's voice was surprisingly fierce. 'You are absolutely *not* a failure. Oh, Hannah, you are so brave. You know what you want and you're doing everything you can to make that happen. How can that be a failure?'

How could she explain? It was so difficult to find the right words. 'But it's not what I want, is it? What I wanted was to get pregnant and be pregnant and have a baby that was a little bit of me and a little bit of David. And that can't happen. That can never happen. I can have a baby that's biologically David's but not mine. I'm really trying not to mind about it, but I do. I really do.'

It was the first time she'd said this out loud and possibly the first time she'd realised how hard it was to know that this child would maybe belong to David more than to her. That the baby would be more his than hers.

'Of course you do. That's totally understandable.'

There was much more to it than that. Much more that, up until now, she'd been ashamed to say out loud. 'But what happens if, after all this, I resent the baby when he or she comes? What if I have a baby girl and she looks just like Katherine and doesn't feel like mine?'

She knew that she sounded like a spoiled, petulant child. Her mother was perhaps the only person she could be honest with about this. Who wouldn't recoil in horror at how awful she was.

Sure enough, her mum didn't even flinch. 'It's natural that you feel like this, sweetheart. But you'll have carried that baby for nine months. Of course they'll feel like yours.'

Hannah hadn't finished. 'But isn't it awful that I'm feeling like this about it? We don't even have a baby yet and I'm worried about being disappointed in it? Does that mean I'm not the kind of person who should have children? I never felt like you were disappointed in me once. Not ever.'

'That's because I wasn't. How could I be? You always worked so hard, tried so hard. I was never disappointed in you and I'm not disappointed now. Everything you're saying is understandable and natural and just proves how thoughtful you are. You had an idea what your baby would be like, about what having a baby was going to be like, and it hasn't happened like that. You need to give yourself time to get over it.'

It felt as if time was something she didn't have. 'There's no point in wallowing in it though, is there? I mean, it is what it is. I can't have a child that's genetically mine, so I just need to get on with doing it a different way.'

Her mum stroked her hand. 'Oh, love. Grieving isn't wallowing. You're allowed to feel angry and upset. I had an idea of what my family would be like too. I wanted three children, maybe four. But it didn't happen for me, and that made me really sad. But then I looked at you and you were so beautiful and wonderful, and I was so glad that I got to be your mum. And you will feel like that too, my darling. When that baby comes, oh, you will have so much love that all these fears will evaporate.'

She wanted to believe that, she really did. 'But what if those fears don't go away? What if I can't let it go?'

'Then I'll be here to help you through it. And you will get through it. And at the end of it, you will be a mum and I will be a grandmother, and that baby will be loved so very much by all of us. Grieving for the baby you thought you were going to have doesn't mean that you won't love the one who comes to you. Just like grieving for your dad doesn't mean that I don't love Tony. Because I do.'

Tony. She hoped that David had got through to him. 'He's been so desperately worried about you.'

'I know. I've given him a big scare. I've had time to think these last couple of hours, stuck in that MRI tunnel. About your father. I'm still grieving him, of course I am. But I also feel like I'm still married to him and that's not fair on Tony. So I've decided, I'm going to accept Tony's proposal. I'm going to marry him.'

Although her voice was certain, she looked at Hannah for

her reassurance, maybe even her approval. It was easy to give. 'I think that's great news, Mum. I really do.'

'Yes, well, I'm going to get better first. The doctor wants me to lose a bit of weight, so I'm going to focus on that. And then you can help me to plan a wedding.' She smiled. 'Who knows, maybe there will be a little flower girl or pageboy by then?'

'You have to get better, Mum. If I have a baby, I'm really going to need you.'

'Of course I'll get better. And it's not *if* you have a baby, it's when. This is a different journey to the one you thought you were on, but the end result is going to be the same. However your baby comes, they'll be so lucky to have you as a mum.'

'And I'm so lucky to have you as my mum.'

This time, when her mum held out her arms, she risked a tighter squeeze. She would need her mum more than ever if she was going to do this. And this scare was a wake-up call that she didn't have the time to wait forever.

Hannah had just about dried her eyes when Tony joined them at the end of her mother's bed. 'I'm sorry, I tried to give you two some time alone, but I couldn't bear it any longer. I needed to see for myself that you were okay.'

His face was so full of concern that Hannah wanted to hug him herself. 'No, I'm sorry we left you outside for so long. Come and join us.'

He was around the other side of the bed in two strides and leaned in to hold her mother in his arms. 'Oh, Gwen.'

The moment was so intimate that, when she heard Tony's deep sob and her mother's soothing, 'I'm okay, you silly thing,' Hannah decided to give them some space. She should go and update David anyway.

And then he could finish telling her about Katherine. The affair. The accident. And what he really thought about using Katherine's embryos.

TWENTY-SEVEN

KATHERINE

Today had been really tough. Even staying in the editing suite was getting too much for her. It was hard to concentrate on the hours of filming of every tiny insignificant thing that was happening in the houses when she just wanted to scream at them about the unimportance of it all. How had she done this for so long and managed not to lose her mind?

The final straw was being called in to see Helen in the Human Resources department. Helen was young, petite and terribly efficient.

'Thank you for coming in, Katherine. Can I get you anything to drink? Tea, coffee, water?'

'I'm fine, thanks. I really need to get home. Is this urgent?'

Helen smiled. 'I just wanted to check in with you. Some of your team have concerns about you. Obviously, they may not be aware of your fertility treatment, but it's been noticed by quite a few people that you don't seem yourself.'

It was hardly surprising. She'd shouted at Jeremy last week for forgetting a signature on a non-disclosure. He'd looked like a wounded animal. Even her boss, Becca, had sent her an email gently suggesting she might want to moderate her tone in written communications to the accounts department. Then Mandie, one of the make-up artists, had caught her crying in the toilet. She could only imagine the rumours that were going around about her. 'I'm fine.'

'Are you though?'

Was the lean forwards, the head tilt, the soft voice, part of her HR training? Irritation curled at the edges of Katherine. Lying at home and lying at work was getting too hard. One of them was going to have to go.

'Actually, I have been considering the right time to give in my notice.'

That made her sit back. Katherine had to smother a smile, the first she'd had in days. Helen moved the papers around her desk. 'Oh. I see. Have you talked to Becca about that?'

'Not yet. But I'll send her an email as soon as I get home. How quickly can I leave?'

Was it bad that it gave her pleasure to see how flustered Helen was getting? 'Er, I'll have to look at your contract.'

Katherine stood. 'If you can do that and let me know as soon as possible, that would be great. Have a nice evening.'

As she turned on her heel and left the room, she enjoyed – just for a moment – a flash of her old fire coming back to the surface.

By the time she got home, she was beginning to worry about what she'd done. How the hell was she going to explain to David that she'd left the job she loved? Could she get away with not telling him? But she had so little in the way of savings of her own, what was she going to live on? And even considering that raised the big question that she wasn't ready to think about.

All those thoughts were driven from her head when she walked through the door and found him waiting for her. 'I've booked us a table at the Lebanese place you like. You've got ten minutes to get changed.'

The restaurant was warm and the spice in the air tickled the back of her throat. As always, the waiters were all smiles and quick to find them a seat. 'I do love it here.'

David grinned, pleased with himself. 'I know. That's why I booked it.'

Watching David read through his menu, frowning as if he was making choices when they both knew he would choose – as he always did – the lamb kofta, made her match his smile with her own. She pushed away the thoughts about work and her treatment and what the future held; for the next hour, it would be just her and David. Like it always had been. Except before, she would have taken a meal here for granted. Tonight, she was going to enjoy every single moment.

David seemed to be in the mood to enjoy himself too. He ordered a good bottle of red wine and, while she merely sipped at hers, he was onto his third glass by the time dessert arrived. Which is quite possibly why the conversation took a turn as soon as their bowls had been collected.

'It's been really nice tonight.' David smiled at her over his wine glass.

It really had. 'I know. It feels like ages since we've done this.'

For the last few weeks, the load she'd carried had grown heavier and heavier. Tonight, she'd set it down for a while. Allowing herself this evening with him, before she picked it up again tomorrow and began the final part of the journey. The part that would break his – and her – heart.

'Yeah.' He stared into his wine, then took another large sip. He was starting to seem a bit fuzzy. 'Before I call the cab... can we talk about it all?'

She felt the hairs start to rise on the back of her neck. 'About what?'

'About children. We haven't had a proper conversation about it since the first round of IVF failed. I don't expect you to put yourself through all that again unless it's what you want. But there are other ways to have a child. We could adopt.'

The precious moments of pretending that all of this wasn't happening were slipping away like sand through an hourglass. Was it now? Should she tell him now that she was leaving? She wasn't ready. 'No, David. I don't want to adopt.'

He looked as if he was picking every word carefully, tiptoeing towards whatever he wanted to say. 'You have to help me out here, Kat. You said that you wanted a baby. We both did. We talked about it before we got married. We both felt the same.'

It broke her heart to see him like this, though she wasn't brave enough to push him away altogether. Not yet. But she had to make a start. 'I've changed my mind. Like I told you before, since my Media Award. I've had a lot of offers I'd like to pursue. Actually, I've handed in my notice this morning. It's time for something bigger and better.'

David swallowed. 'Handed in your notice? You haven't mentioned wanting to leave your precious show. When were you going to tell me about that? About the same time you told me you want to put our family plans on hold?'

People on the table next to them were starting to glance over. The last thing she needed was a scene, so she lowered her voice. 'I'm not putting the plans on hold, David. I don't want a child. Not now. Not ever.'

He reeled as if she'd slapped him. 'But what are we going to do about those embryos that we have in storage?'

Was he even expecting her to answer that question? He looked so broken, she could barely face saying it again. Though she'd rehearsed this so many times in her head, she hadn't expected it to hurt this much.

And it was only going to get worse.

TWENTY-EIGHT

HANNAH

When they got home, Hannah sank into the sofa and closed her eyes while David put the kettle on. She was exhausted, yet wide awake. There'd been so much to think about in the last twelve hours that she barely knew where to start. David, Katherine, her mother: all of it swirled around her head, and it was difficult to grasp at the thoughts as they spun past. Except one. There was one thing that she was certain about and she wanted to tell David before the day ended.

He passed her a mug of tea and slid his onto the coffee table. 'Can I get you anything else?'

She shook her head. 'No. Just come and sit down for a while.'

The seat of the sofa gave way a little as he sat next to her, and she leaned towards him so that her head rested on his shoulder. He adjusted his position so that he could wrap his arm around her. 'Well, that was quite a day.'

'It certainly was. I feel like I've run a marathon.'

She closed her eyes, needing just a few moments of calm before speaking again. David was quiet too. Maybe thinking about their conversation earlier. Wondering when to bring it up.

It was only fair for her to go first. 'I talked to my mum. About how I was feeling. About the treatment.'

She felt him stiffen a little beside her, but his voice was calm. 'That's good.'

'I told her that I was feeling worried about whether we were doing the right thing, using Katherine's embryos. And I also told her that I was worried about how I would feel. About the baby, I mean. Knowing that he or she is biologically yours and Katherine's.'

Somehow, retelling her conversation with her mother was easier than saying these things directly to David. Like her kids at school, when speaking to a teddy bear or their dog was easier than trying to speak to their teacher or friends.

Before she could say anything else, he took hold of her hand. 'I'm so sorry for the way I was earlier. I know this is much more difficult for you than it is for me. It's no excuse, but I think it just brought everything back. I'm so sorry.'

'It's okay. Really. But it's hard for me to understand when there's still so much you haven't told me. When you say "it just brought everything back", what do you mean?'

Of course she knew he meant Katherine. But she needed him to be specific. At least now he seemed ready to do that.

'The thing is, I don't really know. We had both wanted children, we spoke about it before we got married. Like everyone does. Like you and I did.'

Hannah nodded. They'd both been open about their desire to be parents. When you met someone at their age, that question was pretty much a given.

'When we found out that there were fertility issues, Katherine approached it the way she approached everything in life: head-on. Apart from the fact she didn't want to tell anyone, there was no reason for me to believe that she didn't want this as much as I did.' He paused and took a deep breath. 'And I really wanted it, Hannah. Ever since my brothers had kids, and then my friends, I knew I wanted that for myself. I wanted to be a dad.'

She knew this already. 'So what happened?'

'Like I said, I don't really know. Everything was going well. The initial treatment was tough on her, but Katherine was determined. We were both optimistic and talking about what it would be like when we had a baby.'

He stopped then and looked at her. Perhaps gauging how much to say. But she was beyond that. 'Go on.'

'The first round of IVF failed. But the doctors said the prognosis was good, that we'd just been unlucky. So I was shocked when, after enough time had passed that they'd let us try again, she suddenly said she wasn't ready. I didn't push her obviously. I wanted a baby, but it was her body that had to do the difficult part. And then, I don't know, everything seemed to fall apart. She was suddenly working away all the time. When she was there, she just snapped at me, and then one night she just told me outright. She didn't want a child.'

Knowing what he'd said about an affair, Hannah could put two and two together to work out why. But what would have happened about the embryos if Katherine hadn't had her accident? What if the someone else she'd met had – or hadn't – agreed to use them? It was all so complicated.

'Did you talk about the embryos that were left? I mean, what do you think she would have wanted to do with them?'

David held out his hands. 'That's an impossible question. But she made it clear that she didn't want them for herself.'

TWENTY-NINE

KATHERINE

Two weeks after Katherine's appointment with Dr Williams, his prediction came true. The nausea made her want to take to her bed and not get up again.

When David's alarm had gone off that morning, she'd pretended to be asleep. Now, she lay in bed with her eyes closed, listening to him getting ready for work. He was such a creature of habit. As soon as he got up, he put the coffee machine on downstairs, then came back up for a shower, dressed, downstairs again for coffee and toast, which he'd eat while standing up and reading the headlines on his iPad.

Work had accepted her resignation without a murmur; she must have been a complete nightmare to work with recently. In fact, she'd only had to work a week's handover with Jeremy and they'd let her go. He'd been emotional on her last day. They'd hugged and she'd looked him in the eye. They'd become quite close in the last year, and he saw her more often than anyone other than David. Did he know that something wasn't right?

As soon as David was gone, she pulled herself out of bed, needing a mug of the coffee he'd made before it went cold. They'd barely spoken since the night in the Lebanese restaurant. They were like housemates who didn't really get along. They'd been polite but distant, neither wanting to finish the conversation they'd started.

Was he still hoping that this was a phase? To be fair, she had plenty of form with changing her mind. Was he staying out of her way to give her time to realise that she wanted to try for a baby after all?

The only time they'd spoken yesterday was when he'd reminded her that they'd agreed to go out with Priya and Luke tonight, to celebrate Luke's dental practice. He'd been opening a bottle of beer, something he was doing every evening at the moment, and not even looking at her when he asked, 'Shall I call and cancel?'

She knew that it would be awkward if they did. Questions would be asked. It was easier just to go. 'No. It's fine. Let's go.'

He'd nodded and left the kitchen.

Yesterday, she'd been shopping for some new clothes with Hayley, in the hope that they would make it less noticeable that she'd lost weight. She'd cut her hair for the same reason. Hayley had been pushing her to talk about what would happen next. She was right that she couldn't stay here much longer; dragging it out like this was just causing David the pain she'd been trying to avoid. Hayley's flat was too small for the two of them, so they were going to rent somewhere with two decent-sized bedrooms. Hayley's job was looking for somewhere not too far from the hospital. Katherine's job was to try and find her share of the money.

'I just don't have anything in my savings. There's a joint ISA and there's money in the house, but I don't want David to have to sell.'

'Of course not.' Hayley was almost as adamant as Katherine that David should be spared any suffering possible in all this, although Katherine knew that she still thought David should be told. Last night, on the phone, she'd brought it up again and

Katherine had been forced to relive the last months for her dad, until she'd reduced Hayley to tears.

She'd also called to make an appointment with her solicitor for this afternoon. Because she wanted to check something about her will.

The appointment with the solicitor was very straightforward. After a brief conversation, he'd confirmed that the documents they'd signed at the fertility clinic were legally binding. If anything were to happen to her, David would be able to use the embryos; there was no need to add anything to her will. He would be able to decide whether to donate them to a couple who wanted to start a family or even – although she couldn't quite imagine a set of circumstances where this might occur – use them himself.

It wasn't until she'd left the solicitor's office and found a bench to rest on in the park that she actually began to think about what that might mean. It was one thing talking about the embryos in legal terms, in a theoretical manner, but quite another to think about them in terms of possibility. What they could become.

The early afternoon sun was warm on her face as she closed her eyes and tilted her face towards it. She'd always loved the sunshine. David was more of a winter person. He loved to ski. But she was the one who followed the heat like a sunflower. She enjoyed nothing more than a beach and the sight of the sea.

The embryos were made of both of them, her and David. Summer and winter. Hot and cold. Dark and fair.

The fertility treatment had been tough. Much tougher than she'd thought it would be. She was tough too; that's what everyone thought. But that didn't mean she didn't feel pain the same as everyone else. And then she'd barely had a chance to process the disappointment of their failure before finding out about the tumour.

Only now, when it would never happen, did she realise how much she'd wanted to have a baby with David. What would he have looked like, their child? They would have had a son; she was sure of it. Maybe he would have looked just like David, with thick blonde hair and beautiful blue eyes. Or dark like her. Would he have been daring or timid? Academic or creative? Or both?

Her eyes stayed closed, but tears squeezed from under her lids and down her face. This was no more than a dream. She would never get to be a mother. Never get to hold her child, their child.

David might have a child though. Hard though it was going to be for her to leave him, she needed to do this right. Cutting off his love for her meant leaving him open to meet someone new. Someone who could give him a child. Because he would make the most wonderful father. Of that she was sure.

THIRTY

HANNAH

Asking David that question – what do you think Katherine would have wanted to do with the embryos? – was actually the first time Hannah had thought about it like that.

She'd spent so much time considering what it would mean for her and David to use the embryos that she hadn't wondered whether Katherine would have wanted to use them at all. David was adamant that she'd had no interest in them. But Hannah wasn't so sure. She knew what fertility treatment was like: the discomfort, the emotional rollercoaster, the appointments, the money, the time. Why would Katherine have put herself through that if she didn't want a child?

'What was she really like, David? You must have loved her once.'

'I did – of course I did. But it's difficult for me to remember that sometimes. It's like I have to remember two different people.'

'What do you mean?'

He sighed. 'Katherine had always been ambitious and focused on what she wanted and, sometimes, that meant I got pushed to the side. Our friends would joke about how often she changed her mind and how I would have to just get in line. But I was okay with that. Beneath it all, she loved me and we had such a good time together. But when I found out... when she told me about the affair, all I could think was that I'd been an absolute fool.'

'Why a fool? How would you have known?'

'Because all the signs were there. The working away, the fact we'd stopped having sex, she'd bought new clothes, had her hair cut. And then she just gave her notice in on her job. She said she was going on to something "bigger and better". Those were her exact words. I didn't realise at the time that she meant something better than me too.'

'That doesn't make you foolish though.'

'But I knew, Hannah. On some level, I'd known for a while. I'm not proud of it, but I spent most nights with a beer or a glass of wine in my hand, numbing the way I felt.'

That did surprise her. Other than the rugby weekend he'd had with Ben and Luke, David barely drank anything these days. 'Like I said. It must have been hard.'

'I was drunk the night she told me. The night she confessed to the affair.'

THIRTY-ONE

KATHERINE

Some people can hide it well when they're drunk; Katherine had worked with more than a few functioning alcoholics and knew the sleight-of-hand tricks that help keep it hidden. Breath mints. A shot of brandy in the morning coffee. Drinking a bottle alone in their dressing room before the 'first drink' at the bar with the rest of the crew. David was not one of those people. Until the last few months, he'd only really drunk socially; it was rare for him to have more than one beer at home or the very occasional glass of wine with dinner.

After the night out to celebrate Luke starting his own dental practice, she'd driven home from the restaurant with him slumped in the passenger seat, staring out of the window. Other than the odd cough, there had been silence the whole way home.

As soon as she'd pulled up onto their drive, he'd jumped out of the car. But he was still fumbling with his keys in the lock when she joined him at the front door. Then he dropped them. 'Damn!'

While he bent down to pick them up, she slotted her own key into the lock and opened the door. He staggered behind her, then past her, into the sitting room. He reached into the cupboard where they kept a few bottles of wine and pulled out a half-empty bottle of whiskey she hadn't known they had.

She watched as he poured a generous measure into a heavy glass tumbler. 'Don't you think you've had enough to drink?'

He turned to face her, staggering a little. 'You're not at work now, Katherine. You can't tell me what to do.'

He'd used the same line earlier in the evening when he'd started ordering chasers with his beer. She rubbed at her forehead; it ached and all she wanted to do was go to bed. 'I'm going up then.'

'Who is he?' David's voice was thick with alcohol and agony.

Her heart almost stopped. 'What?'

'I'm not stupid, Katherine. Actually' – he held up the hand that wasn't holding his glass – 'I am stupid, because I've been sticking my head in the sand. Maybe I just needed a bit of Dutch courage.' Now he waved the glass, the dark brown liquid in danger of slopping over the edge.

'You're drunk, David. I am not having this conversation with you.'

She turned to go, and he reached out and grabbed her arm, pulling her back to face him. 'Yes, we are having this conversation. Because tomorrow I might not be brave enough. Who is he?'

She stared at his arm on hers before he dropped it. He'd never grabbed her like this before. 'You're being paranoid.'

'That's what I told myself. When you kept checking your phone for messages. When you were home late twice as often as usual. When you kept telling me you were out with Hayley.'

'So you think I'm having an affair with Hayley?'

'Will you just stop!'

The volume of his voice seemed to shock him as much as it had her. Her stomach twisted at the sight of him. Drunk.

Aggressive. Loud. Had she done this to him? 'I'm going to bed now.'

This time his voice was quieter. 'Please, Katherine. You have to tell me. I've asked you this before, but I need you to be honest with me. Are you seeing someone else?'

It was like a dark, unwanted gift; the perfect out; the final act. 'So what if I am?'

THIRTY-TWO

HANNAH

'Oh, David. I'm so sorry I've made you relive all of that.'

He shook his head. 'No. I should have talked to you about it before. And I'm the one who should be sorry for getting angry at the Clarence earlier. Especially with everything that's happened with your mum today.'

Their afternoon tea at the Clarence seemed as if it was weeks rather than hours ago. So much had changed in her mind since then. 'I was terrified this afternoon when I got that call from Tony. But it has made me realise something for sure. I want to have a baby while my mum is still here to be a grandmother.'

She couldn't keep the tremble out of her voice as she spoke, and David tightened his arm around her. 'Oh, Hannah. I know how scary that was. But your mum is going to be fine. She told you what the doctor said. He wants her to take this as a warning to change her lifestyle. Tony was already writing notes of all the advice the nurse gave her. He'll make sure she does what she has to do.'

Tony would look after her mother, she knew that. His face was a picture of happiness when they'd left the hospital earlier and he'd told her that her mother had accepted his marriage proposal. She was glad for him, for both of them.

She pushed herself up in her seat and shifted so that she was looking at David. 'I know that she's okay this time. But what if it happens again? I want to have a baby while my mum is still here. It doesn't matter how any longer.'

His voice was so gentle, she knew that he was trying hard not to upset her. 'I know I was being... oversensitive earlier. But you were right. We need to be doing this for the right reasons. We shouldn't just rush through it without thinking.'

'But I have thought about it. I've done nothing but think about it for the last few weeks. Adoption will take too long; donor eggs is another whole process we'd need to begin. And whatever happened between you and Katherine, you loved her. These embryos were created out of love. I'm ready to have a baby, David. Now. With you. And the rest of it I can deal with as I go along.'

David pressed his lips together as if he was stopping himself from saying something. Probably, he still thought she was making a knee-jerk decision. But she wasn't. After all her indecision, she was finally sure. When he nodded, she took that as his acceptance.

For the next month, Hannah's world was punctuated with appointments and scans and then injections and hormone tablets and more scans. Nausea and fatigue and cramps were the order of most of her days. 'It'll all be worth it' had become her mantra. She tried not to let her mind add 'if it works'.

After consulting with the embryologist at the clinic, they'd agreed to defrost two of the embryos to begin with; only defrosting a third – or the fourth and final embryo – if the first ones didn't progress satisfactorily. He would call them throughout the morning with updates on how things were going so they knew when to be ready to come in for the embryo transfer.

The night before, they lay beside each other in bed, both unable to sleep. Hannah was too scared to say it out loud, but all she could think about was that, by this time tomorrow, she could be pregnant. 'I want so much for this to work.'

David stretched a sleepy arm around her. 'It will, Han. I know it.'

She closed her eyes and tried to believe it was true.

THIRTY-THREE

HANNAH

The first two embryos were due to be taken out of storage at 8 a.m. Hannah was awake at 5.30.

Somehow, David was still deeply asleep, so she peeled the covers back gently and slipped out of bed. There was no point in two of them pacing the floor for the next few hours.

In the kitchen, the floor was cold on her feet. Ordinarily, she would have kick-started her day with a cup of coffee, but she didn't want the caffeine this morning. They hadn't told her to avoid it, but she wanted her body to be as clean and receptive as it possibly could be.

Instead, she poured a mug of milk and stuck it into the microwave to heat. There was something so wholesome about warm milk that it felt like the right thing to do. Plus it might soothe her jagged nerves.

As she watched the mug turning around through the glass of the microwave door, it dawned on her that this might be a regular occurrence in a few months' time. Would she be up in the early hours, warming milk for a baby? Her baby? Maybe she'd even be able to breastfeed? Dr Nash had told her that, once the pregnancy was confirmed, it would progress like any other. That meant she would produce milk like any other new mother. Her stomach fizzed at the very thought, but she tried to push it down, scared to jinx it before it even happened.

The kitchen clock seemed to go backwards as she sat on a stool by the kitchen island. It was like waiting for Christmas morning to come. After a couple of years of 4 a.m. wake-ups, her parents had made the rule that she couldn't drag her sack of presents into their bedroom until at least six o'clock. She could still remember the feeling of the heavy sack at the end of her bed. She would push her toes towards it, thrilled to feel the presents' wrapping crinkle inside. Then, as now, the clock on her bedside table would be interminably slow.

The gift she was waiting for today would not come wrapped in brightly coloured paper, but it would be the best present she'd ever had.

The kitchen door was pushed opened and a sleepy-looking David appeared behind it, yawning and scratching his head, his eyes still half-closed, as if he was hoping to be able to go back to sleep. 'Hey, you're up early. Can't sleep?'

'No, too much excitement I suppose. My brain was busy the moment I woke up. Sorry, I tried not to wake you.'

'You didn't. I must have reached out for you and you weren't there. You're feeling okay though?'

She smiled. 'I'm fine. You can go back to bed if you want. Honestly, I'm good.'

'No, I'm awake now.' He stretched and his T-shirt rose up so that she could see his toned stomach. It made her think of her own. How that was going to look a lot different soon. Hopefully.

David opened a cupboard to grab a mug. 'Are you okay for a drink?'

She nodded. 'Yes, I'm fine. How are you feeling?'

He shrugged. 'Same as you, I guess. Excited, nervous, hopeful, scared.' He turned to smile at her. 'It's bigger for you though; I've got nothing to do today except hold your hand. How are you feeling about the procedure?'

Surprisingly, that part she'd barely thought about. In the midst of thinking about waiting to see if the embryos were viable and then, afterwards, hoping that they implanted successfully, she'd barely considered the moment at which they would be placed inside her. 'I've not really given it much attention. It's just something that needs to happen.'

Of course, David had been through this part before too. None of this was new for him. Had Katherine woken early on the morning of her treatment? Had they stood in this same kitchen and had a very similar conversation?

She shook her head to move that thought away. This was their day: hers and David's. It didn't matter what had happened before. It didn't.

David held a packet of chocolate biscuits aloft. 'Shall we go and sit on the sofa?'

Even with the help of the biscuits, the time didn't go any faster. They tried to watch TV, but Hannah couldn't settle to anything. Instead, she thumbed through YouTube looking at all the IVF channels she'd subscribed to.

David glanced over her shoulder. 'I'm not sure that's going to help with your nerves.'

'I know. But I can't help it.' It was almost as if she was trying to will it to happen. If she watched everything, knew everything, ate the right food, drank enough water, wanted it badly enough, then maybe, just maybe it would work.

Eventually, 8 a.m. came around. She closed down YouTube and placed her mobile on the coffee table, willing it to ring. By five past, she was practically dancing on the spot. 'They did say 8 a.m., didn't they?'

David smiled; put his hand over her twitching ones. 'Yes.

But it's going to take them a few minutes to actually take them out of storage and then call us.'

How could he be so calm? 'And it was my number that they—'

The shrill ringtone broke into the room. Hannah's heart was in her throat. She looked at David. 'Can you answer it?'

The conversation was brief. 'Hello... Yes... That's great... Thank you... We will.'

He smiled and nodded at Hannah the whole time to reassure her that all was okay, but she still wanted to hear it from him after he hung up. 'Everything is fine? The embryos are out?'

'Yes, my darling. The first two embryos are out of storage. The clinic will call us in an hour to give us an update on how they're progressing.'

She let out her breath. This was happening. It was actually happening.

If she'd thought the early hours of the morning had been difficult, the next sixty minutes were torture. She couldn't turn her mind to anything. She tried to keep busy – the kitchen had never looked so clean in the whole time she'd lived there – but even that didn't help. What was happening in that lab? Were the cells dividing? One of them? Two? Three?

At 8.30, her mother called. 'Hello, darling. I just wanted to wish you luck for today. How are you feeling?'

It was as if she was about to start a new job or take an exam. Except that both of those things she could've prepared for, would've had the power to affect their outcome. This was different; she was absolutely powerless to do anything else to make this happen. 'I'm so nervous, Mum. I don't know what to do with myself.'

'Of course you are. Would you like me to come over? I can wake Tony up and ask him to bring me?'

Much as she was pleased for her mum that Tony had moved

in, she didn't want to picture the two of them lying next to each other in bed. 'No, I'll be okay. I'm keeping myself as busy as I can.'

Her mum chuckled at the other end of the phone. 'You're just like your father. Whenever he was stressed about something, I could guarantee that I'd find him servicing the car or pulling all the weeds up in the garden.'

Hannah loved to be compared to her dad, but today it left her feeling even more agitated. Would this baby be like her at all? Or would he or she be a carbon copy of Katherine? It was too late to think about that. No going back now.

'Actually, Mum, I'm going to come off the phone because I want to leave it clear in case the lab calls.'

'Of course, of course. I'm going right now. I'm here if you need me though. I can be there in a heartbeat.'

'Bye, Mum. I love you.'

As she shut off the call, Hannah's own heart was beating hard. There were thirty more minutes before they could expect the embryologist to call. She really didn't think she could wait that long. Would it be unreasonable for her to call them?

David was in the shower. She'd told herself to wait until the lab had called. If it was good news, she would shower and allow herself to start getting ready to go in. If it was not good news, she would run a bath and stay in it all day.

'Don't think it's going to be bad news. We need to stay positive.' Those had been David's last words before he got into the shower. She was trying to send good vibes out into the universe, she really was. But the fear of setting herself up for a huge fall was too great. She preferred to try and keep her emotions in stasis.

Her mobile rang.

For a moment she just looked at it. Before David had got in the shower, she'd told him that she wanted him to take all the calls; she wasn't sure she could actually string a cohesive sentence together to talk to the embryologist, or calm her mind for long enough to understand what she was being told.

It rang a second time.

They'd thought he had enough time to take a shower because they weren't expecting a call until after nine. Why were they calling early? Did this mean it was bad news? She felt hot and dizzy and sick.

It rang a third time.

She grabbed for the phone so quickly that she almost dropped it. 'Hello? Hello?'

'Mrs Maguire?'

'Yes. That's me.' She couldn't even bring herself to ask if there was news. *Please let them be okay. Please let them be okay.*

'This is Dr Collier. I just wanted to let you know that both embryos have started to divide. So far, it's looking good.'

Hannah's back slid down the kitchen cupboard until she was balanced on her heels. 'Thank you. Thank you so much.'

'You're very welcome. We'll call again in an hour. Take care.'

'Yes. You too. Thank you so much.'

The call clicked off the other end, but she kept the mobile to her ear. Three minutes later, David walked in towelling his hair. Seeing her crouched on the floor, he dropped the towel and was beside her in moments. 'Hannah. What is it? Have they called? What's happened?'

Her throat was so thick she could barely speak. 'It's happening, David. It's really happening.'

He pulled her towards him, and all the anxiety of the morning poured out of her as she sobbed into his chest.

Thirty minutes later, they were back to watching the clock.

Hannah had allowed herself time to have a shower and check the bag for her hospital appointment. She was only going as an outpatient but had packed a change of clothes anyway. She'd also packed a book, a snack and a tube of hand cream.

David had insisted that she eat a slice of toast, but she'd barely been able to push it down her throat. To break the tension, he'd suggested that he pick up some pastries from the shop on the corner; it was only fifteen minutes' walk away, but he took the car so that he could be there and back in ten.

David had the sweetest tooth of anyone she knew. That was why, when the doorbell rang, she assumed his hands were too full of paper bags of doughnuts and pastries to be able to get his key in the lock.

But it wasn't David at the door. It was a woman of about Hannah's age, in a long coat with a pale pinched face and dark red lipstick. 'Hello?'

'Hi.' The woman smiled tightly. 'You must be Hannah? Is David there?'

How did this woman know who she was? 'He'll be back in a couple of minutes. What do you need him for?'

The woman took a deep breath. 'I just need to talk to him about something. Well, both of you really. I'm Hayley. I was Katherine's best friend.'

THIRTY-FOUR

HANNAH

A light drizzle was threatening to turn into something heavier, so Hannah invited Hayley to step into the hall. As she did so, she heard her sharp intake of breath.

Hayley was looking around her at the walls, the stairs, the new carpet on the floor. Up, down, into every corner. 'Sorry, it's... well, I haven't been here since... well, I haven't been here for a long time.'

Hannah wondered if the last time she'd been here, Katherine had been here too. She didn't ask though. 'I'm really sorry, but today's not a very good day. We're in the middle of something important.'

Hayley stopped gazing around and fixed her eyes on Hannah, her expression saying so much that Hannah couldn't read. 'I know. I know that you're planning to use Katherine's embryos. That's why I'm here.'

Now it was Hannah's turn to gasp. Who had told her about that? Was it the same person who'd told her Hannah's name? Lauren and Priya came to mind. She opened her mouth to ask but stopped when she heard the scrape of David's key in the lock.

David was already talking as he walked through the open door. 'They didn't have those apple ones you like so I...' He tailed off as he caught sight of their visitor. 'Hayley? What are you doing here? I thought you were in New York now?'

'Hi, David. I do live in New York, but I'm over here for work. I'm sorry to drop in like this. I've been meaning to call, but, well, I just need to talk to you.' She glanced at Hannah. 'Both of you.'

David stepped forwards to put a hand on Hannah's shoulder. 'It's great to see you, Hayley. But we've got a lot on today; can I call you later maybe? Did you say you're here for the week?'

She shook her head. 'No, I'm sorry. I won't keep you, but I really need to show you something. I shouldn't have waited this long, I'm sorry. But I really think you should see this.'

Hannah felt sick to the pit of her stomach. This was Katherine's best friend. Had she come here to stop them using the embryos? Could she? The paperwork at the clinic had made it clear that they belonged solely to David, so what could Hayley tell them that would change anything?

David also looked confused, but he held out a hand to invite Hayley into the sitting room. 'You know where the sofa is.'

The armchair nearest to the door was the most comfortable seat in the lounge, but Hayley looked as if it was stuffed with nails. Her eyes, which had bored into Hannah earlier, looked down at her hands; the hair that fell forwards onto her face was almost as dark as the clothes she wore: funeral black.

She waved away Hannah's offer of a drink. Clearly this was no time for social niceties. 'Okay. I don't know how to go about this, even though I've had it going around and around my head for months. Well, years really. I need to talk to you about Katherine's death.'

David stiffened beside Hannah on the sofa and she placed a hand on his leg. Even though he'd now opened up about his marriage to Katherine, they'd still never spoken about her car accident. Early on in their marriage, he'd made it clear that the memory of that day was just too painful. Today of all days, he didn't need to be reliving it.

When neither of them spoke, Hayley continued. 'Well, not about her death exactly, about the final few months. Some things she might not have told you.'

David's voice almost made Hannah jump; it was so stern and cold. 'If you mean her affair, I knew. I'm surprised she didn't tell you. She was quite open about it in the end.'

Perhaps it was their recent conversations which made David so quick to anger. As if the feeling was still fresh.

Hayley shuffled in her seat. 'That's the thing. She wasn't. Having an affair, that is.'

But David had told Hannah that Katherine had admitted to it. He'd been absolutely certain. A glance at his face showed that he was just as confused as she was.

'Maybe she just didn't tell you. Because I can assure you that she didn't mince her words telling me.'

Hannah's heart went out to him. How painful it must have been to go through that rejection. To know that the person you loved no longer wanted you. It was her worst possible nightmare.

Hayley shook her head. 'She lied about it, David. She made it up to protect you.'

David frowned and shook his head. 'Protect me? What the heck are you talking about?'

Hannah looked from one to the other of them. This was making no sense at all.

Hayley took a deep breath. 'There's no easy way for me to say this, so I'm just going to come out with it. She was ill, David. Really ill. She had a brain tumour. That's the secret she was hiding. Not another man.'

Beside her, Hannah could feel David jolt as if he'd been

shot. He opened his mouth, but nothing came out. Again, she looked between the two of them. Was this a lie? A last-ditch attempt by one of Katherine's friends to stop the two of them from being happy together?

Hayley was watching David intently as if waiting for the information to sink in. He was shaking his head from side to side, his face flushed. Twice, he opened his mouth and closed it again, until the right words came to him. 'I don't believe you. If that was true, why wouldn't she tell me?'

Hayley seemed to expect that question. 'It's complicated. That's why I needed to come here in person and speak to you.'

The walls of the sitting room seemed to have come closer, and there was less air in the room than there had been only moments ago. David pushed a finger into the collar of his shirt and moved it around as if it was choking him. 'But it wasn't too complicated to tell you? If she could tell you, why not me? And why the hell didn't *you* tell me? Surely you must have known that I would want to know?'

Hayley continued. 'I did know, David, and believe me when I tell you that I begged her to tell you. Many times. But she swore me to secrecy. She didn't want you to know.'

David held out his hands, splaying his fingers. 'But why? Surely when a wife gets ill, the first person she tells is her husband. You know me, Hayley. You know how I supported her in everything. Why would she keep this from me?'

Hayley seemed ready for this question. 'To begin with, we thought she was going to come through it. She said she didn't want to worry you. I know it sounds insane, but you know how persuasive she was. Somehow it made sense.' She winced at the final sentence. Clearly it did not make sense any longer.

David brought his hands up to his forehead, pressing it with his fingers and thumbs. 'Made sense? None of this makes sense.'

'I know. I know. When we found out it was terminal, I said that she *had* to tell you. But she didn't want you to see it. See her deteriorate. Get sicker. She wanted you to remember her as she was.'

'She would rather I hated her than see her lose her looks? That's so messed up. And so incredibly selfish.'

Hayley had tears in her eyes, and she reached out for David's arm, but he shrank away. 'It wasn't selfish, David. Really it wasn't. I don't know where it came from, but she was convinced that watching her die would ruin your life. That you might turn her into some kind of saint, that you wouldn't move on. Wouldn't ever be happy with anyone else.'

She glanced at Hannah as she said that. Clearly, she was the 'anyone else'. Was it true? Would David not have fallen in love with her if he'd known that Katherine had died of cancer? If he'd nurtured her in her final months? Was it only his belief in her infidelity that had allowed him to move on so soon after her death? Had all his friends been right in their silent judgement of their marriage? They'd met nine months after Katherine's accident; if he'd been with her until the end of her illness, perhaps he and Hannah would never have even met?

Because Hayley had looked directly at her, she felt as if she was allowed to say something. 'But Katherine died in a car accident? That's true, isn't it?'

This conversation was so surreal that she was almost expecting Hayley to say that the accident had been a lie too. But Hayley nodded. 'Yes. She was on her way to my flat that night. The coroner's verdict was accidental death. But I guess we'll never know the whole truth.'

David flinched, then stared at her. 'Are you trying to suggest that it was suicide?'

Hayley held up her hands. 'She shouldn't have been driving in her condition. And she knew that.'

David stood up and began to pace the room. 'I just don't know what to do with all this, Hayley. I haven't seen you since Katherine died. You turn up here unannounced. Tell me that she had a terminal illness. That her car accident might not have been an accident and—'

'I didn't come here to hurt you, David.' Hayley looked as stricken with guilt as he did.

Hannah had no idea what to do. David was in pain, but she felt as if she were glued to her seat.

Then her mobile rang.

This time she didn't wait for a second ring – she snatched it up and answered. 'Hello?'

'Mrs Maguire?'

It was the embryologist. The call she'd been waiting for and dreading in equal measure. 'Yes, it's me. How is everything going?' Even as she said the words, a part of her wondered whether it mattered any longer. Was David still going to want to go through with this? With her? After what he'd just heard?

The embryologist's voice was so professionally calm and kind that she knew straight away it wasn't good news. 'I'm very sorry, but one of the embryos is not progressing. So, as per your consent, we've taken another out of storage. It's very normal that not all of them are suitable for implantation, so we're still very hopeful for a positive result.'

Hannah closed her eyes. Half an hour ago, she'd had hope too. But now? 'Thank you for letting us know.'

'Of course. And we'll call back again in an hour.'

'Thank you.'

She let the phone slip from her ear and onto the sofa. When she opened her eyes, David was looking at her. 'One of them is gone.'

His face crumpled. Was he thinking, like her, that this was just the beginning of the end? 'Oh, Hannah.' He sat down on the sofa and took her in his arms 'There are three more chances. One of them has to be fine.'

They were empty words and they both knew it. He had no way of knowing whether any of the three remaining embryos would thrive. She pulled herself out of his embrace and looked at Hayley, who clearly didn't know where to put herself. Rationally there was absolutely no connection between her appearance and the news they'd just received, but now Hannah wanted her out of the house as soon as possible. 'You said you had something to show us?'

'Yes. And I'm so sorry. I know this couldn't possibly be a worse time. I didn't realise that it was all actually happening today. I mean, I knew it was soon, but...'

David kept his arm around Hannah as he spoke. 'What is it?'

Hayley unzipped the bag beside her and reached inside. It was a huge, squashy rucksack-type bag and it took her a while to locate what she was after. Eventually, she pulled out a long, pale blue envelope and held it out to David.

'It's a letter. From Katherine.'

THIRTY-FIVE

KATHERINE

On the top floor of a recent house conversion, Hayley's flat was clean and comfortable, but more like an anonymous chain hotel room than a home. Having often moved cities for her career, Hayley hadn't been too concerned about decorating – 'I'll buy soft furnishings when I've run out of imagination on more fun things to spend my money on' – so it was all the more touching that she'd made such an effort to make her bedroom here comfortable for Katherine so that she could stay overnight whenever she wanted.

Propped up on the bed on extra pillows, Katherine felt well enough this morning to take in the vase of flowers, the framed photo collage of the two of them on a trip to Asia and the pile of paperbacks Hayley had picked out from the bookshop near her office. How grateful she was for Hayley. She'd been an absolute lifeline. In the last few weeks, she'd fielded all the post and calls from the hospital. Helped Katherine keep track of her appointments and – most importantly – helped her to keep the truth of her diagnosis from everybody. Now she'd even rented out her flat for a year so that she could move into a two-bedroom place with

Katherine in a couple of weeks' time. She'd asked for nothing in return.

Until now.

Sitting on the edge of the bed, she waved a pen and paper under Katherine's nose. 'Shall I get you something to lean on?'

Katherine kept her arms folded in protest. 'Why would I want to write a letter? I don't want him to know the truth, so why would I write it down?'

But Hayley was adamant. 'For me. In case I ever need it.'

Hayley had been amazing these last few weeks and Katherine didn't want to be even more difficult, but it made no sense. 'That's what I don't understand. If you're never going to tell David the truth, as you promised me you won't, why would you need a letter from me to him telling him everything?'

She knew that Hayley was struggling with keeping the truth from David; this wasn't the first time they'd discussed it. It wasn't just David either. There was her mum too. But even the thought of watching their faces crease with horror and grief as she told them her prognosis... no, she couldn't do it. Maybe it was partly selfish, but coming to terms with it for herself was about all she could manage right now.

Whenever it came up – which was more frequent in the last week or so – Hayley always ended up at the same questions. 'What will I tell them? How will I explain?'

And Katherine's response was always the same too. 'I'll figure it out. Just not now.' Or, in darker moments, 'Because I'm dying and you're my best friend and it's what I want.'

Now, though, Hayley was turning it back on her. 'What you've asked me to do, the secret that I have to keep, goes against what I think is right – you know that. But I'm doing it. Because you're my best friend and I love you.'

'And because I'm dying.'

She couldn't help herself, but Hayley wasn't in the mood for her dark humour today. 'But there might come a time when I have no choice. When I have to tell him. And I want it to be in your words.'

Katherine frowned. 'Like when?'

Hayley took a deep breath; her reluctance was obvious. 'What if he meets someone else? What if he denies himself another marriage, children, happiness, because of a sense of loyalty to you? What if—'

She stopped mid-sentence when Katherine held up her hand. 'That's a lot of ifs.'

Hayley proffered the pen and paper again. 'Please, Katherine.'

Katherine uncrossed her arms, but waved away the stationery. 'Grab my laptop. If I have to do this, I'm not writing it by hand like a Christmas thank-you letter to my granny. And you're going to need to give me some time to think what to say.'

Hayley's face softened. 'Of course. I'll get the laptop and make you a cup of tea.'

She could do with something a lot stronger than tea to get this job done. Though she'd written countless emails and pitches and budgets on this laptop, a final letter to David was the hardest thing she would ever have to write. She opened up Word and stared at the blank page and the blinking cursor. How could she even start?

It took her the rest of the afternoon and a couple of hours the following morning. Partly because she got exhausted quickly now, and partly because she deleted and rewrote every sentence several times. Eventually, though, she was done, and she passed her laptop over to Hayley. 'Here. Read it through before you print it out or whatever you plan to do with it.'

She'd expected Hayley to take it away. But she sat next to her on the bed, and Katherine couldn't help herself rereading it on the screen at the same time.

Dear David,

Even typing that seems weird. How often does someone write a letter to their husband these days? Especially a letter that you're never likely to read, but Hayley has told me I have to do it and she has been frankly amazing these last few weeks. So how can I say no?

Hayley looked up at her then and nudged her with her elbow. 'Thanks.'

Katherine shrugged. 'It's true. You've been the best of friends, Hayley. I don't know of anyone else who would have been there like this for me.'

She wished she hadn't said that when she saw Hayley's eyes fill up. 'What am I going to do without you? How am I going to bear it?'

Katherine shook her head vigorously. It was too soon for this conversation; too painful. She nodded at the letter. 'Just keep reading.'

I am going to assume that Hayley has told you that I am ill. Terminally ill. All the headaches I blamed on my erratic work hours turned out to have a more nefarious cause. A brain tumour. And not, unfortunately, one that is either benign or operable. Believe me, if there was something I could have done to stay with you, I would have.

One thing you do need to know is that the type of tumour I have is not hereditary. The doctors were quite emphatic about that. I have no idea what you'll do with the embryos we have in storage. Maybe you could donate them to a couple who would like a baby? Make sure that they're nice people. Kind. These last few weeks, dealing with different nurses and people at the hospital, I've realised what an underrated trait that is.

Which brings me to my next point. If, for a reason I can't even begin to understand, Hayley needs to give you this letter, I want you to know that you should marry someone else. Not just date. Marry. You are the marrying kind, David. You are constant and faithful; there is so much love in you, and it mustn't go to waste. Otherwise all of this has been for nothing.

Let her be a kind woman. I don't think I've always been kind to you. I know that you would shake your head at that, but it's true. I know who I am.

But this is my final attempt at being kind. Unselfish. It would be so easy for me to tell you about this tumour. I know what you would do. You would look after me and scour the world for a cure. You would spend every moment you had on my comfort and care. And after I was gone, you would spend years getting over it. I know you, David.

And that's what I don't want. You deserve to be happy. The happiest man alive. So this time I'm putting you first.

I love you, David. Always have, always will. That's why you can't see my death as the end for you too.

Your Katherine

xxx

Hayley closed her eyes as she read the final words. Katherine knew that she was trying not to cry. She bent her head to lean on her shoulder. 'Is it okay?'

She felt Hayley nod. 'It's perfect.'

She couldn't deny that it had been therapeutic to write these words down, but that couldn't have been the reason Hayley would put her through it? 'I still don't understand why you wanted me to write him a letter. I mean, I get what you say about him possibly needing to know the truth at some point – but why can't you just tell him that yourself?'

Hayley tilted her head. Her face was so sad. 'It's not just for him.'

'You're not making any sense.'

Hayley pushed her away gently, so that she could look into her eyes. 'It's for me too, Kat. So that I can read these words and know that I'm doing the right thing.'

For the first time, Katherine understood the weight of her request on Hayley. It wasn't just now that she was asking her to lie to David. Unless one of those 'ifs' came to pass, it was forever.

She leaned forwards and kissed her friend. 'Thank you. For everything. You're the only one I can trust.'

THIRTY-SIX

HANNAH

They'd read the letter silently, side by side on the sofa. Hannah was the quicker reader of the two of them, but she didn't move a muscle; stayed staring at the page until David had finished.

When he got to the end, he leaned back in his seat, defeated. 'Oh, Katherine.'

The way he said her name sent fear trickling down Hannah's spine. She'd only heard him use her name a handful of times and it had always been in a very matter-of-fact way. This was gentle, caring, wistful even. She understood, but, oh, it hurt.

In an attempt to comfort him, she put her hand on his leg. It felt so insignificant. What she wanted to do was grasp him tightly and never let go. But, in that moment, it didn't feel as if he belonged to her. His eyes weren't seeing her; they were remembering Katherine.

He turned to her, yet he didn't look her in the eyes. 'Hannah, I'm so sorry, but I need some air. Just ten minutes. I need to walk. Get my head straight. Will you be okay?'

No, she wasn't okay. 'Of course. I'll call you if I hear anything.'

Now he did look at her, but she couldn't read the meaning in his eyes. 'I'll be back before they call again. I promise.'

Another empty promise. They could call back any minute. With more bad news about the second embryo. Or the third.

Once the door closed, Hannah and Hayley sat looking at one another.

Hayley was the first to speak. 'I can understand that you're not best pleased at me turning up like this. I honestly didn't know that today was the actual day you were...' She flailed around for the right terminology but left the sentence hanging in the air.

Neither Lauren nor Priya knew that today was the day, so Hayley was telling the truth. 'I believe you.'

'And I've wrestled with this for a long time. When I heard that David had met you, and that he was happy, I was pleased. It was as if everything had worked out the way that Katherine wanted it to. But still, it knocked on my conscience. I kept thinking that, if it was me, I would have wanted to know.'

For the first time, anger started to push through the other emotions wrestling for space in Hannah's chest. 'Then why take so long to tell him?'

Hayley's face – and tone – pleaded for her. 'She was my best friend, Hannah. You know what that means. Thelma and Louise. Together till the end.'

She did know what that meant. Or what it should mean. 'So why now? Why wait all this time after Katherine's death to tell David? To show him that letter?'

Hayley nodded her understanding at Hannah's confusion. 'There were two things in the space of a week. Firstly, I read an article about brain tumours. It came up on my social-media feed. I normally avoid anything like that like the plague. It's too upsetting. But this one had a heading which said something about changed behaviour and, well, I read it.'

'And?'

'And it said that, sometimes, with a brain tumour, it presses on the part of the brain that controls your personality and makes you act completely out of character.'

This was starting to make sense. 'I see. And you think that's what happened with Katherine?'

Hayley held out her hands. 'I don't know. That's the problem with all of this. She's not here and I can't ask her what to do for the best. And then I emailed Katherine's mother – we've stayed in contact since Kat died even though I feel like an absolute coward for not telling her the truth either – and she told me about your plans to use the embryos. I was beside myself.'

So she was in the same camp as Priya and Lauren on this. 'You don't think it's a good idea either?'

Hayley leaned forwards. Hannah didn't know why, but there was something about this woman that she liked. 'No. It's not that. I actually think it's a pretty wonderful idea for you and David to do this. He deserves this happiness, and he'll make a great dad. Well, I'm sure I don't need to tell you that.'

Actually, it was good to hear that from someone David had known a long time. Especially after the reaction she'd had from Lauren and Priya. 'So why then?'

'Because...' She looked as if she might cry. 'Because Katherine was a great person too, so how could I let her biological children grow up thinking that she'd cheated on their father?'

Hannah could see her point. She knew she would feel exactly the same if it was Tessa or Charlotte. But she wouldn't have left it so long. 'If it was Marie who told you about it, you must have known the embryo transfer was today? I understand why you would want to talk to David, but why today?' It seemed unnecessarily cruel.

Hayley sighed. 'I honestly didn't know. Marie didn't tell me the date. I didn't even know it was imminent until I knocked on your door this morning. All I knew was that you were planning to use the embryos and I couldn't let you go ahead until you knew – both of you – the truth. Now that I'm here, I'm still not sure I've done the right thing. I'm sorry – I really am.'

Hannah had run out of things to say. She didn't want to talk to Hayley about this any longer. It was David she needed to speak to. 'I don't know how long David is going to be. Maybe you should go.'

Hayley stood and picked up her wet coat, which had left a damp patch on the arm of the chair. 'Of course. Well, I'm staying with my mum for a few days so I'll be close by. If you or David want to ask me anything, you can call me anytime.' She paused. 'I am really sorry.'

After Hannah closed the front door, she didn't have the energy to make it back to the sitting room. Instead, she sank onto the bottom step of the stairs and hugged her knees.

The house felt so big, so silent, so empty: she was totally alone.

What was David doing now? Walking the streets? Thinking about Katherine? His perfect first wife who had even sacrificed her own comfort in the final weeks of her life to protect him. Hannah couldn't even begin to imagine what that must have been like for her, facing the end alone. And it was worse than that. She'd made David believe that she was having an affair; the atmosphere in their house – this house – must have been truly awful.

She must have felt totally and utterly alone.

And that was how Hannah felt right now.

Her mobile was still pressed tightly into her hand. She would call David, but she was terrified that she might miss a call from the embryologist. She stared at the screen, willing it to ring and yet dreading the advent of more bad news.

What would happen if David walked back through that door and told her that he'd changed his mind? About the embryos, about having a child, about her. What if he no longer wanted the replacement wife, now that he knew that the original had loved him so much that she'd sacrificed herself on the altar of his future happiness?

She didn't have long to wait. For the second time in the last hour, she heard the scrape of David's key in the lock.

In the time they'd spent talking to Hayley, the drizzle outside had turned into a full-blown downpour. As soon as David came into the hall, he began to peel off his coat; he was soaked through.

Hannah stayed sitting on the stairs, searching his face for an insight into what was going through his mind. Trying to read his eyes as they settled on her.

He held out his hands to pull her up from the step. 'I need to tell you what happened that night. The night she died.'

THIRTY-SEVEN

KATHERINE

'How can you do this to me?'

She'd never seen David look so angry. Throughout their relationship, it had been her who'd ridden the emotional rollercoaster of highs and lows. Hating or loving. Desiring or rejecting. Chasing or running away. David was the one who'd provided the constancy she needed. He could see the other side to any argument, stayed calm in any situation.

Since the night of Luke's celebration, however, when she'd let him believe that she was having an affair, he'd vacillated between fury, grief and a bid for reconciliation. Now he quivered in front of her in a red-hot rage that was frightening. Fists clenched at his sides as if he needed to keep them under control. She wouldn't have blamed him if he couldn't.

She tried to keep her voice calm and cold. 'Finally. Maybe we can start to decide what can happen now. I've already told you that I don't want the house. I just need money to get myself set up somewhere. We'll need to cash in the ISA you set up and I can be on my way.'

She'd had it all planned out for weeks. She just needed him to agree, having neither the time nor the energy to engage in a lengthy divorce and risk ending up without a penny to play with. Hayley had already found a flat they could rent. It was closer to the hospital, so that she could get to appointments easily for as long as...

No. She wasn't ready to think about that. Not the end. Not yet.

'Do you even care? You look like you don't care.' David's face was contorted in a mixture of pain and anger.

This was hard. Much harder than she'd thought it would be. Now she clenched her own fists, digging the nails into her palms to keep herself focused on what she needed to do. What she *had* to do. 'Of course I care, David. It's the end of our marriage. But I think we both know it's been over for some time.'

A deep sound of grief welled up from somewhere deep within him and came out as a low moan. 'I thought... I just thought that we could work at this. I could have forgiven you, Katherine. Sex. An affair. We could have moved past it. Why are you being so cruel?'

How easy it would be to tell him everything. To take this awful, difficult secret and hand it over to him. *Here you are. This is the reason. What shall we do now?*

But she wasn't about to do that. Not now he was ready to be the one to end everything.

This time when she spoke, she didn't even look at him. Instead, she focused on the wall behind him, just above his shoulder. There was a mark on the wallpaper, a tiny smudge. If you weren't looking for it, you wouldn't even notice that it was there. A rogue champagne cork, five years ago, when she'd got her first producer credit.

'You say that I've been cruel? What about you? I just want to leave and you're...' She waved her hands around, trying to find the right words. 'Doing all of this.'

'Because I refuse to give up on us!' His voice was so loud it made her jump, and she was forced to look him in the face again. That dear face, which she loved so much. How many husbands would react as he'd done to her pretended infidelity? Offering to work at it, try counselling, ask what *he* had done wrong?

Her heart was thumping so hard that she didn't trust her voice not to give her away. She was so close now and one tremble, one falter and she knew that David would sweep her up, hold her close and then... then she might not have the strength to go through with it. Instead, she stared at him, trying to make him understand. *Let me go. Let me go.*

But David was nothing if not tenacious. 'Katherine, I am begging you. Please give this another chance. We have so many good years behind us. We've shared so much. I know we can do this. Please.'

It was agony. He'd done nothing wrong and yet he was begging her for another chance. He didn't know what he was asking. 'No.'

'Katherine. Please. Tell me what I can do.'

There was nothing he could do. Nothing anyone could do. Not the doctors or the herbalists or the dieticians or any of the other people she'd researched over the last few weeks. She had no control over this bastard disease. But she did have control over this. She could control how it ended. When the bomb went off, she could restrict who would be taken down in the impact.

And it wouldn't be him. This wonderful, kind, caring man who had looked after her so well from the moment they met. She would not have him see her deteriorate before his eyes. Would not ask him to hold her while she withered away, became a shadow of the woman he'd married.

She stuck out her chin and swallowed the lump of grief that was threatening in her throat. 'You can let me go. You can give me what is mine. You can step out of my way.'

He crumpled in front of her as if he would disappear and

leave behind an empty shirt and trousers in a pile on the floor. Sitting on the armchair that he only ever used if she was in another room – preferring otherwise to sit together on the three-seater sofa – for a moment, she could see him as something separate from her. Resting his elbows on his knees, he let his face fall into the palm of his hands.

If he started to cry, she might not be able to bear it. She was doing this to save him, not to break him. There was no way to explain that. No way to make him see that this was something she was doing because she loved him. Oh, how very much she loved him.

When he pulled his hands away from his face, his expression was dark and unrecognisable. 'If you're going, you can go tonight.'

For all her planning, she wasn't expecting him to say that. Hayley's American boyfriend was over there tonight. She'd barely spent any time with him as it was; there was no way Katherine could crash their romantic evening. 'I'll go tomorrow.'

'No!' His voice was a roar. 'You can go to him tonight. You want out? Then get out. Don't stay here and torture me with your presence. Get your stuff and just get the hell out of here.'

This was what she'd wanted. His anger. Him telling her to leave. But, right now, she felt terrified. 'David, I...'

'No.' He'd stood up now and he took a step back from her. 'Don't you dare do that. Don't you dare try and make me feel sorry for you. You can't play with me like this, Katherine. Changing your mind back and forth. You want a baby. You don't want a baby. You want me. You don't want me. You're leaving. You're not leaving.'

He was tearing another piece from her with every word. But who could blame him? That was exactly what she'd been like. She couldn't stop the words as they started to spill from her mouth. 'David, I'm sorry, I—'

'No!' He held up his hand to stop her words from reaching

him. 'No more. I can't let you do this to me any longer. I'm going out for an hour. Before I get back, I want you out of here. You can come for the rest of your things when I'm at work so that I don't need to watch you dismantle everything that we built together.'

And then he was gone.

The slam of the front door reverberated through her body, and her legs wobbled beneath her so that she had to sit on the sofa, holding on to the arm to stop the nausea. She couldn't think about this now. Couldn't think about him.

All around the room, their shared history looked back at her. The frames they'd bought from a small shop in Beccles the weekend he'd asked her to move in with him; the glass paper-weight full of bubbles that she'd persuaded him to buy from a glass-blowing factory on holiday in Spain; the paint on the walls which he'd been adamant was too dark, though they both knew he'd give in to her.

Because that's what he did. He gave in to her. Indulged her. Looked after her. Loved her.

Now it was her turn to love him by making sure that he didn't have to go through the pain that was now inevitable.

She pulled herself up from the sofa and took the car keys from the table. Saying goodbye to this house and all of their memories together was just the beginning.

The beginning of the end.

THIRTY-EIGHT

HANNAH

Hannah fetched a towel from the bathroom, and David roughly dried off his hair and face. When he pulled it away, he was pale and there was a haunted look in his eyes. Whatever he was about to tell her, she didn't want to hear it. Not today. Not ever.

They sat beside each other on the sofa, turned towards one another so that their knees pressed awkwardly together. David coughed before he spoke. 'All this time, I thought it was my fault. That she'd left that evening so upset that she hadn't paid attention to the road. I mean, that might still be the case, right?'

Hannah didn't know what to say. Would they ever know if Katherine's death was the accident that they'd thought it was? 'Was there not an inquest after the accident? How come they didn't find out about her tumour?'

David's elbows were on his knees, his head in his hands. 'It was all such a blur. I was drinking... way too much. I had so much anger in me. Anger at her for leaving. Anger at the driver coming the other way, who might have caused her to swerve from the road. All I remember is the coroner recording an accidental death and feeling... furious. The guilt didn't come till much later.'

'Guilt?'

David raised his head to look at her. 'It was hell, Hannah. Those last couple of weeks with her were actually hell. As far as I knew, she was living in our house, but she was seeing someone else. Whenever she wasn't there, I assumed that she was with him, this other man. I couldn't stop this mental slideshow of her laughing and having fun with him, whoever he was. And I was horrible to her that last night. She wasn't planning to leave for good that night. I forced her. I told her she had to go right there and then. Living with that knowledge has been horrific. And now' – he paused, gulped, breathed out slowly – 'now I find out that, whatever it was like for me, it was so much worse for her. She was dying, for God's sake. And she had no one... no one.'

He folded forwards and his shoulders heaved in sobs. Hannah spread her arm across his back, her heart tearing for him. Losing her father had been the worst thing that had ever happened to her; she knew grief and loss. How much worse would it be to lose a husband – or a wife? 'I'm so sorry, David.'

They were interrupted by her phone ringing. They watched the vibration move it across the coffee table in front of them as if it were alive, demanding their attention. Both of them were frozen, not wanting to find out what it was about to say.

Hannah reached for it. 'Hello. This is Mrs Maguire.'

'Hello. Dr Collier again, to give you another update.'

He wasn't launching straight in. He was giving her time to prepare herself. This wasn't good news.

David reached for her hand, giving her the strength to ask. 'Yes. Thank you. What's happening?'

'Unfortunately, I have to tell you that the second embryo is failing to progress. But we've taken the fourth out of storage, and the good news is that embryo number three is still thriving. Please try to stay positive and I'll be in touch soon.'

His voice was kind, but staying positive was pretty difficult right now; her words were almost strangled by her throat as she spoke. 'Thank you. I'll be here.'

David's head had been close enough to hers that he'd heard every word. He reached for her. 'Oh, Hannah.'

She shook her head vigorously; she couldn't crumble, not yet. Not yet. 'Just keep talking, David. Tell me everything.'

He seemed to understand her need to focus away from the embryos. This time, he kept hold of her hand as he spoke, looking her in the eye. 'When I was walking, I realised something. I thought I wasn't enough for Katherine. Most of our marriage, I felt like that. She was this... bright light. Always rushing to the next big thing. Sometimes, I felt like I was just being pulled along in her slipstream.'

Hannah tried not to feel hurt by this; not to feel second best. This wasn't the time for petty jealousy.

'And then she wanted a child and so did I, but when it didn't work out, it became an obsession for her. As if she wasn't complete without a baby. So we rushed into the fertility treatment and then, just as fast, she said that she didn't want a child anymore and I thought, I assumed, that what she meant was... she didn't want a child *with me.*'

Hannah's heart ached in response to the pain in his voice. It recognised the pain, the rejection. 'But it wasn't that. At least you know it wasn't that she didn't love you.'

'I know. But you know what? This is harder. When I thought that she'd cast me aside for someone else, I could hold that against her. But now I know that she was doing it to protect me. Because she loved me...'

He tailed off, looked into the middle distance. Hannah could hardly breathe with the fear of what he was about to say.

His next words were whispered. 'She was right, you know. I wouldn't have got over her.'

It was as if every drop of blood in Hannah had sunk to her feet. He wouldn't have got over Katherine? What was he saying? Her throat was dry, but she had to ask. 'If you had known she was dying, you wouldn't have... you don't...' Why wouldn't the words come out right? Why couldn't she say what was on her mind? *If you knew that Katherine had loved you to the end of her life, you would never have fallen for someone else.* 'You wouldn't have fallen in love with me?'

'No. But I did. And I do. I do love you, Hannah. I love you more than anyone else in this world.'

She wanted to believe it, she really did. 'But these last few weeks, when we've been deciding about the embryos, you've been different. A little cold. Even angry at times.'

He let his head drop. 'I know. And I am so sorry. It just felt as if the same thing was happening all over again. I wanted to be enough for you. I tried so hard and yet—'

'David. Please.' She couldn't bear the pain in his voice.

But he held up his hand. 'I mean it, Hannah. I want so much for you to be happy. And you have been so unhappy. My mind wouldn't let up, whispering that maybe, if we couldn't have a baby, I wasn't enough for you. That I was going to lose you too.'

Hannah's heart physically ached within her chest. In all her desperation to have a child, she'd taken for granted this wonderful man. 'You are enough for me. I love you. Earlier, when you left for your walk, I was so frightened that you were going to leave me for good.'

He let go of her hands but only to pull her close to his chest. 'I will never leave you. Never. I love you so very much.'

She let herself collapse into him for a few moments, over-whelmed with relief and sorrow. It had taken him a long time to get to this honesty; it was time for her to do the same.

With her cheek resting on his chest, she told him everything she could put into words. 'I know that I've been all over the place these last few weeks. I wanted a baby who belonged to me. I wanted someone that no one could ever take away. But that's not how it works. I know that now. You don't have a baby to keep it forever; one day it will leave. People leave, but that's okay. Because if they love you, they come back. It isn't to do with blood or rules or anything else. A family is about love. And you are my family, David. With or without a baby.'

His arms tightened around her. 'It's not that I don't want a baby, Hannah. I really do. I just don't want us to lose ourselves in the process. I don't ever want to lose you.'

She pushed herself up and looked him in the eye. 'You will never lose me. But if one or both of these embryos survive, I really, really want to use them.'

David searched her face as if he was trying to read her. 'Are you sure? After everything that's happened today?'

'*Because* of everything that's happened today. Even though it felt like the right thing for us, I worried that I would find it difficult that our children would have Katherine's DNA. But now, knowing what she did, it's made me want to do this even more. For us. But also... a little bit for her.'

Charlotte's words came back to her. *We adopted them for our sake, not theirs. We wanted them desperately.* Well this baby was wanted desperately too. For her sake, and David's and also Katherine's.

Wrapped in each other's arms, they didn't move from the couch for the next hour. Until Hannah's phone rang for the final time.

THIRTY-NINE

HANNAH

It was almost surreal sitting in the waiting room. Knowing what was about to happen.

It was a good job that David held her hand tightly; like a kite, she felt as if she might be caught in the wind and fly off at any moment, floating above the waiting room, watching the events as they unfolded. Sitting here, right this minute, she wasn't pregnant. But in an hour's time, there would be the beginnings of life within her. It was too much to take in.

'Are you okay?'

David had asked her this at least three times since they sat down. And each time her answer had been the same. 'I'm fine.'

He brought her hand up to his face and kissed it. 'Have you got your lucky socks?'

She patted her handbag and smiled. 'Of course.'

In the many online forums she'd trawled, lots of women had recommended socks for the egg transfer because your feet got cold. And there was a superstition or a tradition – where did one end and the other begin? – about pineapples and fertility. So David had bought her a pair of pale blue ankle socks covered in tiny pineapples.

'Mr and Mrs Maguire?'

It was time.

All of the injections in the last couple of weeks hadn't been particularly pleasant. And the hormones in her body had left her feeling like a stroppy teenager with a tendency to burst into tears at the drop of a hat. But all of that was nothing compared to her nerves now. She'd watched countless videos on YouTube and had asked their consultant to be honest with her, so she was under no illusions about how uncomfortable it was going to be. David had been waiting on her hand and foot the last few days. Having been through this before, he was practically self-flagellating with the guilt that it was her that had to go through all of this, while he just held her hand and told her how brave she was.

Whatever it was like, it would all be worth it if they got their baby at the end of all of it.

If.

They were shown into a private room where Hannah had to change into a hospital gown. Other than that, she was naked – apart from the pineapple socks. 'This has to be the most unsexy conception ever.'

David leaned forwards and kissed her. 'You are always sexy to me.'

A giggle bubbled up from her stomach. After the emotional rollercoaster of a day, her nerves and the importance of what they were about to do, she couldn't suppress it.

David smiled too. 'I love you so much, Hannah. You are incredible.'

She smiled at him. 'I know you do. And I love you too.'

The procedure itself took about twenty minutes. Thankfully, David was allowed to be with her, holding her hand, because she was awake for the whole thing. It was painful. Like a protracted period pain. The tube was inside for a while as the surgeon watched a screen to make sure that the embryos – invisible to the naked eye – had left the tube and were inside her.

Afterwards, she had to stay lying down in the recovery room for another forty-five minutes. David sat with her. He couldn't stop kissing her cheek and telling her how wonderful she was.

The nurse who was looking after Hannah winked at her. 'Do you want me to record this for you so that you can play it back to him when you need to?'

When she was out of earshot, David lowered his voice. 'I mean it, Hannah. Not just the medical side of things. All the other stuff. Katherine. Your mum. It's been such a lot to deal with and you've been—'

'Please don't say amazing again. I'm beginning to feel like a circus act.'

After they laughed, they sat in silence for a few moments. If Hannah could have willed those two embryos to embed themselves in her womb, she would have. They were the only chance they had. There were no more.

Of course, she could go down the egg-donation route, but something had shifted in her in the last few hours. Her conversation with Hayley – and then David – about Katherine had made her feel a strange connection with her. These embryos were even more precious now that she knew more about the woman they'd come from. It was as if they came with an extra layer of love.

David must have been having similar thoughts. 'I know this is going to work, Hannah. I can't explain it, but I just know.'

She hoped that he was right. She was scared to move in case she did anything to stop their safe passage. The next two weeks – waiting to see if the procedure had been successful – were going to be the longest fourteen days of her life.

. . .

For the first couple of days after the embryo transfer, she'd been scared to even walk too quickly, in case something dislodged inside her. But life had to carry on as usual, and she'd been into work and tried to pretend that everything was normal. A few times, David had nonchalantly suggested that she could take a pregnancy test before the two weeks were up, just to see how things were progressing. But Hannah wanted to do everything by the book. If they did everything they were told, and followed every rule, surely that would make it more likely that they would get lucky this time?

Outside of her mother, Tessa, Charlotte, Marie – and now Hayley – no one knew about the fertility treatment. It made it easier to put it out of her mind, so that every little twinge didn't send her into an anxious spiral. When she remembered, the thrill of possibility made her fingers tingle. If even one embryo was thriving inside her, it was her own secret. To the outside world, she was just Hannah. Inside, she was a mother.

Now, though, sitting in the clinic waiting room again, she kind of wished she *had* taken a test. Would it have been better to know for sure? But what if they'd had a positive pregnancy test at home, and then got here and had their hopes dashed? It wasn't only the threat of miscarriage; she'd read enough about chemical pregnancies and how they could register as positive on a test, giving false hope until the day of the scan, even though they would never result in a baby.

There was another couple in the waiting room. Judging by the pile of leaflets they were flicking through, they must be at the beginning of their journey. The tentative hope in their eyes made her heart ache for them. For her and David. For all the parents in waiting, who wanted so much for a baby of their own.

She'd already been seen by the nurse for a urine sample and blood test; now they were waiting to be called back in to see the consultant for her results. The clock on the wall seemed to be going backwards. She and David had given up making small talk. They both watched the minute hand crawl forwards, punctuating the time with a squeeze of the hand and tight-lipped smiles. Eventually, the receptionist called their names and they followed her down the now-familiar corridor to discover their fate.

At the door to her office, Dr Nash greeted them with a smile. 'How are you feeling, Hannah?'

'Terrified?' Hannah smiled back to show that she was – half – joking.

'I'd be more surprised if you weren't nervous. Shall I give you the test results first?' Her eyes twinkled and there was a smile on her face. Surely that was a good sign? *Please let it be a good sign.*

Hannah squeezed the hand that David was holding and they spoke in unison. 'Yes please.'

She slid into her seat opposite them and turned the piece of paper in front of her so that it faced them. She pointed to a word more magical than any Hannah had ever seen: *positive.*

'Congratulations to you both.'

EPILOGUE

April is an unpredictable month. Sunshine and showers can replace one another by the hour. But this April day had been kind, and there hadn't been a cloud in the sky since Hannah had woken her mother at eight o'clock with scrambled eggs and Buck's Fizz.

'Oh, this is lovely.' Gwen pushed herself up in bed and smiled. 'Have you run it past Tony? Is it on his approved foods list?'

'I did indeed run it past the groom-to-be and he has allowed it on this occasion.'

Her mum took the tray from her and rested it on her lap, then patted the side of the bed. 'Come and sit with me.'

Hannah had stayed over the night before at Tony's request. He was adamant that he and her mother would arrive at the church separately, but he hadn't wanted her to be alone all night. They'd spent the evening before watching *My Fair Lady* and drinking tea. Her mother had pronounced it the best hen night she could have asked for.

Now she shuffled to the side of the bed so that Hannah could sit down. She sipped at her champagne and orange juice and reached out for Hannah's hand. 'How was last night?'

'She's sleeping off her first hen night. After waking me up at 2 a.m., and again at 5 a.m.' It had been the first night they'd had away from David since the birth, three whirlwind months ago.

'It was lovely to have both my girls to myself last night, but don't feel like you've got to stay. I can get myself dressed if you want to get back to—'

'Mother. Everything is in hand. Eat your breakfast now, because the hairdresser will be here in an hour.'

The bride and groom hadn't wanted a huge wedding – 'we just want the people we love there' – but it was beautiful none-theless. When Tony had needed to pause in the middle of his trembled vows to blow his nose, there hadn't been a dry eye in the house. And when they gathered in the church grounds after the service, the sun warmed them even further.

Olivia had been her usual contented self during the service, and Hannah walked her over to where Katherine's mother Marie was hovering on the edge of the small crowd. Since Hannah's pregnancy, she and Gwen had met and were fast becoming good friends.

She beamed as Hannah approached. 'Wasn't it a lovely service? It was so nice of your mum to invite me.'

It was almost weird that it wasn't weird for Hannah to have Marie in their lives. 'Of course. You're part of the family now.'

Marie looked younger these days, and it wasn't just because Hannah's mother had taken her shopping and encouraged her to change her hairstyle. Now, with what was likely not her first glass of champagne in her hand, her eyes glistened as she stroked her granddaughter's cheek. 'Don't tell your mum, but I thought Olivia-Katherine was the most beautiful girl in that church.'

The first time Marie had hyphenated Olivia's first and second name, David had been worried that Hannah wouldn't like it. Actually, she hadn't minded at all. 'If it makes her happy, let her do it.' After all, hadn't they made sure that Olivia would know about the woman who had given her life by giving her that name in the first place?

David joined from where he'd been on baby-change detail, and Marie turned to him, beaming. 'And here is the most handsome boy in any room.'

David winked at Hannah. 'Told you I've still got it.'

She laughed. 'I don't think she means you.' Hannah leaned down and kissed the bundle in his arms – their son, Olivia's twin brother, James.

'Hey, you.' She turned at Charlotte's voice. 'Godmothers coming through. Is this the queue for baby cuddles?'

Tessa, godmother number two, was right behind her. 'Oh, yes. Me too please. My own children are over by the buffet, trying to pretend they don't know who I am.'

Hannah and David handed over their precious cargo. Tessa took Olivia, and Charlotte took James. 'It was very kind of you to have two babies so that we could have one each.'

Throughout her pregnancy, Hannah had refused to believe that she was really carrying twins. One baby had seemed a miracle. Two seemed almost greedy. On the day they were born, she and David had both smiled like drunks for hours after the surgeon had lifted them both from her within minutes of one another, and pronounced them the most beautiful set of twins she'd ever seen.

Though they were twins, their personalities were already completely different. Olivia was calm and content throughout the day, but up half the night. James, on the other hand, was on the go from the moment he woke up but already slept through the night for ten unbelievable hours. Hence the reason she'd taken Olivia to stay at her mother's last night while James had stayed with David and Tony and a large supply of expressed milk.

Now James started to fuss, and Charlotte expertly shifted his position so that he was upright and started to jiggle him around.

Hannah's fingers itched to take him back, but she settled for a warning. 'You might want to be careful; he's only just had a huge feed.'

It was too late. As soon as the words were out of her mouth, James belched a mouthful of regurgitated milk down the front of Charlotte's beautiful blue dress. 'Well, that was not very godly, Master James.'

Hannah's hands flew to her mouth. 'I am so, so sorry.'

But Charlotte just shrugged. 'Don't be. Babies are messy. Like families, right?'

Hannah smiled at her friend, holding her beautiful boy. And her other friend, with her equally beautiful girl. And her mother, and her mother's new husband. And her own husband. And her husband's first wife's mother, who was also a biological grandparent to her twins.

Yes. Families were messy. And chaotic. And they came in all shapes and sizes.

But however you came by your family, they were wonderful.

The photographer appeared, followed by a very happy-looking Gwen and Tony. He waved his camera. 'Time for the family shot. Who's in it?'

Hannah looked around her, shrugged and smiled. 'All of us.'

A LETTER FROM EMMA

I want to say a huge thank you for choosing to read *To Be a Mother*. If you did enjoy it and want to keep up to date with all my latest releases, just sign up at the following link. Your email address will never be shared, and you can unsubscribe at any time.

www.bookouture.com/emma-robinson

I have friends whose children have come to them through many different routes – IVF, egg donation, adoption – just like the mothers in these pages, and I wanted this book to celebrate them and their families. During my research, I learned quite early on that the journey through fertility treatment can be very varied. Even if some of the medical details in the story differ from your own experience, I hope that you will appreciate that I did my best to capture the emotional side to the treatment that the women I spoke to were generous enough to share with me.

When writing a novel about a current wife and a former wife, I couldn't help but think of Daphne du Maurier's *Rebecca*. If you've read it, I hope you enjoyed the homage in my opening line. If you haven't, I would wholeheartedly recommend it.

Hannah's dilemma is not one faced by many people, but I hope you loved *To Be a Mother* and if you did, I would be very grateful if you could write a review. I'd love to hear what you think, and it makes such a difference helping new readers to discover one of my books for the first time.

I love hearing from my readers – you can get in touch on my Facebook page, through Twitter, Goodreads or my website.

Thanks,

Emma

www.emmarobinsonwrites.com

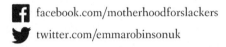 facebook.com/motherhoodforslackers
twitter.com/emmarobinsonuk

ACKNOWLEDGEMENTS

First thanks are always to Isobel Akenhead for being such a fantastic editor and for inviting me to the most enjoyable – and productive! – lunches in town. A special mention to Jenny Geras too for the *What If?* that started me down a rabbit hole that led to this story. Thank you.

The Bookouture publicity team are, as always, a force to be reckoned with. Thank you so much Kim Nash and your team of Noelle Holten, Sarah Hardy and Jess Readett. We're all so lucky that you have our backs.

It takes a lot of people to make a book. Thank you to Gabbie Chant for copy-editing, Laura Kincaid for proofreading and Alice Moore for the cover, which I love, love, love. Thanks also to my friend Carrie Harvey for casting your eye over the final proofs, which swim before my tired eyes.

Huge thanks to Hannah Mills for sharing your fertility journey with me, and to Sarah Howard for an insight into fertility clinics. Any mistakes – or poetic licence – are mine.

Fellow Bookouture writers are an endless source of support. Lizzie Page, for our wonderful windswept walks and for giving me the idea to make Katherine a TV producer – the next lattes are on me. Thanks also to Kate Hewitt, for helping me to thrash out the details of this book on our wonderful writing retreat. Katherine – with one letter changed – was named in your honour.

Despite him usually just suggesting I 'put a shark in it', thanks to my husband Dan for helping me to come up with ways that might suggest someone is having an affair. I'm slightly concerned by how quickly you came up with them. Thanks too to my mum for being there whenever I need her.

Lastly, thank you to everyone who is buying, reading and reviewing my books. I read every review and it keeps me going when I'm burning the midnight oil to write (like now). Thank you.